M000074636

DEADLY
DROUGHT

Also by Gary Alexander

PIGEON BLOOD
UNFUNNY MONEY
KIET AND THE GOLDEN PEACOCK
KIET AND THE OPIUM WAR

DEADLY DROUGHT

GARY ALEXANDER

A THOMAS · DUNNE
BOOK

ST. MARTIN'S PRESS
NEW YORK

DESIGN BY DAWN NILES

Library of Congress Cataloging-in-Publication Data

Alexander, Gary
Deadly drought / Gary Alexander.
p.   cm.
"A Thomas Dunne book."
ISBN 0-312-06331-8
I. Title.
PS3551.L3554D43   1991
91-19048
CIP
813'.54—dc20

First Edition
10 9 8 7 6 5 4 3 2 1

THE AUTHOR APOLOGIZES TO THE SOCIALIST RE-
PUBLIC OF THE UNION OF BURMA, THE PEOPLE'S RE-
PUBLIC OF CHINA, THE LAO PEOPLE'S DEMOCRATIC
REPUBLIC, AND THE KINGDOM OF THAILAND FOR
GEOGRAPHIC DISTORTIONS AND FOR ENCROACH-
MENT OF THEIR BORDERS. TOLERANCE IS ALSO ASKED
FOR LIBERTIES TAKEN WITH THE TOPOGRAPHY AND
THE CLIMATE OF THE REGION.

For Shari, for everything.

For the Caddyshack gang. You know who you are.

CAST OF CHARACTERS:

BAMSAN KIET *(bomb-sawn key-yet)*. Hickorn's Superintendent of Police.

CAPTAIN BINH *(bin)*. Kiet's adjutant.

TUON TRAN *(twon tran)*. Lieutenant commander, commandant of the Royal Luongan Navy.

PRINCE NOVISAD PAKSE *(nove-ih-said pock-see)*. Ruler of Luong.

MADAME SARAVANE *(sarah-vane)*. Luong's foremost mystic.

JEAN-GUY PAKSE. Prince Pakse's illegitimate son.

FENG VU *(fang voo)*. Chinese rice broker.

RED WILLIAMS. American air conditioner salesman.

QUIN CANH *(quinn can)*. Kiet's lover.

HOUPHONG DUC *(hoe-fong duck)*. Luong's Minister of Agriculture.

MARY BETH APPLEBEE. American missionary.

Planting rice is never any fun
Bent from dawn till setting sun
Cannot stand and cannot sit
Cannot rest for even a bit

—*from an old Luongan song*

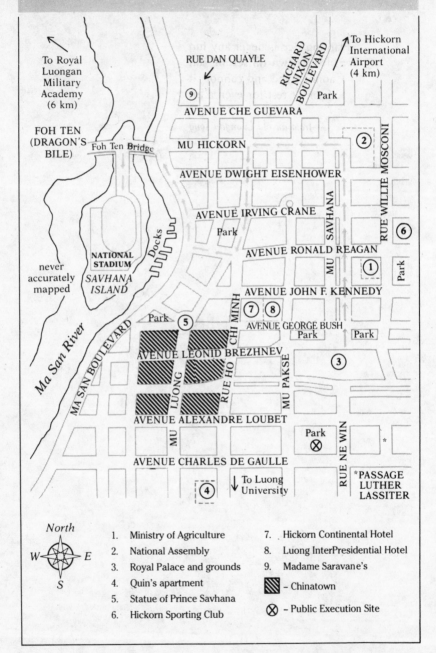

Downtown
HICKORN

To Royal
Luongan
Military
Academy
(6 km)

RUE DAN QUAYLE

To Hickorn
International
Airport
(4 km)

RICHARD NIXON BOULEVARD

Park

FOH TEN
(DRAGON'S
BILE)

Foh Ten Bridge

⑨

AVENUE CHE GUEVARA

MU HICKORN

②

AVENUE DWIGHT EISENHOWER

RUE WILLIE MOSCONI

AVENUE IRVING CRANE

⑥

Park

AVENUE RONALD REAGAN

Docks

NATIONAL
STADIUM

①

MU SAVHANA

SAVHANA
ISLAND

never
accurately
mapped

AVENUE JOHN F. KENNEDY

Park

Park

RUE HO CHI MINH

⑦ ⑧

Park

⑤

AVENUE GEORGE BUSH

Park

Park

MA SAN BOULEVARD

AVENUE LEONID BREZHNEV

MU PAKSE

③

MU LUONG

Ma San River

AVENUE ALEXANDRE LOUBET

Park
⊗

RUE NE WIN

AVENUE CHARLES DE GAULLE

④

↓ To Luong
University

*PASSAGE
LUTHER
LASSITER

*

North
W ✦ E
S

1. Ministry of Agriculture
2. National Assembly
3. Royal Palace and grounds
4. Quin's apartment
5. Statue of Prince Savhana
6. Hickorn Sporting Club

7. Hickorn Continental Hotel
8. Luong InterPresidential Hotel
9. Madame Saravane's

▨ – Chinatown

⊗ – Public Execution Site

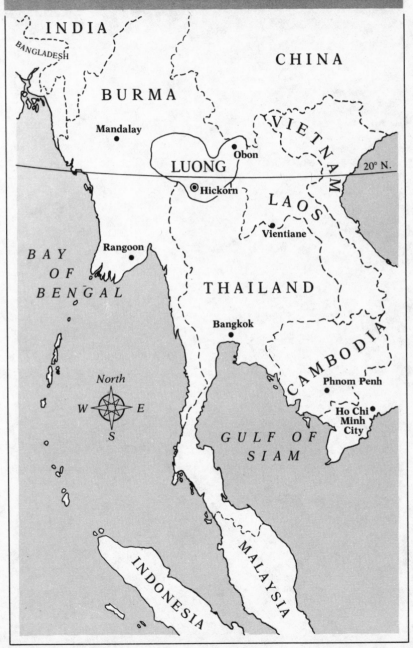

The Kingdom of
LUONG

INDIA

BANGLADESH

CHINA

BURMA

Mandalay

VIETNAM

LUONG ● Obon

20° N.

⊙ Hickorn

LAOS

BAY
OF
BENGAL

Rangoon

Vientiane

THAILAND

Bangkok

North

W ✦ E

S

CAMBODIA

Phnom Penh

Ho Chi
Minh
City

GULF OF
SIAM

MALAYSIA

INDONESIA

PROLOGUE

The Kingdom of Luong and all those who inhabit it are creatures of the imagination. Luong is as real as Oz, although it is often stranger. And since Luong is an illusion, it is therefore not—

1. A Southeast Asian backwater surrounded by China, Burma, Laos, and Thailand.

2. A former French colony that was granted independence in 1954.

3. A constitutional monarchy ruled by eighty-year-old Prince Novisad Pakse, an accomplished neutralist whose true passion is pocket billiards.

4. Mountainous in the highlands, lush and torrid in the southern river valleys.

5. Anchored by its capital city, Hickorn, a sleepy metropolis of 235,000.

6. Formerly self-sufficient in agriculture, an exporter of rice, but now beginning its second year of drought.

7. The jurisdiction of Bamsan Kiet, Hickorn's Superintendent of Police, for whom things never seem to get any easier.

Tuesday, May 19
Tia Nha village
High 94°, Low 79°
Clear

ONE

Bamsan Kiet trudged behind Thanh Dac, inserting tender rice seedlings into the muck at his feet. Two consecutive days of this, he thought; that shall be my utter limit. Any more and I would become a permanent hunchback, as gross and deranged as that Quasimodo fellow in the old movie. But the work that would normally last two exhausting weeks would this year not even take two days. For that Kiet was sad and vaguely guilty, let off the hook by a cruel whim of nature.

Dac, Kiet's brother-in-law, stopped, and threw down his bundle of seedlings. He hawked, spat, and said, "What's the use, Bamsan? I'm fooling myself. Without the monsoon, they'll die. I should have kept them in the beds. They could have died with their own kind."

Thanh Dac was of course right. The muck they were standing in was less mud than paste, a low spot in the middle of Dac's parched paddy. The water Dac and Sini, Kiet's half sister, and their five children poured on the seedlings was fetched in buckets from the Ma San River. Seedlings that would indeed be abandoned to die if the monsoon did not come.

Died with their own kind, Kiet knew, was part bitter humor and part reverence. Dac was not formally religious, but he was an animist, whether he realized it or not. Animist peasants worshiped what gave them life—the sun, the rain, the fruits of the earth. There were nineteen words in the Luongan language for rice, and three were synonyms for sacredness.

The transplantation of doomed rice shoots, Kiet felt, was a reminder to the gods in charge of such things that last year's monsoon had skirted Luong and this year's was a week overdue. Suck moisture off the Indian Ocean, blow eastward, and drench us, damn you! That was Thanh Dac's desperate message.

"Bamsan, are you all right?"

No, as a matter of fact, he wasn't. He was locked in a bent position, canted at an odd angle. He pictured himself in that Parisian belfry, swinging maniacally on the bell rope and drooling. He had not replied because his response would have been a pained grunt, loss of face compounding his physical agony.

"Let me help," Dac said, cupping Kiet by the elbows and wrenching them upward.

"Uhhhh!"

"Better?"

"Splendid," Kiet said, groaning.

"Don't tell Sini, but it happens to me too. Come on, it's time to eat anyway."

Thanh Dac was thirty-seven years old and he looked fifty-seven. He was constructed of wire and leather, a typically sinewy Luongan rice farmer. These country men were strong as iron and could outwork a water buffalo. Then one day, at age forty or fifty, they went to sleep and never awoke. Used up, worn out, nothing left but the husk.

Kiet followed his brother-in-law to the house and their midday meal. He was halfway through a two-week furlough, his yearly escape from urban stress. He had fled the woes of crime, pollution, and high living costs for the purity and agony of manual labor. Rice planting was a family obligation, an obligation woven into Luong's history. But thanks to the drought, this pastoral village twenty kilometers from Hickorn faced a more ominous obligation: survival.

Thanh Dac and Sini's home was on stilts, wooden-framed with a thatched roof. Bamboo partitions divided the interior into children's and adult's sleeping quarters, and the family room. Yes,

4

Kiet thought, you could call it a hut, but it was clean and sturdy. Unlike so many huts in Hickorn's slums, it was not sided with scrap packaging material. No walls of multinational corporate logos. No Coca-Cola, Panasonic, Kotex. Their home had dignity.

Kiet trailed Thanh Dac up the ladder to the door. The purpose of elevation was a dry floor. Although an uncommon occurrence, there had been times when overzealous monsoon rains had washed the Ma San over the dikes. Today, the height kept out the dust.

Sini was squatting beside the brazier, stir-frying vegetables and chicken. Rice steamed in another pot. The food smelled wonderful and Kiet was famished.

"Done already?" Sini asked her husband.

"A fool's chore," Dac said.

Kiet had been the only child of a peasant mother, and a father who served the colonial administration as a clerk, a mandarin to mandarins who processed documents for the French. Kiet's father died when Kiet was sixteen. His mother remarried a farmer, and returned to her origins. Kiet was attending Luong University at the time and remained in Hickorn.

Evidently the harsh simple life of rice farming triggered her fertility. She bore three more children, Sini being the eldest. This generation proved prolific also, leaving the widowed and childless Kiet as a glaring offshoot on a spreading family tree.

Kiet was physically different too. He was, if not obese, plump at the belt line. He towered above his countrymen, as tall as a Caucasian. Half a century old, he could still remember the days when young ladies considered him Buddha-like, an object of quasi-spiritual sexual fantasies that, psychiatric layman that he was, he had not attempted to analyze but merely fulfill.

Further, he did not bring in a crop. He lived and worked in the city, in Hickorn, enforcing city laws and capturing city criminals. He rode in automobiles, spoke into telephones, and took for granted luxuries such as plumbing.

"Where are the children?" Kiet asked.

5

Sini was a tiny, pretty woman who was also growing too old too fast. She did not look up from her stirring. "The village. They have already eaten."

Eaten what? Kiet wondered. On his annual visit he always brought gifts. Last year, a radio, the year before wristwatches. And every year, toys for the children. This year he came bearing twenty-five kilos of rice and three live chickens. The final bird was in the pot, he presumed; he had heard no clucking lately.

He and his presents had been greeted warily. Basic foodstuff was not an appropriate gift. It was charity. Shame.

Kiet explained that the grain and the birds were confiscated property. Just that morning they had raided the warren of a notorious thief. The place was bursting with stolen property, Kiet had said, sweeping his arms for effect. The identifiable goods— the television receivers, the stereophonic cassette machines, and the videotape players—would be returned to their rightful owners. But there are no serial numbers on rice kernels and poultry, are there? I could entrust it to the police property room and risk confiscating it again from yet another criminal or I could bring it here at no cost whatsoever, could I not?

Sini and Thanh Dac said that Kiet made good sense. They accepted the gifts gratefully. No face was lost. But Kiet was lying. He had paid dearly at Hickorn's public market. The chicken seller had bargained as if his birds were the last of their species. And rice had doubled in price in the past six months, moving quickly to triple, the panic of the delayed monsoon boosting the price at a rate of 5 percent a week.

"In the village?" Kiet said. "Playing?"

"Yes. They love the balsa gliders you gave them, Bamsan. They make those little airplanes swoop and soar," Sini said.

More practical than the kites I usually bring, Kiet thought. There was no premonsoon bluster to hold them aloft. The air was as dead as the soil.

"They may have gone fishing too," Thanh Dac added. "You can wade out in the Ma San and pick up shrimp."

6

It was strange how Dac had come around, Kiet thought. His brother-in-law had disliked him, never personally, but for what he was, or what he perceived him to be. What he represented. Kiet was a city boy, a sissy with soft hands who wore shoes and could not live long without electricity and flush toilets.

Before the drought, Dac harvested two crops a year. He fed his family and sold the surplus. Double cropping had provided money, cash in his pockets. "Discretionary income" was how Captain Binh, Kiet's westernized adjutant, would phrase it.

Thanh Dac had saved his discretionary cash income money and had purchased a foot-treadle sewing machine for Sini. Last year, Dac had shown it off to Kiet with enormous pride. He presumed it had been sold. The corner of the family room in which it had been was now so empty a glance would cause an echo.

Without looking at the empty corner, Kiet saw it clearly. There in the void was the answer to Thanh Dac's friendliness. Luongan peasants owned their land, yes, but the moneylenders and rice brokers owned the peasants. The moneylender and the rice broker was usually the same person.

Always operating on a year-late cycle, farmers borrowed on their next crop to pay debts and to have cash on hand for living expenses. When the crops were harvested, creditors took paddy in settlement of debts. Farmers kept the excess paddy, up to 40 percent in a good year.

The brokers barged their paddy to Hickorn, where it was milled and polished into the glutinous white rice beloved by Luongans. Some was sold in Hickorn and some in the highlands. Some was exported. In good years, much was exported. In bad years, some was repurchased by the villagers, on credit, at staggering rates.

Like any farmer, Thanh Dac had been treated unfairly by nature too, but never so cruelly, for so long. That had to be it, Kiet mused, had to be the leveler that flattened the smugness out of his brother-in-law. Thanh had finally realized that circumstances did much to make the man. As a farmer he had subjected himself to the vagaries of weather. He had been humbled by the will of heaven.

Thanh Dac had no control. No more control than Bamsan Kiet had over the decadence of city life. Kiet had been forgiven for his dislike of squatting above a latrine trench and for hands that erupted in blisters at the suggestion of manual labor.

Sini spooned rice into individual bowls with an ice cream scoop. Kiet nibbled at his. Both men should have been diving into the communal pan of chicken and vegetables, chopsticks first. Neither was. Sini looked questioningly at her half brother.

"Thanks, no, Sini," Kiet said. "The food smells and looks wonderful, but I was in the heat too long. It damaged my appetite. A few bites of rice is enough for me."

"Mine too," Thanh Dac said. "It's as hot as it ever gets."

"Yes," Sini said, "now that you mention it, today is warmer than yesterday. I feel woozy."

Good, Kiet said to himself. Everybody is enervated by the relentless sun. Today the children would eat well.

Somebody was coming up the ladder, person or persons too quiet to be the five kids, who usually sounded like an invasion. There was a knock and Thanh Dac said come in.

A young Royal Luongan Navy enlisted man entered, blinked in the darkness, and said, "Superintendent Kiet?"

"Here," Kiet said.

The sailor's heels locked and he assumed the position of attention. "Sir, I have been ordered by Commandant Tran to request that you come with me immediately to Commandant Tran's vessel and ride with us to Hickorn."

"Tran is at Tia Nha?" Kiet asked.

"Yes sir. We arrived moments ago."

The sailor was speaking breathlessly and perspiring. He was dressed in the style of Popeye, the cartoon sailor, the bell-bottoms and short sleeves and the gob's cap that seemed universally the uniform of the military seaman. This lad wore one chevron and a mustache so thin the whiskers could be counted.

"I am on furlough," Kiet said. "I did not drive this year because the roadbed is dried up and potholed as anywhere on Mars. I took the river ferry instead. I could catch the late afternoon boat and be in—"

"Pardon me, sir, for interrupting you, but Commandant Tran was sent by Prince Pakse."

"His Royal Highness needs me?" Kiet said.

"Yes sir. That is what I'm led to believe. He has to see you and it can't wait for a ferryboat."

"Can you tell me why?"

"No, sir, Superintendent. I was only told to hurry!"

Sini's eyebrows raised. Her brother, the important person.

Thanh Dac lept to his feet and helped the still-aching Kiet to his. They embraced, then Dac said, "Yes, hurry, Bamsan. When you see him, ask Prince Pakse to create rain."

No Luongan really believed that their monarch was divine anymore, but it never hurt to try. Kiet smiled and said he would. He went down after the impatient sailor, straining to keep up.

"Urgent," Kiet said to the sailor's back.

The sailor cocked his head. "Sir?"

"It must be urgent business."

"Yes sir."

"Well? Can you guess?"

The sailor did not reply. His arms swung faster. His strides became longer. Enough of this death march. Kiet stopped and shouted, "Well?"

The boy turned and pleaded, "Please, sir, I know nothing except what I have told you."

He slapped his chevron. "I know that Commandant Tran said he would reduce me from seaman third class to seaman recruit if I did not deliver you to his flagship in fifteen minutes."

Kiet sighed and waved, silently saying *go*.

They quickstepped through Tia Nha village. They had it to themselves. It was siesta time, the hellish early afternoon when only fools and children were outside in the heat. And it was *hot*,

9

dry hot. Kiet liked 90 degrees, 90 percent humidity. That was sultry and pleasant. But this—midnineties, negligible humidity. The air was like sandpaper and everything you touched crackled with static electricity.

They walked along the main path that bisected the village of five hundred. They passed concrete pads that served as threshing floors. They passed small shops and the huts in which merchants and village officials lived. They passed the center of the village and the long narrow building that was schoolhouse by day, meeting hall by night. It was Tia Nha's only masonry structure.

They reached the opposite edge of the village. The Ma San River came into view. It struck Kiet then that humans were not the only creatures absent. Not just now, but throughout his visit. He saw water buffalos, yes. They were too important to butcher. They were the peasant's trucks, his tractors. Lose your buffalo and you lost your livelihood. You fed your buffalo before you fed yourself.

It was the smaller animals that he did not see, did not hear. The pigs and the chickens. The dogs and the cats.

Even the rats.

TWO

They walked through gunk that sucked at Kiet's sandals and climbed into a rubber raft. The Royal Luongan Navy's most formidable landing craft, he thought nastily. Suitable for any and all amphibious assaults. The two-man floater was moored as shallow as could be. Tepid river water was not yet lapping against Kiet's ankles and they were easily fifty meters beyond the Tia Nha dock, the outer pilings of which were sunk into fissured clay as hard as stone.

Kiet saw village children playing in the distance, splashing in water that barely came to their knees. They were nearly at midstream. At least drowning, the primary tragedy of monsoon arrival, would devastate no parents today. He saw his sister's five children. The two older ones were dipping for marine life with nets that would in kinder days be utilized to capture butterflies.

The sailor paddled them out to Royal Luongan Navy Commandant Tuon Tran's flagship. It was a twenty-five foot cabin cruiser. The Royal Luongan Navy (RLN) consisted of five such craft designed by their American manufacturers for pleasure. Kiet had seen yacht and boat advertising in Western magazines. The people on board in the photographs were predominantly smiling Caucasian males who were either fishing or enjoying the company of women too young and happy to have been their wives.

The four other ships were also cabin cruisers, although Tran's was the largest. They had become property of the Kingdom of Luong through an obscure transaction with the Socialist Republic of Vietnam, which had inherited them from defunct South Vietnam when the tanks rolled into Saigon in 1975.

They had originally been owned by a fun-loving cabal of South Vietnamese colonels and generals who had somehow cadged them as vital military materiel. They were apparently not obtrusive amongst the millions of dollars per day of aid that inundated the Saigon regime.

The colonels and generals did not utilize the vessels to fire baby depth charges at Vietcong submarines, or whatever the purpose stated on the requisition papers might have been. These fellows, in the parlance of Kiet's adjutant, Captain Binh, were "party animals." They certified the manufacturers' advertisements by cruising the Saigon River with young women who were not their wives and by fishing with hand grenades.

This went on until snipers took the fun out of it. The boats were then dry-docked, and they remained in dry dock until recently, when the RLN began seeking replacements for their aging fleet of similar but smaller ships.

The austere Vietnamese communists dared not float the sleek cabin cruisers. The crafts' scarlet past was common knowledge and anybody who used them would surely be branded a counterrevolutionary and sent to a reeducation camp where no one wore yachting caps and entertained bikini-clad girls. The boats were like new and they were tainted. Kiet assumed the deal had been sweet for Luong.

Although the twenty-five footer had been painted an ugly battleship gray, its stylish lines could not be concealed. Nor had anybody thought to remove the diving board on the bow and the chromium railings. Despite fifty-caliber machine guns emplaced fore and aft, it still looked like it had been made for fun, a suitable home for Binh's party menagerie.

Commandant Tran secured the raft line. He was pear-shaped, in his late thirties, overly serious, and invariably dressed in naval officer whites. He was an avid water-skier, having been introduced to the sport during college study at the tropical American province

12

of Florida. Kiet had seen him once skimming behind one of his warships, wearing wraparound sunglasses and a life jacket around his ample midsection, and decided that he was quite a sight.

Tran liked being addressed as commandant, although it was a toss-up whether he preferred chief of naval operations. In fact, he was a lieutenant commander, the highest rank that could be justified in a landlocked nation with one sleepy river to patrol.

Tran was insecure and ambitious. His movements in handling the rope were typically stiff and grim. For Kiet, he conjured up a constipated albino penguin.

"Superintendent Kiet, thank you for being prompt."

"I know what urgent means, Commandant Tran. I know the what. Can you tell me the why, please?"

Tran extended a hand and helped Kiet aboard. "All engines full," he yelled over a shoulder. "Flank speed."

"Aye aye, skipper," said the sailor sitting in a plush bucket seat at the steering wheel. He shoved twin throttles forward and the boat's nose lifted.

Kiet lurched backward, but grabbed a chromium railing before he toppled overboard.

"Urgent," he said. "Throw me in the water and you can forget your urgent. I do not swim. All I have ever done with water is boil it before I drink it. Talk to me about urgent, Tran."

"Sorry," Tran said. "I forget that you landlubbers have no sea legs. Let's sit."

They sat in the rear, on a padded bench that covered the twin inboard engines. They had to lean forward to talk because of the gunner standing between them, manning a swivel-mounted machine gun. They had to shout because of the full-throttle engine noise. You can have your navy life, Kiet thought.

"We're doing thirty knots," Tran said. "We'll dock in Hickorn in twenty minutes."

"Splendid," Kiet said. "Why do we have to be in Hickorn in twenty minutes?"

13

"My personal staff car is awaiting at the dock. My driver will rush you to the royal palace."

"Splendid. Why do I have to be in Hickorn in twenty minutes to be rushed in your personal staff car to the royal palace?"

"Because His Royal Highness wants to see you."

Kiet groaned. "Why does His Royal Highness want to see me?"

"I am not privy to all the information I should be. I can only guess."

Kiet suspected as much. The chief of naval operations was being employed as an errand boy and he hated it. "Please guess."

Tran swept his arm left and right. "A peaceful setting, isn't it?"

Kiet looked left and right. Flat, brown paddy land as far as he could see. "Peaceful, yes. Dismal too."

"Oh, I'm not referring to the drought. I'm speaking in the context of safety."

"Safety?"

"From danger, from pirates. You wouldn't think to a glance that pirates are a menace, but take my word for it, they are."

Pirates? From where did they lurk in ambush and attack? The land had been worn to the nub by agriculture. An emaciated bandit could hide behind the occasional palm tree, Kiet supposed. He did not reply.

Tran read his silence. "I know what's inside your head, Superintendent. Everybody thinks I exaggerate. You should patrol the Ma San at night. If it weren't for us interdicting the pirates, the barges and ferries couldn't sail the river night or day. Why, two nights ago people from Zhu Vang village were rowing to Tia Nha in a tiny boat to visit relatives. They were going in the evening because of the heat. If not for the good luck of a patrol boat being in the area and intercepting a pirate band, the villagers would have been robbed. The throats of the men would have been slit and the females would have been carried off and raped."

Kiet had a different notion. The likely scenario was a jumpy gunner firing at a noise or a moving shadow, Tran subsequently filing a voluminous report and recommending decorations for

14

heroism. Next day, a peasant would bury his water buffalo before it putrified further, and confront his future very, very afraid.

The fondest hope of Lieutenant Commander Tuon Tran, commandant and chief of naval operations of the Royal Luongan Navy, was to be an admiral. Until he convinced his superiors that considerable expansion of the RLN was necessary, this would not occur. Since there were insufficient numbers of river pirates at which to shoot, Tran was firing salvos of paperwork at the Ministry of Defense.

"Rape and murder," Kiet said. "Terrible. We are fortunate the Royal Luongan Navy never sleeps."

"Exactly," Tran said. "It would not hurt if you relayed that sentiment to His Royal Highness while you have your audience with him."

Kiet sensed an opportunity. "Yes. Certainly. It is obvious that you lack the men and the equipment to carry out your mission to the extent required."

"Helicopters," Tran said, smiling and animated. "Radar and infrared surveillance. We detect pirate activity, we scramble choppers, go in, and vaporize the bastards."

"Scramble?"

"Launch from the carrier. An aircraft carrier," Tran said, flattened palm swooping upward. "A small one for copters."

"Why not a ship that carries jet fighters? Why settle on a small carrier?" Kiet asked, deadpan.

Tran said, "The Ma San is two hundred kilometers long. Fighter planes? Not a *bad* idea, but not budgetarily feasible."

Kiet shrugged, gazed off at paddy infested with sadistic buccaneers, and said, "What do I know? I am no mariner."

"You are insightful. You have a strategic mind."

"I do?" Kiet asked, forcing a smile that pretended delight at the praise.

"You positively do, Superintendent Kiet. You're demonstrating to me the ability to see the situation on a sweeping scale."

Enough, Kiet thought. The flattery was making him nauseous,

as was the boat ride. Luong was a landlocked country, yet he was seasick. The Royal Luongan Navy flagship's engine was screaming and the boat was surging, undulating on the languid surface, slapping it as if jouncing on concrete.

"I will be happy to speak to His Royal Highness concerning you," Kiet said. "On two conditions."

"Name them," Tran cried.

"Slow the boat. I am losing my voice yelling."

Commandant Tran turned to the pilot and cupped his hands. "All back, one quarter!"

"Aye aye, skipper!"

Popeye et al, Kiet thought; the spinach eater led a seafaring life more real than Tran's. "Thank you."

"You're welcome, Superintendent. Except for the urgency, I would have ordered us home at half speed. Landlubbers, no disrespect intended, get seasick in choppy water."

"No, not me," Kiet said. "The second condition is my repeated question, the urgency."

"We're close to port anyway," Tran said, pointing ahead.

The lowered noise was welcomed. The decrease in wind velocity too. Kiet followed the aim of Tran's finger. He could not see Hickorn, but he did see a yellowish haze clinging to the horizon, civilization's signpost.

"Urgency," Kiet said. "I refuse to say that word again."

"You know what I know," Tran said. "As a service commandant, I should be sitting in on joint chiefs conferences. Then I would know what I need to know. I would not have to guess."

"No, I do not know what you know," Kiet said. "I have been at Tia Nha for a week, blissfully isolated from the miracle of modern communications. Please treat me to your guesswork."

"A week," Tran said thoughtfully. "You may not know. The trial and sentence and execution date were set four or five days ago."

"Excuse me? The execution?"

"Yes. It's scheduled for next Monday, May 25."

"Capital punishment was stricken from the Hickorn ordinance book years ago," Kiet reminded him.

"Treason is a federal crime. He was arrested for hoarding and food speculation—"

"Who was arrested?"

"Feng Vu," Tran said.

"The rice broker?"

"Him," Tran said, sneering. "The army, aided ably by a naval detachment, raided a warehouse of his and found tons of rice not listed on his inventory documents. The bastard was licking his lips as the price of rice soared. He hoarded while people starved, waiting for the price to quadruple. Then he'd sell. Feng Vu is unfeeling scum, Kiet. He deserves to die."

Kiet said nothing.

"You and I both know the people want *something* done," Tran continued. "If they cannot have rain, they'll have to settle for blood. Withholding food in a famine earns you a death sentence. Your greed destabilizes your country. They tried Vu the day after they arrested him. The jury found him guilty in thirty minutes. The judge sentenced him to die a week from yesterday."

"Speedy justice," Kiet said. His nausea was recurring. The relapse could not be blamed on rough seas. If he were unable to quell it, he would aim for Tran's white patent leather shoes.

"Correct me if I'm wrong, but regardless of who arrests and convicts, a federal execution is the responsibility of the Hickorn police department, right?"

"True," Kiet said glumly.

"Treason executions are public."

"Yes."

"A firing squad."

"Yes."

"So His Royal Highness no doubt is going to ask you to brief him on your execution plan and protocol. Who is assigned where in the bleachers and whatnot."

Bleachers? "No doubt."

17

"Maybe he isn't," Tran said, nodding solemnly. "There's another situation. I read her column in the paper this morning. You'd be a fool not to anticipate instant ramifications."

"Whose column, please? What ramifications?"

"Madame Saravane's. She saw a comet."

Kiet closed his eyes. The execution had been a horrible surprise. Madame Saravane's sighting was potentially much worse.

THREE

The eighty-year-old man stroked his chin as he gave the triangular cluster of balls a quick study. He chalked his cue stick, aligned it to the white cue ball on a platform of bony fingers, and shot. The ball struck the tip of the triangle with an explosive clap. Balls scattered on the green felt, bumping cushions. The man's follow-through was vicious. His stick arced upward, banging the Tiffany lamp, swaying it, casting psychedelic shadows. Two balls fell into pockets.

The elderly man was short and slight, but deceptively alert and strong. He began to gather the balls and said, "I apologize if I startled you, Bosha. I'm practicing breaks. Nine ball is my specialty, but next month the brother of the Sultan of Yogyakarta is visiting. Although it is not a state visit, he is an important Indonesian and a fine man besides. He's a devotee of straight pool, bless him, and fifteen balls are proportionally harder to scatter than nine. The gentleman shoots a good stick. No point in looking silly if you can help it, is there?"

The billiards player was Prince Novisad Pakse, ruler of the Kingdom of Luong. "Bosha" was Bamsan Kiet, Hickorn Superintendent of Police. They were at the royal palace, in the royal billiards room, a grand rococo chamber centered precisely by the billiards table. Captain Binh, an automobile buff, had once told Kiet that the slate table outweighed on Olds 98.

"Bosha" was colloquial Luongan for "runt," which Kiet had been until late adolescence when his pituitary gland petcock lodged in the open position, giving him a vantage point over his contemporaries and eighteen months of bones and joints that ached so badly that he couldn't sleep. Few people any longer remembered the diminutive; fewer dared repeat it. That His Royal Highness did flushed Kiet with pride, scorching his neck under the collar.

"No, Your Highness," Kiet said. "Commandant Tran mentioned an urgency."

Pakse racked the balls. He had no excess whatsoever. His skin was so taut that at points of prominence such as his jawline it was translucent. He said, "Did Tran ask you to bend me?"

"Yes, Your Highness."

"To put in a good word?"

"Yes sir."

"Everybody who Tran sees immediately before they see me come laden with requests. What, Bosha?"

"An armada commanded by Admiral Tran."

"The usual," Pakse said. He shot. The cue ball collided with force, but accomplished minimal disruption to the wedge and skipped off the table.

Pakse winced and retrieved the ball. "This is why I need the practice, Bosha. I'm lofting my shot and striking the one-ball too high. Helicopters?"

"Yes, Your Highness."

Pakse shook his head. "Tran and his pirates. Were you attacked?"

"Fortunately not. My voyages to and from Tia Nha were in the daytime, the latter under naval escort."

Pakse smiled. "Bosha, whether you realize it or not, you have a wicked sense of humor. I apologize for abbreviating your furlough. Unless it were an emergency, I would not have."

Kiet knew this to be true. Which emergency, he wondered? The drought was ongoing, a conceivable nightmare. Then there were Tuon Tran's revelations. The death sentence imposed upon Feng Vu, the rice broker. The comet seen by Madame Saravane, Luong's preeminent mystic.

"The subject is painful, Bosha."

20

The drought, Kiet thought. Had to be. His Royal Highness anticipating food riots in the streets of Hickorn. "The monsoon has been late before, Your Highness. The rains haven't bypassed Luong two consecutive seasons since—"

"Not that, Bosha. I refuse to fret about something over which I have no control. And the matter is out of my hands, in spite of what some people might believe."

Kiet assumed Prince Pakse was referring to the Luongans who associated their monarch too literally to the mandate of heaven. He ruled with the blessings of the forces of the universe, ergo he had godlike influence. Perhaps the supreme powers refused to pass along their tricks to any earthly king, but they had been historically willing to take out their anger on the subjects. Pakse could speak to Him, It, They, yes?

Earthquakes and floods were bursts of temper, the agnostic Kiet mused. An Almighty's tantrums. A drought was something else again. A drought was slow and measured. A drought was the handiwork of an eternal being with a mean streak.

Luong was a superstitious land, rife with astrologers and numerologists and geomancers and seers and healers and mystics and soothsayers and fortune tellers. You could have evil spirits driven from a loved one or a curse cast on an enemy. There were tellers of the future and suppliers of potions. For a price a vision could be interpreted from the stars, or from chicken entrails. Sheer nonsense, thought Bamsan Kiet.

"Tran informed me that Madame Saravane saw a comet and wrote about the experience."

Prince Pakse sighed, hung up his cue, and sat down. Kiet took a chair and sat opposite him. His Royal Highness looked suddenly tired, as if the sum of his responsibilities had collapsed on him.

"Bosha, Madame wrote and wrote. No astronomer in the world reported Madame's comet, but Madame sees what we mortals do not. The comet portended an ominous future, she said. It crossed the ascending Scorpio on an unpropitious day of the month. Luong is steering a doomsday course."

Madame Saravane's popular following included readers of her

21

column in the *Hickorn Enquiring Mind*, a tabloid and Luong's second-best selling newspaper. Captain Binh said that the *Mind* blatantly ripped off Western scandal sheets. The "supermarket press" he oddly termed it. Their journalistic bailiwick was the woman carrying a space alien baby, spanking judges, and the current activities of Elvis.

"Madame Saravane interprets her visions into predictions too vague to bite her when time proves them wrong, Your Highness. I would not worry."

"Madame and her mysterious comet were uncommonly specific, Bosha. The comet was an angry sign, the taking of offense by whatever is up there. Leadership is the irritant, leadership is at fault."

Kiet groaned. "She is blaming you for the drought?"

"Not in those words. Madame has a slippery pen."

"I should arrest the hag for sedition."

"No, Bosha. Madame, the martyr, would write pure bile from jail and smuggle it out. A cult could form around her and take to the streets."

"You're probably right," Kiet said. "She has too many disciples already. I hope that blame and blood do not become habitual partners."

"Blame and blood. A subtle segue to the topic of Feng Vu, Bosha?"

Kiet nodded.

"Feng Vu is a despicable person."

"He is that. He is also Chinese."

Prince Pakse shrugged. "A scapegoat? Racial tension has always existed between Luongans and Chinese. That is a share of it, but Vu's warehouse was legally searched. Tons of surplus rice was seized. Luongans are hungry and he was hoarding, laying it aside until the price soared yet higher. He violated a federal law, per se. He was given due process."

"Swift due process, Your Highness."

"My nephew saw to that," Prince Pakse said sourly. Prince

22

Pakse's nephew was Minister of Agriculture Houphong Duc, a natty little man in his mid-thirties. "I abhor capital punishment as much as you, and I was delighted when it was abolished in municipal Hickorn, but the national assembly was unanimously opposed to reducing the punishment for treason. Public opinion, I fear, was overwhelmingly on their side.

"Bosha, I have not ruled since independence by often defying the preferences of the majority. I stayed out of it. This is the rare instance when a crime is so heinous that a blood thirst must be slaked. I will not, however, attend the execution."

Kiet regarded Duc as pretentious, a pseudo-intellectual with soft hands who romanticized farming. He had studied in France and the United States, and had been awarded a master's degree in business administration from an American province of Florida university. An "MBA," Captain Binh called it. If you have an MBA, he said, "You've got it made in the shade."

Prince Pakse smiled. "Bosha, you are quiet. I can read your mind. You're thinking about my nephew. Well, I am not fond of the brat either. Nepotism is no virtue, but sometimes a necessity. I have improved in that regard, have I not?"

"You have," Kiet said truthfully. There was a time when every important Luongan office was held by a relative of Prince Pakse. He had naively believed that kinship assured loyalty, but it seemed that every relation not totally incompetent lusted after the throne. There was constant intrigue until Pakse weeded out the most dangerous aspirants.

Enough blood relations were retained to divide family appointees into equal camps of haves and have-nots. In this way, no powerful family coalition could be formed. The have-nots would inform on the haves before their first conspiratorial meeting concluded.

His Royal Highness was a natural compromiser, Kiet thought approvingly. He was a born neutralizer and a born neutralist. His mother must have given birth atop a fence.

"In some respects, he isn't so bad," Pakse said. "Unlike other family members of mine, he isn't stupid and he has an education. Presumably he has read a book or two."

"Your Highness, may I speak frankly, please?"

"I insist that you do, Bosha."

"In his two years at the post, Minister Duc has done little. If he orchestrated the Feng Vu arrest and conviction, it is the first direct action I am aware of. He has no solutions. He plays politics. He is taking advantage of the drought and has made it a political forum. He gives interviews and lectures on Luongan agriculture. He advocates begging for humanitarian foreign aid. He and his ministry would hold control of aid monies and foodstuffs, naturally."

"A plea for aid is a last resort," Pakse said firmly. "Oh, some volunteer aid has trickled in from organizations who have the wisdom not to precede it with trumpets and press conferences. To those kind generous people I am grateful. Most foreign gifts have strings attached that trail back to their capitals. They yank the string and you are dragged along by your nose. Until we have a genuine emergency we do not need them."

"Minister Duc is excessively technical and abstract. Nothing he says ever becomes a deed. Your Highness, the price of rice and politics are inseparable in Luong. By executing Feng Vu he is hinting that speculation and hoarding will cease and that prices will drop."

"What if they don't?"

"Then Duc did what he could," Kiet said. "He had the courage to take a stand. Forces beyond his control prevailed. The weather. Skulduggery outside of his ability to thwart."

"Skulduggery? Who?"

Kiet shrugged. "Other Chinese brokers—future candidates for execution. People in government. Foreigners. Lieutenant Commander Tran's river pirates. Who knows? Duc plays to fears and prejudices."

"Me, an accused skulduggerist too?"

"Perhaps."

Prince Pakse laughed. "Perhaps. Perhaps he wants my job. If

24

he does, he is crazy. No, Bosha. The boy has ambitions. I'm not exactly sure what they are, but I don't imagine my throne is one."

Kiet was growing impatient for what Captain Binh would describe as "the bottom line." "Your Highness, Tran guessed that the purpose of our urgent meeting was execution protocol."

"Did he mention the erection of bleachers and seating assignments?"

"Yes."

"He's been talking to my nephew. Houphong is acting like it will be the World Cup soccer championship. No, Bosha. The arrangements are entirely up to you. You have supreme authority. As superintendent of the Hickorn police department, you are Luong's senior civilian law enforcement officer. You are in charge by statute. I could appoint a replacement, but you are the best man for the job. You will ensure that it doesn't erode into a spectacle."

Kiet closed his eyes. *Entirely up to you.* Which encompassed selecting the site, assigning volunteer patrolmen to shoot guns at Feng Vu, and giving the command to fire. He, himself, nobody else—standing alone like a circus ringmaster. Barking orders. Authorizing his men to kill a fat, helpless, blindfolded Chinese.

"Bosha, you appear restless."

"I do?" Kiet said innocently.

"Your eyes were shut for several seconds and you are fidgeting. You haven't seen your lady friend yet, have you? No, how could you? I practically kidnapped you. Quin Canh, is it not?"

Quin, indeed. The space she had occupied in his thoughts at Tia Nha had multiplied day by day. It occurred to him that Prince Pakse mistook his mental departure as a sexual fantasy. He blushed and said, "Quin, yes. I am very anxious, Your Highness."

Prince Pakse stood, retrieved his cue, chalked it, and said, "You are justifiably anxious. She is a lovely woman. I have delayed explaining what is uppermost in my ancient head because it is relatively trifling. Our kingdom is in peril and I'm selfishly preoccupied."

The prince hesitated. He continued chalking his cue. His back

25

was to Kiet, who thought His Royal Highness might wear his stick through the cube of blue chalk. In Luong, if you introduced a topic while unable to make eye contact, you were in the throes of humiliation and despair. Kiet held his breath.

"My alleged son," Pakse finally said.

"Excuse me?"

"My reputed son."

Kiet wondered whether to play dumb. In the early 1960s, His Royal Highness had participated in a Paris billiards tournament. He had met a Frenchwoman, an olive-skinned Gallic beauty, and had enjoyed a torrid two-week affair. The instant he stepped onto the Air France Caravelle jet and departed Paris, never to return, the relationship terminated. Rumor had it that Pakse had fallen hopelessly in love with her. The night before his departure, he had purchased an engagement ring with a diamond the size of a molar.

Although he had been eliminated from the tournament she had counted on him hanging around as a spectator, not arriving at her home as early as he had. Prince Pakse hoped to surprise, but it was he who was surprised. She was with another man, and that was that. His Royal Highness learned then what everyone else knew, that she was opportunistic and promiscuous.

The woman was an erstwhile countess who married well and divorced better. She had married seven men and divorced six to date. An international banker, an aerospace manufacturer, a prominent winegrower, and a NATO general were among them. They were, on average, twenty years her senior.

A single offspring resulted from the unions, a boy who was born nine months and one week after the Caravelle departed Orly. Prince Pakse, stung by the woman's infidelity, denied fatherhood.

The Frenchwoman was shrill. She threatened a variety of embarrassments. Without admitting fatherhood, Pakse wisely reached a financial settlement. All was quiet until recently, when the child sued in a French court to establish legal paternity—and won.

Prince Pakse's refusal to testify or to even supply a deposition made the opposition's task easy. He had buried his head in the sand. When he came up for air, he was a proud father. That the boy was obviously Eurasian made defense tactics futile anyhow, Kiet supposed.

Since the boy, named Jean-Guy Pakse, was of legal age, no child at all, actually approaching thirty, his mother had no monetary interest in his courtroom maneuverings and certainly none whatsoever in his alleged biological father. She had her own life. Her present husband was a retired American stock brokerage tycoon, a Wall Street magnate. According to the *Hickorn Enquiring Mind*, he was "the sweetest of her seven sugar daddies". *Mère* and her new beau were busily spending the nest egg. Deliriously happily, so advised the *Mind*.

"Jean-Guy is coming to Hickorn, Bosha."

"Why?"

"He claims to yearn for his Luongan heritage. He claims he is coming home."

"Do you believe him, Your Highness?"

"No."

Neither did Kiet. Jean-Guy had a playboy reputation. Extremely spoiled and rakishly handsome, he was an aficionado of fast cars and faster women. Ferraris and blondes, respectively.

"He is coming expressly to see you, Your Highness?"

Pakse shook his head vigorously. He was looking at Kiet again and his eyes were red. "I have not been thusly notified. Rude but irrelevant. I don't care what the Paris court decreed. He is not my son!"

Prince Pakse had had three wives. He was widowed, divorced, and widowed, in that order. The marriages produced no heirs to the throne. Until the French judge wagged a judicial finger, Pakse had been officially childless, unluckily saddled with barren wives.

Kiet thought it ironic that he and His Royal Highness, two mature men who through the years had generously donated their sperm, had conceived one alleged baby between them. Captain Binh had said that just because they were "shooting blanks" they

27

were no less masculine. No sir. Captain Binh then tapped on his wooden desktop and thanked his lucky stars.

A greater irony was Prince Pakse's denial of paternity. Here was the child, the successor, the crown prince he never had. It was the Frenchwoman, Kiet felt. Thirty years had gone by and His Royal Highness continued to love her with all his heart and to hate her with all his heart.

"What are his intentions, Your Highness?"

"I don't know."

"Money?"

"No. His mother is wealthy. She attached herself like the leech she is to her husbands and drained them. She indulged her son. He has money."

"I imagine he will wish to see you."

Prince Pakse racked the balls. "That is impossible."

"Excuse me?"

"Impossible. I am not going to receive him."

Prince Pakse shot. No balls dropped into pockets, though they scattered and the cue ball did not skitter off the table. He said, "An acceptable break, distractions considered."

"What do you want me to do, Your Highness?"

"Whoever he is, whoever his father is, he is a celebrity. Protect him, Bosha."

"And baby-sit him?"

Prince Pakse gathered the balls and smiled. "Oh, you know me too well, Bosha. Yes. Keep him out of harm's way—and out of mine."

"How is he traveling?"

"A private charter flight. He is traveling secretly."

"Why?"

"Because he's considerate? Because he was raised by his loving mother to be a thoughtful young man and to save his homeland from a circus scene? I don't know, Bosha. I really do not have an inkling."

Prince Pakse shot. The balls scattered as if exploded. *Four dis-*

28

appeared into pockets. The Indonesian would have no chance if His Royal Highness played with such ferocity. But His Royal Highness's break was not a billiards shot, Kiet knew. His cue was his penis and he was penetrating Jean-Guy Pakse's mother.

"When is he coming?"

"Tomorrow," Prince Pakse said.

Kiet's mouth went slack.

"Urgent, Bosha. That is why I told Tran *urgent*."

FOUR

Avenue Alexandre Loubet honored a nineteenth-century French priest who romanized the Luongan language. The Chinese-like ideograms of old Luongan were incomprehensible to Europeans and therefore pagan. A Christian bible demanded a Christian alphabet. The conversion was made and the word of God was taken to the natives, thus saving innumerable souls from eternal damnation.

The address of Hickorn police department headquarters was 900 Avenue Alexandre Loubet. Two stories of bulky unadorned stucco, it had served for half a century as barracks and headquarters for Indochina Legionnaires. Its interior was dim and stale, bordering on seedy, the era of French hegemony frozen in time and grime. The place smelled of history and nervous perspiration. Acoustics were strange; footsteps echoed like the boots of ghost soldiers. You could almost hear the arrogant banter and crisp commands, and, toward the end of French rule in Southeast Asia, the softer voices of men relieved to be posted at Hickorn instead of Dien Bien Phu.

Kiet had more than once overheard a visitor to headquarters look around and mutter "creepy." This he regarded as a compliment. He had no intention of tampering with the no-nonsense message the place gave his police officers and reluctant guests alike.

"Superintendent! You're a week early."

Captain Binh was in Kiet's office, at his desk, but no longer in his chair. At the sight of his superior he sprang out of it as if it were afire.

"I was summoned," Kiet said.

"There were those rumors in the grapevine, Superintendent. His Royal Highness was said to have called you home to prepare for the execution. Hey, no sweat. I'm right on top of it."

"That was not the reason."

Binh frowned. How the lad hated to be wrong. He was young, supple, and eager. Dressed in his customary white uniform, his trouser creases were machete sharp. On shoulder boards, gold captain's pips sparkled like jewelry. A Colt .45 automatic was holstered in black patent leather. Kiet could see his reflection in Binh's shoes. What Binh saw was a somewhat wilted and rumpled middle-aged man in sandals, slacks, and white shirt.

Six months ago they had happened upon a ragged, sad-eyed young man shoplifting dried squid at the public market. They nabbed him and it turned out he was an impoverished poet.

The poet gave them a haughty perusal and said they couldn't be policemen, couldn't arrest him. They were human antonyms. Kiet and Binh hauled him in, regardless. The label stuck with Kiet. Human antonyms. He liked it.

"Superintendent, what was the reason?"

"Brief me on Feng Vu, please."

"Well, it was a fed collar. Minister of Agriculture Duc orchestrated the whole ball of wax. He got MPs and a swabbie unit to raid Vu's warehouse and bust his fat ass. They charged, tried, and sentenced him before you could say J. Edgar Hoover. Wham, bam, sorry 'bout your appeal, Sam."

Kiet suppressed a groan. Binh was again lapsing into American cops and robbers slang. He had trained for a year at the United States of America national capital, with their District of Columbia constabulary. He had returned to Hickorn gushing tales of computerized APBs, radio-equipped squad cars, and plea bargaining.

"Vu gets ventilated next Monday, you know."

"I can hardly wait."

"Me neither!" Binh said.

32

Kiet's sarcasm missed cleanly. "Captain—"

"There's beaucoup left to do. Minister Duc has volunteered the resources of his office, but I'd rather we did it ourselves. Now, if it's okay with you, Superintendent, that park four blocks west of here on Loubet at Mu Pakse and Rue Ne Win?"

"A nice park."

"Yeah, well, I figured it would work. It's a full city block and mostly grass and paths. We could contract to have some quickie bleachers—"

"No bleachers. His Royal Highness and I oppose bleachers."

"I guess that's why Minister Duc said we could scratch National Stadium."

"Indeed."

"That fountain in the middle where the water cascades down those big rocks?"

"A sculpture," Kiet said.

"Yeah, except it doesn't look like anything. Whatever it is, one side is pretty flat, straight up and down. We could stack sandbags up against it."

"Splendid," Kiet said. "By all means."

That gibe also sailed past Captain Binh's head. "It's the roomiest side too. We don't want people out in the streets blocking traffic. We could squeeze six or seven hundred in. Some of the sight lines would be lousy, but everyone could see something. The thing is, how do you monitor it? Thousands of people will want to attend. VIPs have to have choice seats."

"Seats?"

"Not bleachers. I was thinking folding chairs for the high mucky-mucks."

Kiet shook his head. "No chairs."

Binh's eyes widened. "Superintendent, Prince Pakse cannot be expected to stand!"

"His royal Highness has other plans that day."

Binh sighed dramatically. "Okay. Fine. The bigshots can stand but they have to stand up front."

"Absolutely," Kiet said.

33

"The problem is, how do we regulate the flow? Everybody and his brother will be trying to squeeze close in. I'm afraid there'll be some rowdy elements, some boozers and wiseasses and rabble-rousers."

"At an execution?" Kiet said incredulously. "We certainly cannot tolerate riffraff. We cannot allow hooligans to ruin the dignity of the occasion. Perhaps engraved invitations are the answer."

This cynical salvo thumped Binh directly between the eyes. "Superintendent, I know you don't believe in capital punishment, but that's no excuse to impede my plans. We really have a lot to do before Monday."

"Sorry," Kiet said.

"Since we're on the death penalty, if you ask me we should reinstate it for murder too. You'll have to admit, it's one helluva deterrent."

Kiet had *not* asked Binh. Nor did he feel a firing squad deterred anybody but the guest of honor, who could commit no additional crimes while dead.

"Captain, please, a moral debate will be lengthy and passionate. Neither will convince the other. We'll waste time and we'll stay angry for the rest of the day."

"Superintendent, Feng Vu is a scumbag."

Kiet said nothing.

"Rice shortages are growing critical. After an example is made of Vu, his kind will think twice before—"

Kiet silenced Binh with a raised hand. "Captain, let me end the discussion by saying that my objection to Feng Vu's execution is based as much on common sense as conscience."

"Huh?"

"Feng Vu dies and his colleagues will be frightened out of their wits, yes?"

"Damn right they will!"

"They will be so frightened that they will accelerate their speculating, transfer the profits to overseas banks faster, and perhaps eventually flee Luong."

"Good riddance to bad rubbish."

"The Chinese and Indians are the merchant classes of under-developed tropical countries, are they not? The engines of the economy?"

Binh nodded. "It sure does seem like they manipulate things, yeah."

"As much as we resent ethnic outsiders controlling our commerce and fattening themselves at our expense, what happens when they leave?"

Binh shrugged.

"After coups d'etat in Uganda and Burma, the ethnic minority tradesmen were forced into exile. The market economies disintegrated. The nations became economically medieval."

"We'll fill the vacuum, Superintendent. This is Hickorn, not Rangoon. Luongans land on their feet."

Binh was retreating behind a wall of clichés and patriotism, ready to fight to the polemical death. Kiet sighed and said, "Very well, Captain. Have it your way."

"We're in the grip of a famine, Superintendent."

"Not yet. No famine yet. Please do not utter that word."

"Soon, Superintendent. We're getting there posthaste. People are hungry and food prices are too high. Those Chinese are out for themselves."

"Conceded."

"We're getting there, Superintendent. We're approaching the 'F' word you ordered me not to utter mucho quicko. Feng Vu and his kind are getting richer by the day."

"Captain—"

"Whether anybody likes it or not, the sentence was handed down and Feng Vu dies in six days."

"Yes, yes."

"Which puts us in a time crunch, Superintendent. The nuts and bolts of an execution are more complicated than you might realize. We've got to recruit shooters from the ranks of our best marksmen. Almost every man on the force volunteered. There are going to be some hurt feelings, those who're aced out. You, personally, being in command, have to follow procedures. I'd advise a rehearsal."

Splendid, Kiet thought, we can kill Feng Vu in practice also. Bamsan Kiet's deepest secret was his aversion to blood and gore. At the sight of violent death, he became dizzy and nauseous. He was virtually useless at a murder scene. He would inspect the victim while squinting his eyes out of focus, then remove his attention from the corpse as soon as he could.

A practice execution he could cope with. But the real thing? Would he as police superintendent be expected to administer a coup de grace, a bullet to the back of Feng Vu's head? He queried his unconscious mind: Were his objections to capital punishment selfish and hypocritical rather than pragmatic and ethical? If he fired his breakfast at Vu instead of a lead slug, the humiliation, the loss of face would be beyond human comprehension. His inner self did not reply, and that was just as well.

Kiet changed the subject. "Madame Saravane wrote an inflammatory column in the *Mind*, I understand."

"I don't normally read that rag," Binh said. "I read it when police business requires me to."

A necessary preliminary, Kiet knew. A disclaimer. The trashy periodical was unfashionable among upwardly mobile Hickornites, but most read it, at least portions that appealed to a specific interest.

Captain Binh was single, a lady's man who proclaimed monogamous intentions, who tumbled hopelessly in love twice a month. Kiet had more than once surprised him in his office as Binh was underlining passages in the classified personals column. *Scanning for suspects who match felony warrants, Superintendent. Yes, splendid, continue the good work.* Felony suspects who were single Luongan females, age twenty-five, desiring to meet sincere, professional gentleman, et cetera.

Kiet, a closet reader too, though intermittently, regarded the tabloid as entertainment. Midgets birthing triplets and homosexual Martians were wonderful escapism.

"Did you by any slim chance make an exception and read it on the day that column was printed?"

"*Everybody* read it, Superintendent. I was informed by someone who had and, yes, I read it myself. Inflammatory is too mild a word."

"She blamed His Royal Highness for the drought?"

"Not verbatim, but you could easily draw that conclusion. Her and her goddamn comet. Superintendent, we ought to throw that grungy old bitch in irons."

"Is she advocating a leadership change?"

"Well, her gods or whatever the hell it is she consults, they wouldn't lose any sleep if there was a coup or a royal reshuffle."

"Which raises a vital question."

"Is she being prompted?"

"Exactly."

Binh shrugged. "It would seem so, but I don't know by whom. She's a nutbar, but she's always listened to her own drummer. She doesn't stick her neck out unless there's something in it for Madame. I can't picture her in cahoots with anyone, but I guess I'm gonna have to rethink that point."

"Indeed."

"Next question. With whom? Answer. Damned if I know. My ear's to the ground, Superintendent. If that old douche bag is playing politics, I'll find out. That's why His Royal Highness brought you home from furlough, isn't it? He's got to be a little afraid of her, Madame and her curses. Madame the healer. Ha! She can give you cancer and she can cure it. If you ask me, unless she has you psychologically whipped, she couldn't cure a hangnail. Her curses are a joke too. She couldn't make a bird crap on your car."

"I agree, but thousands of faithful would call us reckless fools."

Binh shook his head. "Go figure."

Kiet summarized his conference with Prince Pakse.

Binh's eyes widened. "Jean-Guy coming to Hickorn? You gotta be putting me on."

"Putting you on what, please?"

"Shucking me. You know, jiving me."

Oysters and swing music? Kiet looked at him, musing sadly how a single year in America of colloquialisms and lazy speech had linguistically stunted him.

"Sorry. Guess I slip into the informal when a bulletin knocks me on my keester."

"Indeed. And the slippage continues. You are disputing Jean-Guy Pakse's motives?"

"Sure am, Superintendent. He's an item in the Hickorn press, and not just in the *Mind*. The legit media goes bonkers over him too. Jean-Guy gets more ink than Madonna and Tom Cruise rolled together."

Kiet had never heard of either of those presumed celebrities, although the first may have been a religious figure, a Western world television preacher perhaps. No matter. "The secrecy puzzles His Royal Highness."

Binh looked suspiciously at Kiet. "Wait a second. It's starting to sink in. Prince Pakse assigned us to protect his son?"

"Alleged son."

"They got His Royal Highness dead on the blood tests, Superintendent. No 'alleged' about it."

"Judging by what you have read, what do you think of the young man?"

"I think I don't much like the idea of the media calling him crown prince, although he technically is. He's never set foot in Luong."

"Your general impressions of him, please."

"Well, of course I don't know him personally. I don't need to. He's a spoiled brat. He's never done a day's work in his life. He's useless as tits on a boar."

"Jean-Guy is an authority on Italian sports cars," Kiet said, attempting to be casual.

Binh was a car buff who had still not forgiven Kiet for selling their previous department staff car, a red Mazda RX-7 convertible confiscated when its former owner, an opium-dealing gangster, had retired from a life of crime because of his sudden death. He had died from a bullet wound to the head beside the automobile. Better than inside it where blood would have permanently stained the upholstery, said Binh. The only decent thing the dude did in his scumbag life.

"He digs Ferraris, Superintendent. Sure, that definitely indicates that he has taste. Then again, it's a snap to have taste if you've got the bread. C'mon. Protection? What are we talking about there?"

Kiet cleared his throat. On the taxi ride from the royal palace, Kiet had searched his vocabulary for euphemisms. "Captain," he said, "How would you like an added challenge, a greater responsibility?"

"Uh, Superintendent, just before your departure on furlough you appointed me department procurement officer. I appreciate your faith in me."

"You deserved the appointment," Kiet said. "You are maturing splendidly, possessing abilities and potential that—"

"Excuse me, Superintendent. In all due respect, can we cut the crapola?"

"Captain, it is my pleasure to appoint you as special security liaison."

"Shit," Binh said. "You're making me baby-sit him. How long?"

Kiet sighed. "You may join His Royal Highness and me in wishing we knew."

FIVE

Captain Binh retired to his office to sulk.

Kiet anemically assaulted the paperwork that had swollen in piles on his desk like malignant tumors. He couldn't force himself to plod through the memoranda and documents. He despised the paper aspect of the job any time, and since he was still officially on furlough, doubly so.

Make that triply so. Binh was sulking loudly, destroying Kiet's fragile concentration. He could be heard quite plainly through bunkerlike walls, slamming file cabinet drawers, yelling into the telephone, kicking his wastebasket.

Please, Kiet thought. He trudged out of his office. It was late in the day and he was through. Should be through, that is. Should be buying flowers and surprising Quin. A left turn and he would be outside, looking for a flower vendor and his love. But he veered right instead, grunting as he pulled the iron handle of a massive door.

He went in a small anteroom, location of jail dispatch, and returned the head jailer's salute. He paused as the jailer, a sergeant, jumped up from a stool where he was reading a gun magazine, unlocked an inner door, and swung it open for his superintendent.

Kiet nodded thank you and entered a narrow corridor, which bisected communal cells. They were at average capacity, about two-thirds full, approximately eleven men per. The noise—shouts, curses, and unintelligible jabbering—was a din. The cell block smelled awful.

Kiet, however, detected no unusual anxiety in the clamor and whiffed no putrefying flesh, an irrefutable clue to mayhem. His guests were, yes, unhappy—should they be kept in a state of euphoria?—but they were being treated acceptably humanely and were behaving in kind.

At eleven men to a cell, you had the roster of a soccer side, though barely the space of a goal mouth. But they weren't stacked like cordwood either, as he had heard they frequently were in Western jails with their drug addicts. And as far as Kiet was concerned, the enforced community living was perhaps beneficial to sullen criminals who had been deprived of formative social contact earlier in their miserable lives. Western penal critics and their Black Hole of Calcutta quips regarding Southeast Asian detention facilities had a lot of room to talk!

Kiet was not ashamed of his jail but it was nonetheless making him sick. At the far end of the corridor was another door. He hurried through it into an isolated block of single cells. An average Luongan adult could extend his arms and touch walls. The bunks were sheets of plywood the dimensions of coffin bottoms. Toilets were holes in concrete. There were no windows and bare light bulbs in the hall burned around the clock, like an Arctic summer.

Prisoners in the general population would give anything for such spacious comfort, although they, by and large petty criminals, did not envy the offenses charged to colleagues in luxurious isolation. Murder, rape, armed robbery. As comparatively swanky as the private cells were, the sentences would be interminably long, therewith removing some luster from the accommodations.

The isolated block presently housed but one inmate. He would not be there interminably. He would vacate his cell next Monday morning. Not a man in the main cell block envied him.

Kiet motioned the officer on suicide watch to leave. A callow youth, the officer was unnaturally haggard and visibly pleased at the break. Kiet knew the prisoner's zeal and skill for verbal abuse.

The prisoner smiled an icy smile and said, "See, Kiet, I'm still alive. No blood on my wrists. No bedsheets tied around my neck.

42

This boy is doing his job. I mustn't cheat the ghoulish. I mustn't cheat you."

"You aren't," Kiet said. "But thank you for your concern."

"You were away from Hickorn. You missed the excitement, didn't you?" Feng Vu said. "Luongan justice moved in a dizzying blur of efficiency and vengeance."

Feng Vu squatted at the center of his cell. If he had been upright before, he surely dropped to his haunches when Kiet approached. It was as if he were receiving an underling or supplicant in his office. Feng Vu rose to his feet for no man unless there was something in it for him. Kiet said, "So I am told."

Feng Vu laughed. "I won't cheat you, Kiet. I love my life too much to extinguish it voluntarily. That deed shall be left to you. I studied the law. The ordinance binds you to put a pistol bullet in my head after the riflemen have their fun. You love me as much as most Luongans do. Aren't you looking forward to it?"

Vu's laugh was mocking. Kiet couldn't help but think that the Chinese had intuited his secret squeamishness. Vu penetrated you with his eyes and his mirthless cheer. He was a man who tore secrets from your essence and spent them like loose change.

Kiet pictured himself at parade rest in Vu's office. "Get up," he said. "Get on your feet."

"Oh, are you going to beat me? You can't wait for your coup de grace to hurt me? Ah, but by then I will feel no pain. Torture and flog me now, Kiet?"

Kiet looked him up and down. Vu was an obese bull, a brute with thick wrists and skin creases where a neck would normally reside. His scalp was bare. At age forty, he had not experienced premature baldness. His hairstyle was intentional, depilatory, strand by painful strand plucked, along with his whiskers. It saved him the time of a daily shave, time better utilized to make money.

The noncoiffure suited him. It increased his menace quotient; a potential for volatility was usually advantageous in shady business dealings. Feng Vu looked to Kiet like the Chinese villain in

43

political thrillers filmed before the Nixon rapprochement, when the People's Republic was Red China, a heartless empire of ChiComs and yellow hordes. He was the heavy who would, if permitted by the scriptwriters, joyously garrote the male lead and launch the ICBMs.

"I am not going to touch you, Vu. Squatting is bad for the leg circulation of fat people like you and me. We cannot have you contracting gangrene."

Feng Vu did not move. "My legs amputated, you leaning me up on my stumps for the firing squad. That would not look good for the kingdom, murdering a cripple, would it? I like you looking down at me in this manner, Kiet. You could square your shoulders, though, and clasp your hands behind your back."

Feng Vu, scooping out your secrets. Kiet groaned and said, "Very well, I will invite your chaperon back in. I will ask him to bring friends. I presume you have been a delight to everyone who has been in contact with you during your stay as our guest. They will be happy to assist you."

Vu leaped to his feet, shockingly agile for his age and bulk. He laughed again and said, "See what happens when you ask politely, Kiet? All right, we are face to face. You're still looking down at me, but now because you are taller, and that is to your benefit, isn't it? We are acting silly, aren't we, like diplomats bickering over the shape of the negotiating table? I promise to grow up if you do."

Kiet said, "I came to listen to your version."

Vu smirked. "And find a loophole, prove my innocence, and save me?"

"The process is out of my control. I am merely curious."

Vu's mouth had seized in a hateful grin. "Read the transcripts and the arrest reports. You have access. Why bother me in my final days? Curious is a synonym for morbid."

"You withheld foodstuffs from the marketplace despite extreme shortages. You hoarded rice while the price shot up like holiday fireworks. Troops raided your warehouse and found the evidence.

44

People could starve and the rice would go moldy for all you cared. The grain would not be released until it reached whatever cost per kilo you desired."

Kiet stared at Vu, silently requesting a reply. Yes or no, true of false, guilty or innocent?

Feng Vu folded his arms, puckered his lips, and turned his head. Kiet remembered filmclips of Mussolini, on a balcony, posing, offended, pouting as a prelude to the disclosure of some injustice or another he would rectify with bombs and soldiers. It was uncanny, the resemblance. Add a fascist uniform and round eyes and he could pass for Il Duce.

"Us Chinese in Southeast Asia, Kiet, what is it we are known as?"

Kiet shook his head no.

"Don't pretend ignorance, Kiet. Vietnam, Indonesia, Luong, Malaysia. Chinese residents of substance, successful hardworking types, there is a phrase for us. You know."

"I didn't come here for a lecture on racism," Kiet said.

"Aha! You admit it."

"I admit nothing. I came for information, not a sociological berating."

"If you won't say it, Kiet, I shall. The Jews of Asia. We are ambitious and we love a profit more than a fuck. The Jews of Asia. It rolls off Luongan lips as if they had just licked the sidewalk. Jews. Hitler said the word the same. That madman Libyan and the homicidal priest who ruled Iran, they said the word the same, like their tongues were coated with dog shit. We would sell our mothers, we would rob graves, we would do anything for money. Jew. Jew. Jew of Asia. Is that so, Kiet? Is it?"

"That does not apply to every Chinese. That does not apply across the board to any race. In your case, Vu, perhaps. You *would* sell your mother."

"My mother is dead."

Kiet smiled warmly. "All the simpler. Hire a coolie with a shovel."

45

"You cannot insult me, Kiet. I have been debased every day of my life."

"Feng Vu, an ethnic martyr?" Kiet said, eyebrows raised. "Are you the wealthiest person in Luong? Gossip asserts that you are."

"What goal is worthier?" Vu said, spreading his arms.

"Besides being the biggest rice broker in the country, you have done splendidly in real estate."

Vu raised a finger. "Buy low, sell high. Remember that wisdom, Kiet."

"The new Luong InterPresidential Hotel—"

"Luong's finest."

"As you wish. You owned the land—"

"Bought low, sold high. Kiet, do you want a financial statement? I also own grain barges, a fleet of pedicabs—"

"Which you rent exorbitantly to drivers. When their bodies wear out at an early age from exertion, you discard them and rent their—"

"Me, a slant-eyed Jew, a kike gook, exploiting the indigenous masses. Get to it, Kiet! As loathsome a creature as I am, am I not entitled to peace in my remaining five days in this cruel world?"

"Guilty or innocent, please?"

"Innocent."

"You were framed?"

"I was."

"The contents of your warehouse, Vu? If your shelves had been bare, no army of conspirators could have loaded them with false contraband and gotten away with it."

"Oh, I had rice in inventory, but it was imported. Not raw Luongan paddy, not even milled and polished Luongan rice. There isn't much of that around."

"Imported from where, please?"

"You know the legend of the origin of rice, don't you, Kiet? There was always the rice plant, the *Oryza sativa*, but its ears were bare of grain. Along came a goddess. Each Asian country has its own name for her. She squeezed her breasts over the plants. Her milk dripped into the ears, and that was the beginning of rice. How sacred and passionate this common grain is to us, Kiet, don't you agree?"

"I remember the tales from primary school. The rice, please?"

"Thailand and America are the world's two leading exporters, respectively. I buy Thai rice. It's convenient. Kiet, did you know that in our traditional cultures the sacredness of rice is second only to that of kings and the Buddha?" Feng Vu pounded his chest with beefy fingertips. "A stupid bland little grain is the cause of hand-wringing emotionalism. That is why your boys are going to shoot holes in me and why you will check to see if they did their jobs and then shoot another hole in me for good measure."

"How much rice?"

"I can store five thousand metric tons in my facilities. This so-called raid seized two hundred tons." Vu lifted a shoulder, as if two hundred metric tons were a pile of husks. "Nowadays, you buy what you can buy when you can buy it."

"Nearly half a million pounds," Kiet said. "You were hoarding?"

Vu gazed upward, beady brown eyes searching the heavens for deliverance from fools and unfairness. "Kiet, I am a businessman. I retain a commodity on the short term when it is advantageous to capitalize on upward price pressures."

"Whether it be Luongan paddy or polished Thai white, Vu, you were hoarding."

"No, no. By short term I mean *short* term. Listen to reason, Kiet. I can't hang on to my investment too long. The rumors about foreign aid? It's coming if the monsoon doesn't, whether Pakse's pride is—"

"Prince Pakse."

"—whether *Prince* Pakse's pride is bruised or not. The first photo of a child with a distended belly that makes the pages of a Western news magazine—Kiet, you watch—relief planes will be stacked above Hickorn International, layered into the stratosphere. Can your policeman's brain comprehend the effect on prices? The bottom would fall out. I'd lose a fortune."

"A horrifying prospect, so echoes my policeman's brain."

"Amusing. I buy and sell at lightning speed. The rice was in my central warehouse less than a week."

"You can prove it?"

"The rice was delivered in 100-kilo bags printed with the logos and brand names of the exporting firms," Feng Vu said. "The Thai are more mechanized than we are. They rely on forklifts and trucks, we on strong backs and pedicabs. My men transferred the rice into fifty-kilo bags."

"Luongans carrying on their breaking backs sacks printed with the prestigious Feng Vu name?"

"That insufferable prick, Houphong Duc, led the plunder. He took it as evidence of hoarding of the remnants of the last Luongan crop."

"You had the old 100-kilo bags as evidence that you were not hoarding, yes? And invoices and bills of lading to verify date and quantity of shipment of the Thai rice?"

"Yes, I had them then. No, I did not at my trial. Duc disposed of the bags and the accounts."

"Your employees?"

"My coolies and clerks have been compromised. They refused to testify in my behalf. They pled ignorance. Hickorn International Airport personnel who witnessed the rice unloading lost their memories too."

"Your Thai suppliers?"

"Loyalty is transitory, Kiet. They knew they would never do a lick of business with me again. Their allegiance to a minister of agriculture supersedes any to a condemned convict."

"What is Minister Duc's motive? Why did he frame you?"

Feng Vu threw back his head. Laughter rattled through the eerie acoustics of the cell block. "Kiet, you find out. You're the detective. Leave me alone and do your job."

They parted without salutations. Kiet walked out, puzzling over Feng Vu's peculiar bravado. Vu's clock was ticking down, yet he was defiant, fatalistic. He should have been despairing, humble, wheedling a postponement, begging Kiet to seek a deal, any deal.

Vu's life was the deal, the hustle, the money game, demand and offer, buy and sell.

Had Vu given up, resigning himself to his fate? Or was it something else? No, Kiet thought, shaking his head. Couldn't be. On the other hand, this was Feng Vu, the richest, greediest man in Luong. Had he discovered how to take it with him?

SIX

No sooner had Kiet retreated from the jail stench than another rank odor slapped him in the nostrils. It was an olfactory cocktail of perfume and alcohol. Binh had told him that Western professional athletes derived lucrative supplements to their incomes by advertising the stuff in magazines and on television. Kiet was smelling aftershave lotion and/or cologne, and the smell was coming from his office.

"Superintendent, I though you were gone for the day."

Binh rose from Kiet's chair easily and naturally, none of the earlier caught-playing-at-the-grown-up's-desk panic evident. He was, of course, fully involved in his snit about the Jean-Guy Pakse assignment and Kiet owed him, owed him plenty. And he was not alone.

"Captain—"

"Oh, hi. You gotta be the grand poobah."

The person speaking was the fountainhead of the aftershave lotion/cologne fumes. He was standing beside a wall, measuring tape in hand. Kiet looked at Binh.

"Uh, Superintendent, Superintendent Kiet, it is my pleasure to introduce you to Mr. Red Williams."

Mr. Red Williams retracted his tape and clipped it onto his belt in one neat motion, like a gunslinger holstering his shooting iron. He proffered a handshake and grasped Kiet's hand as it was still moving forward. An impatient man, Kiet thought, a man with things on his mind, things to do; not necessarily an admirable trait.

He was a large man, taller and heftier than Kiet, ten or fifteen years younger, with a thinning reddish brushcut, and that Caucasian skin disease known as freckles. Complimenting the male perfume were wash-and-wear slacks, white shirt, and Rolex watch. Mr. Red Williams wore the uniform of the Far East carpetbagger. He also wore a warm sincere smile, although the affability in his bloodshot blue eyes struck Kiet as not so much honest congeniality as a running joke, the punch line of which nobody else was privy.

"Boy, is this a pleasure or what? Your acting superintendent told me all about you and—"

Kiet said to his adjutant, "Acting superintendent as in *acting* superintendent?"

Binh blushed. Red Williams said, "Heck, when the starter takes a blow, goes to the bench to suck up some oxygen, boy, it's unusual that the second-stringer can go right on in and the ball club doesn't lose momentum. Binh's one of those kind of guys who gives you 110 percent. You can hear the shoulder pads pop. You got a right to be proud—uh, what's your first name? You can call me Red."

Kiet answered, his eyes on Binh. "My first name is Superintendent. Captain—"

"Red loves sports metaphor. It's super common in the States."

The "States" as in the United States of America. Kiet suppressed a groan. Binh continued, "Red was a big-time football star in college. Mo-bile, a-gile, and hos-tile. Iowa, Red?"

"Iowa State. And, come on, I wasn't that big a deal," Red Williams said, head bowed, a precise dose of modesty dispensed.

"Soccer?" Kiet asked.

Red Williams laughed. "No. *Real* football. The gridiron, three yards and a cloud of dust. Blitzes, post patterns, play action, audibilizing, crossbucks, and forearm shivers."

They were referring to American-rules football, Kiet concluded. He had seen videotape demonstrations. *Football* was a misnomer. The participants competed in brightly colored paramilitary garb,

52

and the emphasis was on throwing an oblong ball that would not roll properly, run with it, and push one another onto the ground. A foot was rarely employed, the ball rarely kicked, and then only by an immigrant midget—perhaps an unemployed circus performer—who entered the match for that unique purpose.

"Red was all-conference," Binh said.

Kiet sensed idolatry and he didn't like it. He had no idea what all-conference meant, nor did he give a damn. "All-conference. Splendid. Congratulations."

Red Williams looked at his feet and shook his head. "Nah. I was actually second team, All–Big Eight. Outside linebacker. Compared to some of those hosses we went up against, I was a runt."

Red Williams slid a finger down the bumpy ridge of his nose. "Busted it nine times in my football life, twice in my senior year alone. But, heck, we had to play Oklahoma and Nebraska every season. That says it all, doesn't it?"

"Indeed," Kiet said, eyes frozen on Binh's for an explanation, solid answers preferably, that failing, a semiplausible orientation on this surrealistic experience.

But it was Red Williams who wiped his wide flat brow and spoke. "You boys look at the thermometer today? Heck, that mercury's gotta be clippin' a hundred. I'm based outta L.A., you know, Los Angeles, and I'm used to scorchers, but this heat wave of yours, it'll whip your average fat-assed white man like yours truly down onto his knees, his tongue hanging out, big as a salami and dry as a bone, begging for the cooling rains, just like you Luongans are, and, hey, I tell you what, I'm on your side, praying for that monsoon.

"I'll give this to Hickorn, you might have the humidity, but you don't have L.A.'s smog. Heck, their air's so cruddy you could bag it up and sell it to the tourists if you had the demand, which you don't because they all come to go to Disneyland and see movie stars.

"You folks here, in these little countries, you don't have that serious pollution. Hickorn's got itself a sewage problem when the wind's blowing the wrong direction, that's no secret. But you're not gonna have smog problems till you suck in the foreign capital and throw up the smokestacks."

Kiet said, "And you, sir, are a—"

"A humble observer of the human experience," Williams answered. "The point I'm driving at in regards to this heat and humidity—I'm not trying to remind you of your misery, I'm not that insensitive—is that air conditioning is pert'near the most important invention of the twentieth century, ranking right up there with the A-bomb and the face mask."

Red stopped talking and grinned, a comic's pause for laughter. Binh laughed. Kiet stood motionless and emotionless.

"Anyway," Red went on, "it's no accident the developed countries are up there in the temperate zones. Man, you're pedaling uphill to make your mark in the world when sweat's rolling off your nose. Heck, Einstein and Salk and JFK and Vince Lombardi, they weren't always sticking to their shorts when they were doing their thing."

"Envinced what, please?"

"Vince. Vince Lombardi was a legendary and immortal football coach, Superintendent," Binh said.

"Football," Kiet said. "Of course. Thank you."

"How I got it scoped is that the developed world's got an eighty-year head start on you third worlders. You're asking how I came up with eighty years, right?"

There was nothing more insulting to Kiet as a Luongan than the reference to his homeland as third world. It was like a pat on the head. He said, "No. I am not."

"Air conditioning was invented around eighty years ago. In Hickorn, what I've seen of it, air conditioning could've been invented yesterday. Your foreign embassies, some of them, they've got it. That new hotel, the Luong InterPresidential, they got it. The Hickorn Sporting Club too. The bartender there, he makes a mean Singapore Sling, doesn't he? I'd match it against the Raffles' any day of the week."

"I would not know. I am not a member." The Hickorn Sporting Club was Luong's most exclusive private club. Kiet had never been inside it.

"Yeah? Somebody in your position—well, the bottom line is that thanks to modern technological advances, air conditioning is affordable to everybody. You folks, you can be playing on a level field. All you got to do is make a commitment."

"Playing field?" Kiet asked. "Are we discussing air conditioning or football?"

"Just an expression, Superintendent," Binh said.

"This conversation has been a string of expressions," Kiet said.

"Nobody has to tell Red Williams when to shut his big yap," Red Williams said. "I got to scoot anyhow, boys. I have the measurements I need and we'll be in touch. We'll do lunch."

"Right on, Red," Binh said, exchanging thumbs-up signs with the departing Williams.

"Who is he, please?"

"Red's new in Hickorn. He sells air conditioning systems. I thought that was rather obvious."

Kiet hated Binh's tone of voice. "I thought he was merely treating us natives to a sermon on progress."

"That was uncalled for, Superintendent. So was your rudeness to Red. He's a heckuva guy."

"Superintendents of police are paid to be rude, Captain. On to business, may we? I was not gone for the day. I had a chat with Feng Vu."

"He's a sweetheart, isn't he?"

"Do you find his conduct peculiar?"

"His obnoxiousness? Yeah. He's acting like Feng Vu, which, I agree, is strange. He's condemned to die inside a week. That should humble anybody. Not Feng Vu. He's been riding the guards heartlessly. Little subtle digs, you know. He zeros in on a weakness and doesn't let up. Like Officer Second Class Ky."

"The lad with the acne?"

"Yeah. Vu calls him Officer Pizza Face. He reminds him of his skin condition endlessly. I've had to post the suicide watch unarmed. They check their sidearms with the head jailer. I'm afraid somebody will shoot him."

"Somebody will," Kiet said.

"Shoot him before his date with destiny," Binh said, cracking a smile. "You know what I mean."

"Has Vu had visitors?"

Binh raised an index finger. "One. Luong's richest man is without friends. I don't blame them. Feng Vu is bad news and bad luck."

"Who was his visitor?"

"Madame Saravane. She came while I was out. She logged in for one hour the day after Vu was sentenced. The old bitch chased my guard out of the cell block for the duration, so we don't know what went down."

"Interesting."

"Red's an interesting character too, speaking of interesting, isn't he, Superintendent?"

"Interesting," Kiet said. "Yes. Why do I not know him?"

"Well, like I said, he's new. I met him, I guess, the day you went on up to Tia Nha on furlough."

"How did you meet him, please?"

"He, you know, came here, to headquarters."

"Selling air conditioner machines?"

"Uh, well, that's what, you know, he does."

Kiet stared at his adjutant.

Binh licked dry lips and said, "Red's exclusive Luongan distributor for the top lines. Working out of L.A. Trane, Carrier, Lennox, General Electric. I saw the brochures and order sheets. You're in the market for the best quality brand names, you operate through Red. As department procurement officer, it behooves me to keep track of the marketplace, right? This is super timing for investing in imported durable goods, Superintendent. The zin is going to drop like a rock because of food shortages. We'll never have a more attractive exchange rate on the dollar than we do now."

Kiet closed his eyes. Mr. Red Williams had hustled the impressionable young adjutant, had him prattling like an amateur economist. Binh deserved elevation to department procurement officer, yes, but the title was also a psychological unguent. Due to budgetary poverty, annual salary increases were minuscule. *Department procurement officer.* Kiet and his budget would pay, dollars for pennies or pennies for dollars, however that Americanism went. "Are we contemplating buying through Mr. Red Williams, Captain?"

"Well, you could probably say that," Binh said, "Red was making a service call."

Oh no, Kiet thought. "A service call?"

"Measuring your wall. For installation of your unit. They're on order and quite reasonably priced."

"My unit? *They?*"

"You don't even have a window, Superintendent. The French Legionaire commandants were so paranoid about communist sappers lobbing in satchel charges, the weenies. You need fresh air, ventilation. My office will have one too, as will the booking area. Red promised to modify the wiring free of charge so we don't blow fuses."

"I'm going home immediately," Kiet said. "I'll have ample air and ventilation."

"Cooling, invigorating air is what I'm saying and you know it. Ninety degrees and no wind isn't ventilation."

"Captain, I hate air conditioning. It makes my teeth clatter and it gives me colds. My mucus membranes evaporate to dust and my arm hair stands straight up."

Binh sighed heavily. "Superintendent, the units are adjustable."

"Adjust mine," Kiet said, walking out. "Adjust it so it doesn't escape the carton."

SEVEN

"Bamsan, should I go home?"

"No. Please, no. Stay."

"I loved you surprising me by coming home from Tia Nha early. I love the flowers. I love you. I don't love your mood," Quin Canh said.

"Policemen bring their moods off duty with them, Quin. I love you incredibly and I am a policeman. We serve and protect, and we cannot help but live our jobs," Kiet said, hating instantly his last sentence and the rancid taste the unctuousness left clinging in his mouth.

"Nurses bring their worst experiences home too," said Quin, a nurse and nursing instructor at Luong University. "Is that any excuse to brood and hold it inside?"

"No," Kiet admitted. They were at his villa, in his bed, recovering from the ardor generated by a week's separation. They had decided the moment they shut the front door behind them that conversation could wait.

"No? Just no?"

"Very well," Kiet began, relating the events of his day, taking his time, sparing few details. The hardships endured by his sister and her family. The summons by Prince Pakse. The boat ride with Lieutenant Commander Tuon Tran. Notification of the Feng Vu execution. The Jean-Guy Pakse baby-sitting assignment. Interviewing Feng Vu. Making the acquaintance of Captain Binh's fast friend, Mr. Red Williams.

"Mm, you did have a plumper day than I. Usually not, but today you did." Quin got out of bed and walked to the dresser.

Quin Canh was Kiet's first serious romantic interest since Tien, his wife, perished in the 1966 cholera epidemic. Quin was a forty-four-year-old woman who looked even better nude than clothed. She was slim and supple. Black hair traced with gray fell below her shoulders. Delicate lines radiated from the corners of her eyes.

Quin stood at the dresser mirror and brushed her hair, saying, "Bamsan, no, not a plump day, a horribly bloated day. May I say what I think bothers you the most about your dreadful day?"

A fastidious woman who hates snarls in her hair, Kiet thought, staring at her naked backside. She was a compulsive brusher, but she also knew how the nude hair-brushing process aroused him.

He loved her perfections and her flaws equally. His devotion was across the board. Her smile, her breasts, her feet, her temper, her cheekbones, her cunning, her navel. Her cellulite. Without understanding or caring why, he loved the tiny ripples on her thighs.

Binh had told him of thirty-minute commercial programs on American television in which viewers were persuaded to telephone at no cost to themselves a "1-800" number and to subsequently recite their credit card numbers. Among the products that could be purchased via this electronic ritual were miraculous engine additives, the inner secrets of gurus who became fabulously wealthy by informing acolytes how to buy the houses of others without giving them cash money, and, oddly, cellulite-elimination lotions. An inscrutable extravagance, he thought.

"Bamsan."

"Excuse me?"

Quin glanced at his groin and giggled. "You amaze me. You should be snoring. What I believe has really irritated you, may I tell you what I think it is without making you grumpier?"

"Yes. Of course you can, and I am not grumpy. I am in splendid humor." Kiet smoothed the sheet. "Come here and explain your theory."

"No, thank you. I'll keep a safe distance. The drought and His Royal Highness' son and that hideous man you are executing, those problems would drive anybody to insomnia."

Kiet patted the mattress. "Sing me a lullaby."

"Red Williams and Binh."

"Red Williams? I mentioned him in passing. The fact that Binh bought his air conditioners annoyed me."

"You mentioned him in passing, but your voice rose when you did."

"He addressed us as boys. The French addressed me as 'boy.'"

"You *were* a boy those days."

"The French addressed my father as 'boy' too."

"I forget that I am very much younger than you. I don't remember anything before independence."

"A mere child, yes. Come. Rock this old geezer to sleep."

"Binh admires him."

"He admires what he perceives Williams to be. American giants, two-legged elephants, play a game they have entitled football, although it is not. Red Williams was an expert player and my young adjutant deems that a special talent."

"You're jealous, Bamsan. Binh worships you and you're worried that someone else has come along that he venerates too."

There were instances when Kiet regretted falling in love with a woman so insightful. He continued watching her, thinking how well she fit in here. He had lived alone in this small villa on the corner of Rue Willie Mosconi and Avenue Che Guevara since Tien's death. He lived alone, that is, except for a mangy cat who had adopted him several years ago, a salacious and malodorous tom he had refused to name because of its arrogance and disdain for its nominal master.

Divorced a dozen years, Quin lived with her mother, Le, and grown son, Bao. Lovemaking at their apartment was out of the question. Quin would never cease being her mother's daughter, and in the old lady's view unmarried girls who coupled were unconditional sluts. Quin was justifiably afraid to sneak an hour of heavy breathing with her Bamsan when they had the apartment

61

to themselves. Her mother was as adroit at detecting clues—from bedding, from clothing donned hastily, from guilty faces—as Kiet was at a crime scene. If fornication were a felony, Kiet mused, Hickorn would need a jail as large as the city and Le Canh would be superintendent of police.

Le Canh was no fan of Kiet's either. From what he could gather, she did not especially dislike him, but she loathed his profession. She lumped him with the French colonial *prefecture de police* who, where the natives were concerned, did not always remember that they were public servants. A cop was a cop was a cop.

Charitably *and* maliciously, Kiet attributed her stubborn prejudice to narrowed brittle arteries which supplied insufficient blood to her brain. However he analyzed his relationship with the woman, though, whatever the roots of their mutual enmity, one fact was constant: If Quin and Kiet married, Le would be her own dowry.

Quin and Kiet had never discussed marriage. The prospective mother-in-law was a specter, yes, but of greater significance, these were two mature people accustomed to freedom. Yet, Kiet thought, how ideal an addition to his home, how glorious a life with her would—

"Bamsan, you didn't answer me."

"What was the question?"

"I didn't ask a question. I said that Binh esteems Red and that you're jealous."

"Perhaps."

"Yes or no? Your perhaps isn't perhaps. When you say perhaps, you have already made up your mind, yes or no."

Damn her perception, which was instinctive, intuitive. He dared not say *intuition*, as in feminine intuition. They took it as a quotient of biology, like menstrual cramps, a quaint weakness they could not overcome.

She was not liberated in the sense of the Western woman who, two decades ago, burned her brassiere for television news cameras or her latter-day sister who commanded army regiments and cor-

62

porate divisions and sat at the head of the table during power lunches, but Quin was her own woman and would not hesitate to whack Bamsan Kiet across the nose with a rolled-up newspaper if he patronized her. He said, "Maybe."

"I'm teasing." She knelt on the bed behind him and kneaded his shoulders. "I'm through annoying you. You have had a dreadful day."

"Yes, yes. Yes I have."

"We've had two beriberi cases this week," she said. "Children from the country whose village doctors brought them to us."

Beriberi. A nutritional disease, Kiet remembered. Thanks to Luong's agricultural self-sufficiency, beriberi and its cruel kin were just hygiene class topics studied in school, medical definitions memorized for examinations. He recalled feeling abstract pangs of sympathy for parts of the Orient where people did not have enough to eat. "Thiamine deficiency?"

"Yes. I had never seen a case before. Those poor babies were weak and half paralyzed. They looked horrible. They were close to death when they came in. I hope I never see another beriberi patient."

"Unless it rains, I fear you will. How are the kids?"

"They will recover. We received them soon enough. We're feeding them properly and supplementing their diets with megadoses of Vitamin B complex."

"They weren't getting enough rice to eat?"

"Not so simple," Quin said. "We Luongans prefer polished rice. The bran containing the vitamins and minerals is milled off. Farmers raise poultry, fish, meat, and green vegetables too. Those foods offset vitamin deficiencies in white rice, but you can't grow animals and plants of any kind without water."

"Tia Nha," Kiet said, visualizing dead earth and the absence of creatures.

"When the monsoon comes and we've returned to normal, the medical school staff is going to campaign against white rice. Unhusked brown rice spoils too rapidly because of the oils in it, but we're going to preach parboiling. Steep the harvested rice, allow the bran's nutrients to soak in, *then* mill it white and pretty. I hope they don't lose interest when everyone has full stomachs and good health again. I won't let them!"

Kiet thought it incongruous that in this milieu of nudity and hormone secretion they, man and woman, were discoursing upon nutrition like professional types. Or to an extreme, foreign developmental specialists, experts on third world poverty, those gentlemen who flew in with lucrative grants and all the answers.

We should be in a climate-controlled Range Rover, driving through the countryside, jotting recommendations on clipboards. And they were, he and his imagination, involuntarily conjuring a field trip to Tia Nha. Littered by the road were empty rice bowls and doomed children.

Kiet did not have to gaze downward to confirm that his manhood had hibernated. Children were starving, the Ma San River valley was a graveyard of dust, and he was frustrated because untidy fantasies prevented him from making love to his woman. Guilt washed over him like the tardy floodwaters. He hadn't realized how tired he was. Stupid tired. Punchdrunk tired. Silly tired.

"Feng Vu claims that he lost two hundred metric tons of Thai rice in the raid. Half a million pounds in fifty kilo bags. Four thousand bags," he said.

"Hoarded Luongan rice. That was the verdict at his trial."

"Whichever. I wonder where it is. Five hundred thousand pounds of rice could feed many, many, many people. We could eat it or we could possibly sell it to Thailand whether it was grown there or not. We could swap for poultry and vegetables."

"Who are you going to ask?"

"Luong's paramount agricultural wizard, His Royal Highness' nephew, Minister of Agriculture Houphong Duc."

"He wears suspenders, Bamsan? Did you know that?"

"I did not."

"Don't tense up. I didn't rip his clothes off. I don't even know

64

him. I saw him on the street once. At an angle you can see them under his suit jacket."

"Luongan men do not wear suspenders."

"Duc does. Oh no, I forgot!"

"Excuse me?"

"Your cat. I was to feed your cat while you were on furlough."

"You forgot to feed him? Don't worry. He becomes too hungry, he eats what is in front of him. A dog, a produce stand, a fish market, a Japanese tour group, an automobile."

"No, I didn't forget to feed him."

"Then he is happy. Did you give him a saucer of beer in the evening? That makes him bearable."

"Bamsan, what I forgot to tell you is that he isn't here. I haven't seen him."

Wednesday, May 20
Hickorn
High 96°, Low 83°
Clear

EIGHT

Kiet awoke with a liquorless hangover, a product of fatigue and stress. An abundantly miserable morning after, he thought. The ailment without the satisfaction of self-abuse.

Fortified by aspirin and a long shower, he headed to the Ministry of Agriculture, an architecturally unimpressive three stories of stucco, arched windows, and tile roof. Located on Rue Willie Mosconi, it was in a thicket of ministries and agencies.

The French had built it as headquarters for a proposed rural development agency, and dedicated it in 1954, a day after the Vietminh overran Dien Bien Phu. Lukewarm interest in rural development cooled arctically. Colonial civil servants began looking into steamship schedules and postings to Algeria. Luongan independence was forthcoming anyway, so the natives themselves, or the barefoot Marxists, could tend to rural development. The French utilized the building as a document warehouse for other departments until independence. The communist hordes never invaded but the Luongan bureaucracy did.

Kiet announced himself at the lobby and asked for Minister Duc. An attractive woman at the reception desk called Minister Duc's administrative assistant, who came downstairs. He was a haughty young man who stated in a choppy monotone that Minister Duc received no visitors without an appointment, that was his policy. Kiet asked the lad if he knew who he was. The answer was yes, he did recognize Hickorn's superintendent of police, and so what. Kiet then explained in a sweet voice that he was neither here on a social call nor to pick up the minister's laundry nor to be rebuffed by a flunky. May I see him, please. Thank you very much.

Civility had its rewards. The administrative assistant went off in search of his master. So stirred was he by Kiet's splendid manners that in his hurry to comply he threw open an inner door with such force that it stuck open.

Kiet observed bays packed with clerks. Their desks were loaded with precarious piles of documents. Ceiling fans shoveled slabs of warm air. Employees underneath processed the material with rubber stamps, paper clips, and methodical precision, no matter how long it took.

The ministry seemed to have grown in direct proportion to the plight of Luongan agriculture. There was less rice to complete more useless forms on, more nonexistent programs to implement, more stunted crops not to administer. Kiet could not see the upper two levels, but he could almost hear floorboards groaning under the weight of reams of typing paper, photocopy machines, and associate deputy assistant undersecretaries. The men, and the occasional woman, of influence were replicas of that peculiar North American subspecies known as Yuppie. He wished that just one of these agricultural prodigies had once upon a time been a farmer.

Duc's assistant returned and informed Kiet that although Minister Duc was presently out of his office, the superintendent was invited to join him at the club where he was having tea and a game of tennis.

"The club?" Kiet asked.

"*The* club," he said, smirking, cocking his head to the northeast.

"The Hickorn Sporting Club," Kiet said.

"Which other club could I be referring to, Superintendent Kiet, sir?"

Which other club or *club*, indeed. The smarmy youngster gave Kiet a quick vertical survey, condescending eyes perusing sandals, twice or thrice worn slacks, and white shirt (cleaned and pressed). He obviously failed muster and was doubtlessly unsuitable regardless of dress.

70

Kiet was curious how the youngster's pouty lips and lifted brow would respond to pain. Involuntary facial muscle spasms, perhaps. He smiled benignly and said nothing.

"You do play tennis, don't you, sir?"

"No," Kiet said. "I do not."

"Minister Duc is anxious to confer with you on important items too. He says he will save a set for you if you desire, but since you don't play, well . . ." A petulant pause.

"Well what, please?"

"Nobody in Hickorn can string a racket properly. I thought you, being a policeman, might have a recommendation. You people have ears and noses poking in—"

Kiet walked out before he committed a violent crime, a felony against person. The Hickorn Sporting Club was on the opposite corner of Willie Mosconi. It occupied a city block and was shielded on all four sides by espalier—a living green fence taller than two men. The club was purported to be a close facsimile of a French country manor, and Kiet could just see twin roof peaks from the sidewalk. He recalled from secondhand descriptions that half the property was building and veranda and courtyard, the remainder swimming pool and tennis courts. The colonial ambience knotted his stomach, reminding him why he had avoided it. An irrelevant snub, he confessed; annual membership dues exceeded his yearly salary.

The staff did not speak Luongan while on duty; this was an unwritten rule, an elitist, pre-independence tradition that had been preserved like an endangered species floating in a laboratory jar. They spoke English and French, and there was a rumor that employees with ambition were studying Japanese on audio cassettes. A thriving anachronism, Kiet thought. An enclave of health and wealth.

Kiet went through an iron gate and announced himself to the doorman, who wore the whites and high collar of a colonial manservant. He instructed Kiet in French to stand by, and closed the door on him. Kiet stood by, on a brick entryway, sandwiched by roaring stone lions, wishing he could arrest people for rudeness.

71

He would tack on a supplemental charge of smugness, making it a compound offense. They would serve long sentences in remote penal colonies, clearing jungle growth that grew back as fast as they chopped it down. The tropical equivalent of the Western penitentiary rock pile.

Kiet was smiling, basking in the fantasy, when the boy reappeared and said in French, but yes, Minister Duc is expecting you at his table. In Luongan, Kiet said, sorry, I do not comprehend. The message was repeated in English. Kiet, who had a fluent command of both languages, shook his head helplessly.

The boy flushed, swallowed in distaste, and reiterated in his own language. Kiet said "ah so," patted him on his white uniformed shoulder, and trailed him to the dining hall and Houphong Duc's table. Kiet's boozeless hangover was gone. Now that he was having a little fun, he felt chipper. Minister Duc's *courtside* table, the boy qualified as he slid out a chair to seat him. In case the monolingual barbarian cop was blind as well as uneducated and crass.

The table was a leaden slab of glossy teak. Kiet caught a vague whiff of lemons. The tablecloth and napkins were starched linen, the dishes bone china, the flatware sterling. He estimated that a nimble-fingered criminal in a baggy raincoat could grab three months pay before water glasses were filled.

The room was a roughly even mix of empty and full, Luongan and foreigner. Kiet saw, among the Luongans, army generals, top ministry officials, and some of Hickorn's sharpest businessmen. He surveyed the last category and counted no Chinese.

Kiet ordered a Golden Tiger beer and gazed through screening at the courts. There were eight, and four were in play. Duc was on the near side, in stylish white togs, swatting a fuzzy green ball back and forth over a net. Duc's opponent was vaguely familiar. A chief deputy of the minister's, perhaps.

Duc's opponent's strategy confirmed his subservience. Kiet knew as much as he cared to about tennis—nil—but common sense indicated that the deputy minister was going in the tank.

While Duc attempted to bat the orb where his adversary wasn't, the return shots invariably were aimed at Duc.

Hitting the ball to each other seemed to Kiet to be eminently practical gamesmanship in a game devoid of rationality. Energy was preserved. Chasing it idiotically from side to side in the dreadful heat was madness that could bring a sportsman to a sudden cardiovascular end.

The ball sailed past the deputy for the last time. Duc raised his arms in triumph. They shook hands at the net and went inside to change. Twenty minutes later, Minister of Agriculture Duc appeared at the table.

"Sorry to delay you," he said genially, shaking Kiet's hand. "I had presumed you played, I'm always ready for an extra set."

To play, to perspire and to strain until blood vessels ruptured like defective plumbing? No, thank you. "No, I am not a tennis player."

Houphong Duc was spiffy: gray linen suit, tie striped with the colors of some British regiment, and, yes, suspenders. His narrow triangular face blushed from his exercise and shower. He was eyeballing Kiet distantly, not quite concealing his amusement.

Kiet decided that the gaze was practiced, a gambit to establish superiority. Perhaps it was curriculum in the American, made-in-the-shade MBA school. They had indeed taught Duc mysterious things. They had graduated him and sent him home with a fat vocabulary and an evangelical reverence for paper projects and theoretical proposals. They had made him a state-of-the-art mandarin, an exemplary chief clerk.

Kiet answered Duc's eyes with a counterattacking ploy, a sip of beer and a yawn. The agriculture minister lifted an arm, snapped his fingers, and said, "Your stopping in at the ministry was providential. I had been hoping to touch base before Monday. You abbreviated your furlough. No family emergency, I trust."

"No. No family emergency," Kiet said, giving him all he was going to, then playing dumb, "Monday?"

73

Duc made a pistol with his hand, cocked his thumb, and said, "Bang. The execution."

His finger snap was answered. A waiter poured glasses of hot tea. A second waiter rolled in a cart of napoleons. Duc patted a flat stomach and pointed to a slab of pastry. "That one. I burned a calorie or three in advance. My associate deputy minister wasn't world class competition by any stretch, but I'm entitled. You?"

Kiet said yes please and selected two pieces of layered heaven. Crack wise about my girth and the calories I did *not* burn, you twerp, he thought. Please do.

Duc read Kiet's face accurately and would not be baited. "Preparations are proceeding?"

"Yes."

"Flow patterns that anticipate unexpected contingencies?"

"Certainly."

"I offered the resources of my ministry to your adjutant. The offer stands."

"A generous offer," Kiet said. "But you have done so much already. Captain Binh is proceeding and flowing nicely, thank you."

"I'm not disputing you, but this is not an everyday situation and we're working on a skinny time frame. Glitches are bound to arise. I have connections. I can grease some wheels. Getting those bleachers nailed together and on line has got to be a hair-puller. Give me the name of the carpenter you awarded the contract to and I'll—"

"No bleachers," Kiet cut in.

"Where will the important—"

"His Royal Highness has asked me to ensure that the execution of Feng Vu does not become a spectacle. He himself will not be attending. No bleachers, no chairs, no engraved invitations, no live television coverage. We will have a plain, cozy, simple execution."

"Uncle Novie isn't coming? He didn't tell *me*."

Uncle *Novie?* Blasphemy. "He will be indisposed next Monday."

74

"Doing what?"

"Anything except attending an execution."

"How do *you* know? When did you see him?"

Kiet slowly savored a gob of custard and jelly and chocolate, and Houphong Duc's jealousy.

The minister drummed manicured fingernails on the tabletop. A response would surely be forthcoming when the lumpen cop masticated the food that was puffing his cheeks. You presumed *some* social graces. Eat like a pig, and balance gluttony by swallowing your food before speaking.

Kiet gulped and patted his lips with a cloth napkin. "Delicious."

Duc moaned and threw down his expensive silver fork, clinking an expensive Limoges plate.

"Careful," Kiet admonished.

"Uncle Novie is hidebound, Kiet. Maddeningly old-fashioned. He resists change per se. The twenty-first century is just around the corner, and his foreign policy is frozen in the simplistic artifice of naming and renaming Hickorn's downtown streets."

The kingdom of Luong was militarily weak and symbolically strong. His Royal Highness had made the latter so by hammering in street designation as his principal foreign policy plank. Every street in the grid was named for a person and, except for Prince Pakse's billiards idols, no man's immortality was secure. Kiet had learned from his ruler that the delicate manipulation of the human ego was the secret of neutrality. Cause the wrong man to mope and you could awaken some fine morning to paratroopers and tanks.

Some years ago, for instance, China briefly fell from favor. Avenue Mao Tse-tung became Avenue Ronald Reagan. This occurred during the reign of the American actor, during a period in China when hardline Maoists were a detriment to the establishment of Kentucky Fried Chicken franchises and were therefore bad elements. No harm done. Six months later, Rue Souvanna Phouma relinquished to Rue Chou En-lai. Phouma was gone and Laos posed no threat to Luong's borders. Chou was venerated in China, impervious to political wind changes. Everyone of importance was happy.

"I refuse to debate His Royal Highness' wisdom with you. Please answer a question. Why is the execution so important to you?"

"That should be obvious," Duc said. "We're sending a message to our benighted Chinese sharks. We're sending a message to our people and to the rest of the world."

"Excuse me, the rest of the world?"

"Agriculture is global in scope, Kiet. You have to take a geopolitical tack. We're international, and not just Pacific Rim. World community is the scale I'm talking about here. B-school case studies taught us to think big, think problem solving, think progress."

B-school as in MBA, Kiet supposed. Duc wore his diploma like insignia. "The firing squad will fire shots heard around the world?"

"To a limited extent. The message is that we're dealing with our deficiencies. We are people of the soil and no treachery by man or the elements will overcome us. A developing nation does not become a NIC unless it is agriculturally mature."

"A NIC?"

Houphong Duc sighed. "Newly Industrialized Country. We cannot take that step until we have stabilized agriculturally and positively impacted the flood and drought cycle."

"Of course," Kiet said. "Kill the Chinese and the farmer prospers. Easy. I am a simple man, Mr. Minister. Taming the landscape seems a bit harder."

Duc shook his head resolutely. "Challenging, yes. Impossible, no. My staff and I are blocking out a feasible Ma San River dam and irrigation project. It has the potential to triple Luongan rice production."

"Ah, so that is what everybody at your ministry is busily doing."

Duc sidestepped the dig. "It takes money, significant sums of money. Billions of U.S. dollars or the counterpart in yen, marks, whatever we can obtain. Foreign aid is the bottom line and it will come when we've demonstrated we're on track. Uncle Novie will have to be persuaded to accept the aid, but he's a problem I can eventually resolve too. My destiny, Kiet, is to modernize Luongan production and commerce through sound business practices and enlightened management."

"Could we shrink the scale from global and geopolitical and billions for a moment, please?"

Duc smiled. "Certainly. You're obviously more comfortable with the trivial and the mundane. You are my guest and I want you to be happy."

"Two hundred tons of rice is not trivial if you are hauling it on your back."

"The contraband we seized in the Feng Vu raid?"

"Yes. Where is it now?"

Duc fluttered his fingertips. "We immediately distributed it to every food seller in Hickorn at below-market price. A drop in the bucket, but it did relieve the supply and demand situation on that particular day."

"Feng Vu asserts that it was imported Thai rice and that it was a recent shipment."

Duc made a hand pistol again and held it to his temple. "Who wouldn't lie to save his own life? Vu bought the rice from river pirates who robbed and stashed paddy from our last good harvest. He milled it and sat back, licking his fat chops as the price rose. We know the score. My men conscientiously inspect the millers and brokers, and tax their incoming paddy. Kiet, I never regarded you as a bleeding heart. Could it be you are a sob sister, worrying over that chink?"

Chink. Kiet digested the epithet. Chink, nip, jap. And the nonspecific Asiatic slur: gook, slope, dink, zip. Not to be forgotten—lunk. Lunk for Luongan. Did Feng Vu label Duc a lunk? Doubtlessly.

"Detective's curiosity," Kiet said, thinking *conscientiously inspect*. Luongan agricultural inspectors were notoriously corrupt. For a bribe they routinely recorded short weights on paddy shipments, thus reducing the miller/broker's taxes.

77

"I can relate to that, to anybody diligently doing his job. Join me for lunch? They serve soon."

Chink was rising in Kiet's gullet, like heartburn. He stood. "No thank you."

Duc pointed at Kiet's empty napoleon plate and then to his midsection. "You ought to. The club has an outstanding salad bar."

NINE

Bamsan Kiet hailed a pedicab outside the Hickorn Sporting Club and asked the driver to take him to Chinatown. The ride was leisurely. It could not help but be. The pedicab operator was small, his fare large.

Kiet took the time to ruminate about Houphong Duc and the club. Duc and his NIC and his proposals and his salad bar. A zillion dollar-mark-yen-pounds worth of concrete damming every Ma San tributary wider than a trickle. He imagined a peasant urinating twice in the same spot, qualifying it for a hydroelectric grant.

Duc and his next NIC phase, his Newly Industrialized Country of Luong. Red Williams's smokestacks. A flat, acrid Hickornscape of industrial parks belching out videotape recorders and jet engines and automobile transmissions and deadly fumes. Would there be money in the foreign aid generosity funds earmarked for Mr. Red Williams's "sewage problem?"

Duc and his grandiose fantasies. The lad was deluded. Not stupid, though. Yet possibly dangerous. His "destiny," of "eventually resolving the Uncle Novie problem," he might be reaching beyond reality, but he was reaching with both hands. Minister Duc deserved special police attention, Kiet thought.

And what was a salad bar? You ate salad greens and you drank at a bar. Salad bars were perhaps avant-garde recipes, raw vegetables marinated in booze. Brandied bean sprouts. Bok choy drizzled in warm gin. No thank you.

There was in Kiet's mind also the question of Duc's tripled rice production. Irrigation dams could dot the countryside like archeological megaliths, and production would not triple, not according to his sister and brother-in-law, who were actual bona fide farmers.

They told a parable of the miracle rice, the new strains that grew faster and resisted pests such as their nemesis, the stem borer, an evil worm that gobbled the innards of the rice stalk. The weight of the rice head then made the weakened plant topple over into the paddy water and rot. Lodging was the technical term for the toppling and rotting; disaster was the end result.

Miracle rice, the green revolution, came to the Ma San rice villages in the 1960s. The peasants resisted it partially because it was new. They resisted it partially because Hickorn shoved it down their throats, like the old French missionaries peddling their Jesus of Nazareth.

The peasants who were convinced to plant the seed harvested double the normal crop of paddy. The peasants were moderately pleased, albeit visibly exhausted by the added burden of a bumper crop. The Hickornites were delighted. They had introduced a program that worked. The peasants now possessed "discretionary income," which could be spent on consumer goods sold by Hickorn merchants. They could also be taxed at a higher rate.

Next planting season the peasants cultivated half as much land, toiled half as hard, and brought in the same as the previous harvests. The Hickorn agricultural advisors and the social scientists who accompanied them like pilot fish were puzzled. It was finally pointed out that rice farmers had no car payments, no electrical bills, no alimony, no cable television fees.

Progress and tradition compromised. Miracle rice was allowed to be mildly miraculous. Leisure and output increased proportionately, in modest increments.

Kiet did not feel he was negligent in not reminding Duc of the miracle rice difficulties. For the same reason he failed to mention Quin's beriberi patient. He doubted if there was a pro-

80

vision for malnourished children and slow-paced farmers in the minister's B-school, case study, NIC destiny.

There had to be an answer to the crisis. Save for a drenching monsoon, Kiet didn't know what it was. He just knew what it wasn't: Houphong Duc.

Hickorn's Chinatown was six city blocks framed by Avenue George Bush, Rue Ho Chi Minh, Avenue Alexandre Loubet, and Rue Deng Xiaoping. An eclectic bunch, Kiet thought. Three heads of state and a missionary. Sit them down at a table for cocktails and how long would it be before voices rose?

Kiet instructed the driver to turn in on Mu Luong, Chinatown's north-south bisector and main commercial thoroughfare. Visitors who asked Kiet directions to "inscrutable and colorful" were aimed toward Chinatown's Mu Luong. The unfathomable Orient. This was it.

For three Chinatown blocks, Mu Luong was a bazaar of strange chatter, pungent odors, and ideographic shop signs. Sidewalks and streets were as always energetic and teeming.

Kiet paid the pedicab driver and began walking. People looked at him oddly, those who knew him as police superintendent and those who just recognized him as a Luongan. He wasn't the only Luongan on the Chinatown streets, but because of the Feng Vu case he was definitely in the minority. He had never been able to place an undercover man in Chinatown. He had no Chinese officers and an ethnic Luongan would not have been more conspicuous if he had had three eyes.

Binh had talked nonchalantly of covert police operations in the District of Columbia. Why shouldn't he? Installation of a police spy would be ridiculously simple. Their police department enjoyed the advantage of keeping the peace in a society where everybody looked alike.

The Chinese sold everything here and they hawked their wares loudly. Kiet detected no shortages at the grocery stores. They sold rice in barrels and the barrels were heaping. Scoop out what you want, make the scale creak, but bring money. Rows and columns of barbecued pork slabs and whole chickens hung in windows. Mountains of fresh produce were displayed in bins. Tinned meats. Bakery goodies. Bottles of cooking oil. Candies. Soda pop by the case. Exotic imported foods in colorful packages: Hamburger Helper, Bisquick, Jell-O, Froot Loops, Gaviscon.

Luxury-item shops proliferated too. Jewelry, clothing, shoes, electronics. They specialized in counterfeit merchandise manufactured out of country. Piaget, Gucci, Apple; nine chances in ten it was a phony. Tourists knew, they didn't care. They bought cheap, cheaper even than Hong Kong, the knockoff capital of the world. They were buying the label and the logo. They went home with three thousand dollars worth of image on their wrists, junk purchased for ten dollars and the people they hoped to make envious would be none the wiser.

Kiet gazed at the Chinatown architecture, unruly rows of two and three story buildings. Entrepreneurs lived above their businesses with their families. The Chinese work ethic was inviolate and everybody in the household contributed. An eighty-hour week was par, so there was no sense wasting time commuting from an outside neighborhood where you were hated and resented.

Kiet saw broken windows and obscenities bleeding through glossy wet paint. Here and there, a random smattering, yes, but vandalism it was. Luongans were too sweet-tempered to riot; it was in the genes, he believed. You would have to explain why rioting was beneficial and then assign them specific tasks, like Molotov cocktail tossing and police barricade attacking. You would have to supervise the fracas step by step, prompting them to be violent and idiotically furious. Otherwise they would sneak off to a café to eat and drink with their foes.

Young Luongan males in buddy cliques were the exception. Primed on alcohol, given the Feng Vu quasipatriotic hysteria, the youngsters had been racing through Chinatown in the late hours, in and out fast on Honda motorbikes, tossing their stones, slathering "FUCK YOU CHINK" and "DIE CHINK" on walls. The

Feng Vu death sentence had provided an unneeded jolt of testosterone.

The air tingled. It seemed to get worse every day. If the parching heat persisted and food prices continued to rise, the juvenile delinquents would have allies. Given a chain reaction of angry outbursts, gentle Luongans were surely capable of rampage. Burn a fuse to the powder and anybody was. He knew it could happen. An agnostic, he prayed to any deity who would listen, praying for rain.

Kiet headed westward on Avenue Leonid Brezhnev. As ironic a street designation as we had, he reflected. Brezhnev, the stolid preperestroika fellow. He associated the dead general secretary with news film of hard winters and workers bundled in scarves and coarse coats, enduring long lines to buy potatoes and vodka.

The Chinatown segment of Avenue Leonid Brezhnev was the inverse of a socialist paradise centrally planned economy. It was the Chinese commercial zone. A laissez-faire, caveat emptor hive of profitability. Proof that His Royal Highness, Prince Novisad Pakse, had a wonderful sense of humor.

The street and its storefront facades were austere. There was no neon, no shouting vendors. Low profile, Binh would say. Chinese power in Luong was economic and Kiet was walking into the engine. Bland stucco wholesale houses distributed grains and other bulk commodities. Firms identified solely by rusty street numbers on doors were moneylenders who lent money to moneylenders. Swank retail jewelers came to Brezhnev to haggle for their stock of rubies and star sapphires.

Foot traffic was light, primarily middle-aged Chinese men. They were the engine's gasoline. Kiet attempted eye contact. They would not reciprocate. They studied their shoes and scuttled off, crablike. They knew Kiet, who he was.

Kiet badly wanted to brace one of the low-profiling tycoons, smile, speak softly and politely, pin him to a wall and say talk to me, please, be free to speak candidly and elaborate on questions I pose.

They would obey, they would reply. They were honest, polite, law-abiding citizens. But they would lie and evade in Chinese, a language Kiet didn't speak. He was a cop and he was a Luongan. He was an outsider.

Kiet came to Sincere Rice Co., Ltd., Feng Vu's rice brokerage corporation. Windows and a tiny brass sign above the door had been painted over. Freshly.

He knocked. No answer. He tried the doorknob. It turned easily. He entered darkness and fumbled for the light switches. Overhead fluorescent lamps flickered on.

Vu's Sincere Rice Co. was a godown, a warehouse. There was a framed-in bank of offices to the right, on ground level. Everything else was structured for paddy storage. Loading docks in the alley, platforms to store the bags, forklifts to move the cargo, desks and calculators and telephones and computers in the offices to expedite shipment and payment.

Sincere Rice Co. Ltd. was bare. Not a grain of rice remained. Not a mote of dust, not a film of talcum powder. Luongan loved their rice *white* and talc embellished its whiteness.

Kiet understood why Feng Vu's godown had been picked to the bone. It was not thievery. Sincere Rice Co., Ltd. had been stripped by business associates, creditors, and by those few who might have felt affection for him.

Guilt or innocence—that was immaterial. Feng Vu had dishonored Hickorn's Chinese by becoming a condemned felon. He had erred and the majority Luongans, who despised him, pounced. The community had lost face.

Kiet thought of Vu's lone jail visitor, the redoubtable sorceress, Madame Saravane. She was tricky, yes, but it was not within even her power to expunge the sin that most greatly offended his peers. Feng Vu was bad luck.

TEN

The communiqué beat Kiet to his office by five minutes. Printed in a tiny hand on royal palace stationery, to wit:

Bosha,
   He is due at 1430 hours. The charter co. is expensive, and reliable. His hired aircraft is an unmarked Hercules. A penthouse suite is reserved at the InterPresidential under an assumed name.
   In your debt.

The note was unsigned, no signature necessary. Binh had taken receipt of it and was hovering anxiously. Kiet glanced at the wall clock and said, "We have one hour."

Binh adjusted the gig line on his immaculate uniform, sighed, and said, "Well, if we have to, we have to. We'd better saddle up."

Saddling up meant Binh driving them to Hickorn International in the departmental staff car, the oxidized-blue 1968 Volkswagen Beetle.

The deceased opium gangster's Mazda was too ostentatious for Kiet. He replaced it with this Beetle attached by the Hickorn police department when its owner, an aspiring pimp, could not pay his fine. Prostitution was illegal in Hickorn, but condoned if there was not excessive flash or public disturbance. The downtown whores in their clinging, slit Suzy Wong dresses appealed to visitors, who paid with hard currency.

The pimp had been arrested not for pandering, but for assaulting a customer, a Japanese tourist. The pimp denied his occupation and testified that the lecher had encountered his niece on a street corner and had accompanied her to his Hickorn Continental Hotel room where he drugged her and committed unspeakable debauchery on her virginal body. Soon thereafter, on the sidewalk outside the hotel, at the intersection of Rue Ho Chi Minh and Avenue John F. Kennedy, the foreign devil, an insatiable sadist, attacked without provocation both the young lady and her uncle.

The Japanese testified that the girl had confronted him in panic, asking him to aid her elderly mother who was suffering convulsions in a nearby hotel room. He rushed upstairs with her, he a happily married man and inveterate Samaritan, whereupon he discovered no convulsing mother. Lo, instead a lifting of the Suzy Wong dress and a lewd proposition, which he indignantly rejected.

The Japanese asserted that his wallet vanished sometime during the beginning of his effort to perform a good deed and an hour later when he returned to the sidewalk. He waited for the harlot, followed her to her pimp, and made a reasonable demand for his stolen property.

Kiet had monitored the trial. It was so lengthy and so infested with lies that he cared not about the verdict. Right versus wrong, this was not at stake; degree of culpability and sleaziness was the sole issue. Behind chambers, agreements were made, Kiet in attendance. The tourist went home, his marriage intact. The pimp received a suspended sentence and forfeiture of his automobile. Justice was done.

Binh said the car was "so gutless it couldn't move out of its own way." To Kiet, engine lethargy was the automobile's prime attraction. That Binh could stomp his gas pedal foot through the firewall and achieve a speed no higher than forty miles per hour was to Kiet assurance that he might not prematurely join his ancestors.

"This is degrading," Binh said, clashing the gears.

"Excuse me?" Kiet had not been in the car since returning from furlough. Leg room was never generous, but his knees were pressing against the dashboard. Had he grown? Had the car shrunk?

"Really, you know, Superintendent, despite this assignment, the special security liaison crapola, being a royal pain in the ass, pun intended, we ought to do it right."

"Absolutely," Kiet said, extricating his knees sufficiently to massage them.

"What I'm getting at is that the little turdbird is the crown prince—"

"Please avoid honorifics," Kiet interrupted. "The verdict in a French court and Luongan reality are two—"

"I'm just repeating what I read in the *Mind* this morning. Again! They're in a super frenzy. They caught wind of rumors of Jean-Guy Pakse coming to Hickorn, but they can't verify them. What was I pissing and moaning about? Oh yeah. Whatever Jean-Guy is, he's a VIP. Going for him in this crate is degrading and embarrassing. Somebody should've sprung for a limo whether Prince Pakse shuns him or not. Don't you agree, Superintendent?"

"Ah," Kiet said, touching a louvered box mounted to the bottom of the dashboard. "This contraption is responsible for my discomfort and potential incapacitation. What is it, please?"

Binh cleared his throat and said, "Uh, Red, he's a helluva guy, you know."

"Red? Mr. Red Williams?"

"Yeah. We were having a couple brews last night and Red was talking football. Boy, he's got stories! Listen to this, Superintendent. They're playing a top ten team, see. Blowout City, right? The Vegas spread is twenty-eight points. You can guess who they're laying the points on, can't you?"

"I can?"

"Nobody but nobody beats this ball club, especially on their home field, which is where they're playing. Red's super proud of the guys on his defensive unit. They may not have won too many games but they play smash-face football."

"Smash-face?"

"Take no prisoners, you know. Kick ass."

"Of course," Kiet said. His knees were cooling, numbing.

"Well, the game's in the fourth quarter and Red's Cyclones are down by thirty-five—"

"Cyclones?"

"The team nickname. Groovy, huh?"

"Splendid."

"The top ten team is leaving their starters in to run up the score so they can move up in the polls. They were like number four that week, but if they ring big-time points on the board they can maybe climb to three or two or even one, particularly if number one's upset. That's as chickenshit as the day is long."

"Reprehensible," Kiet said, comprehending nary a word. He pinched his calf and felt no pain. Could one experience a spinal cord injury without knowing?

"Well, they've got this tailback who's a Heisman candidate and he's already rushed for a hundred and eighty yards. They're trying to push him over the two hundred mark so they call his number on a draw play. Red read it from the word go and shot the gap when the offensive guard and tackle faked pass-block and gave him some daylight. He drilled this superstar so hard he spit out his mouthpiece, which landed past the far hashmark. Dislocated his shoulder too. Out for the season. That cost the swines two losses and the national championship. Is there a moral to the story or what?"

"Indeed there is. I am an improved human being for having heard the story. Why, please, am I paralyzed at and below the kneecaps?"

"It's the, uh, air conditioner, Superintendent. It cools, but something's haywire with the fan. Cold air just kind of drifts out of

88

those vents instead of blasting out and cooling the entire car, although as far as I'm concerned it's damn preferable to not having air. It's a secondhand unit and we've got a fan motor on backorder."

Kiet groaned. "An air conditioner. Where did it come from?"

Binh turned switches. "I'll shut it down. Maybe we shouldn't be using it at all until we change blowers."

"Where did it come from, please?"

"Red."

"Mr. Red Williams would be one of my first five guesses," Kiet said. "This is part of your headquarters purchase?"

"It's not costing us a zin, Superintendent. Red is expressing his appreciativeness for our business. A harmless gratuity."

"Harmless if my legs can be saved," Kiet said.

Binh sighed theatrically. "Superintendent, Red scrounged all over Hickorn to find this unit. It's the only air conditioner in town that could be retrofitted to this disgusting shitbox, unlike the RX-7, which was equipped with factory air. We wanted to surprise you upon your return from furlough, Red and I. While you were off on your Feng Vu tangent, Red paid premium wages to mechanics to work overtime and complete the job. Obviously I did surprise you, but not in the happy manner I intended. You have my profound apologies."

Binh's words were fifteen degrees colder than Kiet's knees. His young adjutant had a disconcerting knack for reflecting constructive criticism back at his accuser, like a scowl in a mirror. Further, Kiet had not chastised the lad, he had merely made a snide remark.

The sarcastic comments and bad feelings must cease, Kiet thought. Face will be lost, vital police work will be disrupted, and Binh will drive faster, lose control, crash, and transmit Kiet to a premature reunion with his ancestors.

He said, "How does one properly address an illegitimate alleged son of a monarch. Is there a protocol?"

Binh laughed. "We could call him Romeo. He's a super slick ladies' man."

"I think we shall settle on Mister Pakse and sir."

"Suits me, Superintendent. How did things go with Minister Duc?"

"Inconclusively."

"Yeah, I can relate. Duc's an okay guy, but he's sort of stuck up and he lives in a dream world. How'd you like the Hickorn Sporting Club, Superintendent?"

"Opulent."

"Yeah. Understatement of the year. I hear they have a dynamite salad bar."

"Indeed," Kiet said.

Hickorn International Airport was four kilometers from town, on the north end of Richard Nixon Boulevard. As they passed the shabby stucco terminal, Kiet again noticed the "H CKO N" above the main entrance. He wondered if there would ever be allocated funds or enthusiasm to replace the missing letters. They went onto the tarmac and stopped beside the control tower. Binh's hand was on the ignition key, ready to kill it, when Kiet pointed at the western sky.

Binh peered through aviator sunglasses. "Good eye, Superintendent. Four engines. Turboprop. In the pattern, gear and flaps down. Yep, a Hercules. It has numbers, but no lettering. I'll bet it's one of those hush-hush charter outfits that haul anything anywhere if the price is right. Must be our guy."

Kiet swiveled his head. Traffic at Hickorn International was not dense. No lineups for takeoff, no widebodies stacked in holding patterns. The Hercules was on final approach. When it landed the immediate airspace would belong exclusively to the birds. "Must be."

Binh glanced at his watch. "Jesus, they're half an hour early!"

Air travelers flying in and out of HIC commonly experienced delays. An airliner was as likely to be days late as hours or minutes. "Remarkable."

The airplane touched down with a squeal and a mist of burned rubber and taxied to the transient apron. The deceleration of

90

the propellers from a blur to four-bladed paddles, huge vertical ceiling fans, fascinated Kiet. He was unashamed that he felt childlike.

Binh drove out and parked next to the plane's nose. The policemen waited for a door to open, a staircase to drop. No; the airplane just squatted there as if a monstrous and dormant insect. Binh and the pilot seemed to be engaged in a staring contest, eyes concealed from one another by fly-boy spectacles.

Binh sighed and turned to Kiet. "He gonna stay up there till we sprout hemorrhoids?"

"Is that a rhetorical question, Captain?"

"Yep. Unless you have an answer."

"Perhaps. Come."

Out of the car, Kiet presented his badge to the pilot, arm extended like a Nazi salute.

The pilot replied with an upraised thumb. An electric motor whirred. The rear loading ramp slowly lowered.

Binh said, "Open Sesame, Superintendent. I'm impressed. What was the secret?"

"Proof of authority."

"That we are police officers?"

"And that we are not newspaper reporters."

Off the ramp onto the tarmac strode Jean-Guy Pakse. He was lithe and tall for a Luongan, his height midway between Kiet's and Binh's. He wore brown loafers, pleated white slacks, tangerine shirt unbuttoned to a hairless chest, mirrored wraparound shades, and a leather cap that matched his footwear.

Kiet was assaulted by goose bumps and butterflies; the resemblance to His Royal Highness was undeniable. The delicate jawline, the elevated cheekbones, the aquiline nose. Handsome, yes, but not as pretty as a sissy boy. No wonder a French court had awarded Jean-Guy the Pakse name.

Kiet and Binh stepped forward, presented their badges, and introduced themselves.

Jean-Guy examined the shields, folded his arms and looked

around. His mouth and nose joined in a twitch, as if he had been deposited on a toxic waste dump. "What stinks?"

Kiet and Binh shrugged in unison. Kiet said, "Perhaps your airplane is leaking fluids. We smell nothing unusual, sir."

"Sewage, exhaust fumes, and flowers," Jean-Guy said. "That's nothing unusual?"

Foreigners and their olfactory imaginations, Kiet thought. The power of suggestion, the third world squalor syndrome. "Captain Binh will be your special security liaison, Mister Pakse. He will be responsible for your security and will assist you however possible."

Jean-Guy removed his glasses. His eyes were green. *Green.* Tabloid photographs were black and white, and coloration other than brown hadn't occurred to Kiet. But why not, he thought? His haughtiness favored his French heritage, so why not eye color too?

Jean-Guy smiled and said, "My baby-sitter? I accept. A man traveling incognito requires a protector and confidant. Isn't my father going to greet me?"

"Not to my knowledge, sir," Kiet said.

"Alienation from Father is my fault," Jean-Guy said. "I should have consulted him before initiating the lawsuit. I owed him the opportunity to accept me or reject me. The trial was ugly and sensationalistic. Mother urged me to sue. She loves publicity. She has wrinkles in these, her middle years. Gossip photographers prefer to aim their lenses at milky skin and breasts that do not sag. Of course, a juicy story can magnetize a camera. An exiled prince, an heir, and so on. I'm entering the country secretly so I can adjust, plant my feet firmly on the ground, before the god of celebrity raises its ugly and overrated head and shines a spotlight in my face."

"May I ask, sir, the purpose of your visit to Luong?"

"It is not a visit. To pass through like a tourist is not my intention," Jean-Guy said. "I am immigrating to my natural home, to the world of my ancestors.

92

"When you are two colors, you are essentially the darker of the two. That is who you are. A mulatto is regarded as black. That is racism, but it is in the heart too. A man's duskiness is the coffee. His whiteness is cream and sugar, rich and cloying, but subordinate. I am a Luongan and I am home."

Eloquently done, Kiet said to himself. And artificial. The monologue was too perfect, the metaphor instantaneous. It smacked of rehearsal. Had it been from the heart, he would not be wrinkling his face at alleged vapors of hydrocarbons and excrement. He would be on his knees, kissing the kingdom of Luong.

"Eloquent," Kiet said. "And touching. You have a suite reserved at Hickorn's newest hotel, the Luong InterPresidential."

A crewman inched backward on the ramp, guiding a handtruck loaded with suitcases. He and another crewman carried out a steamer trunk.

"My apologies," Kiet said, gesturing to the Volkswagen. "We neglected to arrange for your luggage. Our staff car is inadequate."

"Not to worry," Jean-Guy said. "I brought along my own transportation. Everyone owns a possession they can't leave behind and this is mine."

Jean-Guy squatted and waved at the Hercules maw. A horn beeped. A wide, low sports car rolled onto the tarmac. It had massive alloy wheels and a baritone of an engine, an intimidatingly muscular rumble Kiet associated with aircraft power plants. The automobile was vivid red, except for windows, which were tinted black.

"Superintendent, a Testarossa!"

"Excuse me?"

"Ferrari! Ferrari Testa—Testa—Testarossa!"

Binh was inhaling, exhaling, inhaling, exhaling, eyes straining at the sockets. The precise medical term for the attack evaded Kiet, but he remembered the cure.

"Be calm, Captain. I'll go to the terminal and bring a paper bag for you to breathe into."

"No, no, I'm okay, Superintendent. The magnificence of it sort

93

of just temporarily blew me away. I never dreamed I'd see a Testarossa outside of a magazine. Twelve cylinders, four hundred prancing horses under the hood, three hundred kilometers per hour top speed. God, isn't it beautiful?"

Binh, heretofore sullen, was suddenly in the thrall of a machine. An impressive machine, Kiet had to admit. "Beautiful. Unquestionably."

Jean-Guy opened the driver's door and motioned. "Do the honors, would one of you? Needless to say, I don't know the town. The air crew will arrange to have my luggage brought to the hotel where I am registered as Pierre LeClerc. Clever, eh?"

Binh looked at Kiet, wordlessly asking permission. Kiet said, "Anonymity is important to Mister Pakse. This Testa-what automobile is not exactly inconspicuous."

"No sweat, Superintendent. The windows are as black as the ace of spades. No way could anybody see inside. We'd best scoot too, before the press is clued in. I'll keep in contact."

"Splendid logic," Kiet said. "Go."

They went, expanding the definition of Binh's *go*. Kiet conjured four hundred horses in harness, his euphoric young adjutant cracking a whip. Jet fighters launching from aircraft carriers should *go* like the red Testa-something.

A disappointing day, Kiet concluded. An irrational, meaningless, unproductive disappointment of a day. Minister of Agriculture Houphong Duc and his tennis and his salad bar and his double-talk. Chinatown and its incommunicative citizens and the void within Sincere Rice Company, Limited. Jean-Guy Pakse and the Luonganness pulsing in his heart. Assuming a stupid, silly, singsong French nom de guerre. Incognito in a snarling red sports car that might attract less attention than a flying saucer.

"Pierre LeClerc, Pierre LeClerc," he muttered, recollecting musical rhymes sung eons ago at *lycée*.

Kiet climbed into the VW, thinking that disappointment verged on ominous. Unlucky, accursed, fateful. The sensible thing would be to drive directly home and curl in the fetal position under his bed until his luck changed.

But I am not superstitious, Kiet told himself; I am a modern man in control of my own destiny. Armed with that questionable premise, he started the car. He revved eight fewer cylinders than Jean-Guy's Testa-who and headed for Madame Saravane's.

ELEVEN

It was an ordinary street, a quiet street perpendicular to Avenue Che Guevara, not far from Bamsan Kiet's villa. It was a strip of shops and flats inhabited by the Luongan middle-class. Their standard of living might be classified by a Western sociologist as "working poor," but they were unaware of their poverty; they lived indoors, had clothing to wear, food to eat.

The street had been renamed more frequently than any three others combined. Rue Adlai Stevenson to Rue Ngo Dinh Diem to Rue Sukarno to Rue Lin Piao to Rue Alexander Dubcek to Rue Edward Kennedy to Rue Nguyen Van Thieu to Rue Jimmy Carter to Rue Yuri Andropov to Rue Ferdinand Marcos. It was now Rue Dan Quayle.

Redesignations had been forced by death and/or fall from grace. Outsiders regarded the pattern as strange and ironic, a bizarre chain of bad luck. Residents of Rue Dan Quayle held a different view. Their celebrity neighbor possessed the magic to concoct luck, good and bad.

She conjured malevolent luck by flinging whammies across time zones and continents at the politicians. Believers concluded that the dooming and damning was a manifestation of a sense of humor, although no living person ever reported seeing a smile on her lips.

A moldy wooden placard tacked above the stairway adjacent a noodle soup café announced: Mme. Saravane. Quayle was typically congested with pedicabs, bicycles, and automobiles, but

Kiet had no trouble parking right beside Madame's understated sign. Good fortune, perhaps. There was usually a crush of limousines and European luxury cars. Only fools parked their vehicles on that side of the street, which Madame reserved for the convenience of wealthy and powerful clients.

You had money and influence, you came to Madame for advice. Taking a trip? Marrying off a daughter? Receiving an important guest? Selecting a piece of jewelry? Changing your hairstyle? Those crossroads in your life, you brought the decisions to Madame. She foretold through numerology and astrology and the configuration of chicken intestines what you should do and whether you should do it at all.

Kiet walked up the steps, remembering Binh on Madame Saravane. That old douche bag. Binh's intelligence-gathering ear to the ground. A naive and impossible promise. Gossiping and rumor-mongering were as natural to a Hickornian as taking a breath, but ask anybody and you would be informed that Madame Saravane confided only with the supernatural. Further, the idiot who dared whisper of her and malign her was asking for permanent canker sores.

Nonsense, Kiet thought. Wondering too, What did she do with her money? She was a notorious miser, an inconspicuous consumer. He instructed himself to snoop into her finances, her worldly mammon.

At the top of the stairs, Kiet knocked on a curtained glass door and was told to enter.

"You," said Madame Saravane.

"Me?" said Kiet.

She was seated in one of two bamboo chairs in the center of the rank, ill-lighted room. She wore layers of black silk that concealed feminine curves Kiet doubted she had anyway, a black bandanna, and a ransom in bracelets and necklaces and rings. Bony and wrinkled, with hard eyes encased in leathery bags, what teeth remained in her head were stained as black as her witch's costume from a lifetime of chewing betel nut. Outside of a museum sarcophagus, Kiet had never seen a human being as old.

98

"You have no appointment."

"I do not have an appointment," Kiet agreed.

Madame Saravane lighted an Emerald Queen cigarette from the one she was smoking. Emerald Queens were manufactured in Hickorn. They smelled like a car fire and were said to be as carcinogenic as plutonium. Madame had no cough and spoke in the voice of a woman half a century younger. Magic? "I admit no one without an appointment."

"Forgive me, Madame," Kiet said without much feeling as he reached for his badge.

She waved a bejeweled claw, saying, "Leave that tin trinket in your pocket, Kiet. I know who you are. You want your fortune told? Get out of here and make an appointment. See the lady in the noodle soup café. She sets my appointments."

"I do not want my fortune told, Madame. This is official police business."

"I have no business with the police."

"The police have business with you. A few questions, please."

"Five minutes. My next client needs me badly."

Kiet took the second chair. "His Scorpio is ascending erratically?"

"Impertinence counts on your five minute allotment."

"Explain your rogue comet, please."

"Not my comet. A comet's streak that revealed a streak of the future."

"And a caution regarding the present."

"How do you separate past, present, and future, Kiet? Today is yesterday's future and tomorrow's past."

"The comet was invisible to everybody else. The astronomy community. Everybody."

Madame exhaled Emerald Queen smoke that was the hue of a storm cloud and crooked a gnarled finger to emphasize her point, saying, "Astronomers see with their eyes. Astrologers see with their inner selves."

"Carl Sagan did not see your comet, Madame. Isaac Asimov did not see it."

Madame Saravane lighted an Emerald Queen and dropped the spent butt. It hissed in the foul water in the coffee can beside her chair. "Their eyes are . . ." she said, touching hers, then thumping her sunken chest, "not—"

"Ah, then it was not a trick to vindicate a political position, to slander His Royal Highness and blame him for the drought?"

"You are a vile and misinformed man, Kiet."

"Thank you. Why, please, did you in your tabloid column viciously attack His Royal Highness?"

"What is your date of birth?"

"Excuse me?"

"Your date of birth, Kiet. I'll tell your fortune, free of charge."

Kiet shook his head. "No. No thank you."

"Afraid?"

"Agnostic."

"Falfoux was my client."

Madame's eyes bored in on Kiet. He couldn't hold her gaze. He examined his fingernails.

"The Henri Falfoux who built the villa in which you have lived a substantial portion of your adult life. Yes, him," she went on. "The number on your gate is out of sequence, isn't it?"

"It is."

"510 Avenue Che Guevara. You live at 510 Avenue Che Guevara."

"So?"

"You should be at 580 or 590. The homes to your west should be 510 and 540. Falfoux was deeply troubled. I solved his problems numerologically. The mid-fives were crushing him sexually and personally. By my calculations, his master number was 5-1-0."

Kiet looked up from his fingernails.

"Falfoux couldn't perform. His wife's boyfriend could. The lover was Luongan, a double humiliation to a French cuckold."

"I trust your adjustment corrected his problems."

"Marvelously. His wife and his manhood returned to him. A year later, the lover boy was discovered flagrante delicto with the

100

Eurasian mistress of a Moroccan legionnaire, who blew them apart with one shot from an Enfield elephant gun. Why haven't you changed the number to its proper sequence?"

"Grandfather clauses in the Hickorn ordinance book permit a house number changed prior to revision of the code to remain as is."

"I know the law, Kiet. You recited it incompletely. 'To remain as is if altered on the recommendation of a competent astrologer in order to change the property owner's luck.' "

"An archaic, superstitious, nonsensical law."

"Why haven't you reverted your number to its proper geographic sequence, Kiet?"

Damn her, she had him rattled. His cheeks burned and he could not remember *his* question. If he had indeed left off at a question before Madame's departure into street numbers and voodoo. Onward. "You visited Feng Vu at my jail, did you not?"

"I did."

"He is your friend?"

"No."

"Client?"

"Give me your date of birth, Kiet. You're acting like a toad, an antisocial goon whose master number may be far different than 5-1-0. We can find you a suitable house number. Who knows, positive numerological alignment may give you decent manners. Reveal it to me. Your five minutes are disappearing."

"I never changed the number because of the paperwork, the replacement of identity documents and the like."

"You *did* change it," she said. "In excess of twenty-five years ago. You changed it and changed it back."

Kiet had not been lying. Not exactly. He had stashed that period of his life in a corner of his memory set aside for the horrible. The screams of his nightmares blew the dust off them. "Yes."

"You changed it to 5-8-0. The cholera epidemic of 1966 struck weeks later. Your wife died in your arms at 580 Avenue Che

Guevara. She was cremated and you, a widower, lived ever since at 5-1-0, now carnally consoled by that little nurse."

He had perhaps then believed that his innocent orderly action had knocked Tien's luck askew. He had also prayed to gods he hadn't believed in. It should not have surprised Kiet that Madame knew everything about him and that she turned his own demons on him. Her occult potency was derived from her ability to snoop and her prodigious memory, a mental card file of closeted Hickornian skeletons.

"Is Feng Vu your client?"

"I don't discuss my clients. They expect confidentiality."

Kiet groaned. "Madame is a doctor or a lawyer? You read birth certificates and entrails. How much do your clients pay you?"

Madame Saravane laid her hand over her forehead and closed her eyes, as if gauging a high fever. "Madame is sickened by your uncouthness."

"Splendid. How much did Feng Vu pay you for what? He seems at peace with his fate. Did you babble an incantation granting him eternal life?"

"One minute, Kiet. Then be gone. I can bear your cynical stench no longer."

"But you extended me a free horoscope offer."

"Yes. My promise is the hardest currency. End the insults and give me your date of birth."

"No. Instead of evaluating my numbers and heaping upon me a lifetime of wondrous luck, do this. Predict the future. Stories about Jean-Guy Pakse's immigration to Luong circulate. Are they true? Is he, and when?"

She shut her eyes tightly. To concentrate, Kiet thought, on the unseeable. "The rumors are untrue. The crown prince loves twelve-cylinder Italian sports cars and blonde Caucasians. He will marry the daughter of a Marseilles Lamborghini dealer."

Madame had answered too snappily, too assuredly. Madame, omniscient Madame, pleading ignorance of Jean-Guy's presence in Hickorn. She was therefore involved at some level in the peculiar migration of Jean-Guy Pakse.

102

Compounding this lie that ridiculed his intelligence was the hag's lacerating reference to Tien's death. Plus the insinuation about Quin's morals. Kiet was angry. People kowtowed to Madame and she trampled them. Not Bamsan Kiet. No thank you.

"Liar," he said.

Madame threw up her arms. Jewelry clanked like wind chimes. "You people, you police and ministers and businessmen, you come to me when all else fails! I am reviled and feared. Conversely I am afforded no respect."

"We pay you money, myself excluded. Where does it go? Swiss banks? Or do you sleep on a mattress bulging with banknotes?"

"You dare accuse me of miserliness and fraud?"

Kiet summoned a Binh Americanism. "If the shoe fits, shove it."

"Kiet, which do you care less to putrify agonizingly, what is between your ears or what is between your legs?"

"Thank you for asking."

"Which?"

"Ah, you are imposing a curse on me?"

"I am. Which?"

"Madame, exercise your good judgment."

"I shall," she said, glaring at his crotch. "I shall."

"Nonsense," Kiet said.

Madame Saravane smiled.

Thursday, May 21
Hickorn
High 97°, Low 81°
Clear

TWELVE

"You're walking funny, Superintendent. Like you've been riding a horse."

"Never mind," Kiet said, jabbing a thumb at the red Ferrari parked at his door, the Testa-something. "Captain, why are you not guarding our esteemed visitor?"

"No sweat," Binh said. "Jean-Guy, I never clocked him as a hermit. I didn't expect the incognito phase would last thirty minutes. I was prepared to make the sacrifice of escorting him on a chippy-chasing mission. I mean, what's a baby-sitter for? But he's holed up in his suite and has shown no inclination to wander. He just stares out the windows. Go figure."

"He is unguarded?"

Binh sighed. "Superintendent, he is *not* unguarded. There's just one way out of that suite and I've got my two best plainclothesmen posted. We slipped him upstairs yesterday through the side entrance. Everything's on the qt. Besides, it's 8:00 A.M. Jean-Guy is sound asleep. He's never been up at eight in his life."

"You have his car."

Binh grinned. "Sure do."

"With young Mr. Pakse's permission?"

"Yep. He said last night to me, be a buddy and go take it for a spin twice a day. It's good for the mechanisms. A Testarossa's made to be driven. Testarossa is 'redhead' in Italian, you know."

"Logical," Kiet said. "The car is redder than red."

"That's not it, Superintendent. Testarossas come in black and other colors. The cam covers are painted red."

"Logical," Kiet said.

"Would you believe that the glove box is electric?"

"I believe."

"Disc brakes. Twelve-point-two inches and vented. They're the size of pizza pans."

"No trunk space," Kiet said.

Binh shook his head, his instructional efforts hopeless. "Superintendent, I never said it was a practical car."

Binh was being highly informative but Kiet hoped that he would not launch on the benefits of "blowing out the carbon." To blow out the carbon and extend engine life required throttling said engine to capacity. Binh blew out carbon on Luong's only four-lane divided highway, the four kilometers of Richard Nixon Boulevard that linked downtown Hickorn to the airport.

Binh had raced mundane coupes and family sedans to speeds in excess of 150 kilometers per hour. What velocity was within the capability of the Tessa-Roasta? Kiet could not imagine. A tire failure, a collision, and he would bid hello to his ancestors wearing a Ferrari dashboard as a funereal headdress.

"Where are you taking me?"

"Just on back to the hotel."

"Good. Splendid."

"Hop in."

Kiet did, resting his butt on black leather that was disturbingly close to the ground. The glass, opaque from the outside, admitted light and images, and Kiet was mildly surprised. He asked, "What do you think of Jean-Guy, generally?"

"Not a bad dude. Once you get to know him, once he loosens up and mellows out, he's okay. One on one, he's not really the asshole we encountered at Hickorn International."

"Is he confiding in you?"

"About, like, how come he's in town, what his game plan is? Nope. Not yet."

"This automobile is a peculiar form of transportation for someone who craves privacy to adjust."

"Yeah, it is. I was brutally pissed when you stuck me as his baby-sitter, you know."

"I suspected."

"But things can work out for the best, can't they?"

"Yes," Kiet said, puzzled.

"Too much is happening too fast and out of the blue the alleged crown prince pops in on us secretly. The *Mind*, those illiterate dodos, they haven't a glimmer."

Binh took today's issue of the *Hickorn Enquiring Mind* from under his seat and held it up for emphasis. Kiet scanned the headlines. UFO EXPERT SAYS FLYING SAUCER TO LAND AT WIMBLEDON. WORLD'S FATTEST BRIDE EATS ENTIRE WEDDING CAKE. HICKORN HEAT WAVE CONTINUES.

"So far so good," Kiet said.

"Right, okay, at first that special security liaison bullshit was security-weighted as opposed to intelligence gathering."

"Indeed."

"Pretty smart of you, Superintendent. You were looking ahead, predicting Jean-Guy as some kind of critical role player."

"Yes. Yes, I was," Kiet said, trusting that it did not sound like a question.

"Only one man could be trusted with this job. Me."

"Absolutely," Kiet said. "Positively."

"Like Red would say, on third and goal at the one yard line, you give the ball to the hoss who ain't gonna fumble, right?"

Kiet nodded blankly. "Of course. We are going to the hotel to awaken Jean-Guy for a specific reason?"

"Nope. I'm taking you to the missionary."

"The missionary?"

"She's also a guest at the Luong InterPresidential."

Kiet suppressed a groan. Binh and his non sequiturs. "What missionary, please?"

"The missionary who flew in last night on this ratty cargo charter loaded with relief supplies that customs turned around and sent off with its freight still on board and her raising a big stink and

109

refusing to leave with the plane and finally customs saying okay, fine, lady, then calling headquarters and dumping her on us, but by the time our officers get to the terminal where all the hell is being raised, she's gone off in a taxi to the InterPresidential, and they say the hell with it until they pass on the glad tidings to me inside of one hour ago at Jean-Guy's suite, so here I am, coming for you before going to interview her since a potentially sticky situation like this, well, I thought you'd like to be in on it."

Binh's vast rapid-fire sentence was a symptom of anxiety, of a plate heaped with dilemmas. It was spoken in a *single* breath. Were Binh a Micronesian, Kiet thought, he would be a prosperous pearl diver.

"There's just too damn much going on, Superintendent. I need this missionary flap like I need an ingrown toenail."

"His Royal Highness is discouraging drought relief aid."

"I'm on his side, Superintendent, 100 percent, and Minister Duc is dead wrong on this issue, because you give charities carte blanche, they'll turn Luong into a raggedy-assed soup kitchen, although this missionary we're talking about, named Mary Beth Applebee, that's a middle-American monicker dripping with Mom, apple pie, and Chevrolet by the way, an old blue-hair lady I'll bet, she's affiliated with some nickel and dime Bible-walloping outfit out of Seattle."

"Prince Pakse gratefully accepts humble gifts donated in kindness. I am no champion of missionaries, but—"

"Yeah, you were around when they were—oops, sorry, Superintendent, I'm not ragging you about your age. You were a young pup in those days, right?"

"An early adolescent at Independence, yes," Kiet said. "Most of the missionaries departed with the French. Perhaps they were afraid of being eaten."

"Well, you never talked about them to me a lot, but I envisioned them as pushy."

"They were authoritarian," Kiet said. "Especially in the country. The peasants had less education than city people. They were

110

easier to sell. Trade them your superstitions for theirs. Rural people believed in animism and its variations. They were pagan, savage, atheistic. Happily, some still are. Try as they might, the French didn't completely obliterate our heritage."

"They were pretty authoritarian, weren't they? Embrace Jesus or else?"

"They were shrewder than that. They instituted schools. The schools provided, besides a European education by rote, meals, clothing, and medicine. Cooperation was rewarded."

"That's like those gospel missions in the States, Superintendent. They do good deeds, sure, but on their terms. You eat their meal, you listen to the sermon first."

"Our prejudices aside, why did customs not allow the Applebee woman's plane to unload?"

"Just between you and I and the fencepost, Superintendent, there wasn't diddly on board worth stealing. You know customs. Half those guys would roll out the red carpet for a hydrogen bomb if you greased their palms."

"Hasn't it been our experience, Captain, that anything is worth stealing?"

"Yeah, but this was too goofy," Binh said. "She'd apparently organized this run from Bangkok in a super rush."

"A rush? Why?"

"I don't have anything solid. I actually don't have zilch. She can maybe tell us what the hell is going on."

"What was on the aircraft?"

"Edibles, though edible is using the term loosely on part of the stuff. She scrounged an oddball load. You can buy whatever you can pay for in that town. She brought bulk foodstuffs, Western and East European origin, bagged and case cans, both. When you wheel and deal for that kind of bulk in Southeast Asia, well, you can be reasonably safe in assuming it was foreign aid to begin with."

"Destination elsewhere?"

"Yeah. Toss a dart at a globe. Those customs scumbags have

111

a sharp eye for contraband. You couldn't give the canned goods away. Creamed corn. Borscht. Bean soup. Spaghetti and meatballs. Yucch!

"This crap went out the back door of aid agencies who couldn't pay folks to eat it. Poor dumb old Applebee, they probably screwed her on the deal. The bagged goodies weren't any better. The potatoes were sprouting. The wheat had green stuff growing on it. The rice was brown, three crops old, and rancid.

"Applebee's manifest was a Chinese fire drill. She was definitely in violation of import-export laws if you're gonna be picky. She didn't have the money to pay a bribe or the decency to import stuff worth skimming, so to hell with her was the bottom line."

Traffic was as usual a mess. It was the morning rush hour, a human-powered crush of pedestrians, bicycles, pedicabs, and the rare motor vehicle. Kiet regarded it as a merciful mess. Binh was restrained to a walking pace, an impatient dance of clutch-brake-gas, fingers all the while thrumming the steering wheel. Passersby stared at their metallic beast and squinched unseeing into the blackened windows. Their expressions were uniformly incredulous, like Wimbledon UFO watchers.

Kiet reported his audience with Madame Saravane. He spoke frankly about her curse. He did not mention the side effect, however, the slight discomfort and hardly unnoticeable limp Binh observed and inaccurately referred to as "walking funny." Moments before the adjutant's arrival, while examining himself with a hand mirror—a reasonable precaution—he had strained a groin muscle.

"That old bitch and her voodoo, Superintendent. What hogwash! What a bunch of happy horseshit!"

"I agree. Sheer nonsense."

"Uh, you're feeling okay today, aren't you?"

"Yes."

"No headaches? No trouble peeing?"

"Captain, am I in the company of a believer?"

"No way, Superintendent. My point is that the human mind is potent. It can play tricks on you. People get well on placebos

112

because they believe they'll get well. Same when it comes to getting sick. Madame's big-time in the local occult scene. She says your dick's gonna rot off, your subconscious is listening."

"Thank you," Kiet said.

"You could carry garlic around with you. Or a crucifix. Those things could help. Mind you, I don't buy any of that bunk for an instant, but where the supernatural and the unconscious psyche are concerned, it doesn't pay to take chances."

"Captain—"

"You know, I really wish you hadn't confronted her, Superintendent. I guess I've made it clear where I stand on Feng Vu. You needlessly jeopardized yourself on account of that worthless scumbag."

"Captain—"

"Say, yesterday when we were talking about the execution, I can't remember, did you give me an answer on my request for a rehearsal?"

"No, I did not. Captain?"

"Yeah?"

"We passed it."

"Oops," Binh cranked the steering wheel, U-turning the car.

His policy on sudden changes of course was swerve now, observe later. Kiet clenched his eyes until the one-eighty was accomplished. Remarkable. The Ferrari was intact. Neither innocent persons nor property had spilled onto the pavement.

The Luong InterPresidential was as pretentious as its name. Six floors of precast concrete and diamond-shaped windows, it was back to back to the venerable Hickorn Continental, the fallen king of the city's hostelry.

For half a century you could sit at the Conti's open-air *terrasse*, lazing under ceiling fans, sipping cocktails, gossiping, seducing, dealing. But now the money had moved across the alley to teak trim, marble floors, and velour sofas in the lobby and elevators; liveried foreign domestics, hot water, functional telephones, satellite television, and, yes, air conditioning.

Financing of the InterPresidential was convoluted, ownership

113

indeterminate. The money and string-pullers were rumored to be: Japanese, Hong Kongers fleeing 1997, Golden Triangle opium warlords, Elvis.

Kiet despised the place. Except for the delectable fried shrimp they served on the *terrasse*, he was no lover of the Continental either. Schemes originating at the landmark often entangled him. The Conti was at least Luongan, neocolonial Luongan to the hard-nosed nationalist, true, but Luongan nonetheless. The Luong InterPresidential spurned the indigenous climate and culture. Its architecture and decor was antiseptic, alien.

An Indian doorman in brocaded tunic and visored hat smiled, and said, "Welcome to the InterPresidential, Sahib."

He parted the thick glass doors. The lobby air conditioning slid out like a block of ice and clobbered Kiet.

Binh led the way, tugging at his uniform shirt, saying, "ahhh!" Kiet trudged behind, making a manly effort not to shiver. At the sight of Hickorn's top two cops, easily a dozen people rose from overstuffed velvet. They were not tourists, they were reporters.

"How do we handle them?" Binh asked.

"You evade, I lie."

"Is the crown prince in Hickorn?"

"No comment," said Binh.

"Who?" said Kiet.

"Jean-Guy Pakse. The Ferrari. We've seen it around town. Jean-Guy owns a Testarossa. Is it his?"

"No comment," Binh said.

"No, it is not his, whoever you are talking about," Kiet said.

"Whose is it, Superintendent?"

"Somebody else's."

"Who does it belong to. We have the right to know."

"Elvis."

"What are you detectives doing at the InterPresidential?"

"No comment," Binh said.

"Investigating pilferage of dining room silverware. Excuse us, please."

114

The desk clerk had a suitably snotty demeanor, but he recognized Kiet and Binh. He did not exhibit his nostrils.

"Miss Applebee's room number?" Binh asked.

"Room 202, gentlemen. Oh."

"Oh?"

"She isn't in her room. She's having breakfast with Mr. LeClerc in his suite."

THIRTEEN

Jean-Guy Pakse's penthouse suite was the largest of three. A brass placard on the door identified it as "The Victorian Suite." Binh had dizzily explained this oddity in the elevator, saying that besides the increased square footage of the unit, they could charge heftier bucks—you think the InterPresidential takes the Luongan zin, you're dreaming—because of the old world classiness, since the other suites and the rest of the rooms, to some extent, were done in a Vegas motif that borrowed heavily from the interiors of American luxury cars. Not that he was criticizing. Different strokes, you know.

Two uniformed officers saluted and admitted them to The Victorian Suite. Kiet's puzzlement did not abate. The anteroom ceilings were coved. The wallpaper was busy, the carpeting busier, the ornate furniture busier still. Dark wood moldings trimmed everything immovable.

"Wild pad, huh?"

"I am contracting vertigo," Kiet said.

"A harpsichord next to the armoire would be a nifty finishing touch," Binh said.

"In here," Jean-Guy yelled.

They followed his voice, entering a small corner room that featured windows overlooking ministry buildings and the royal palace. Prince Pakse's alleged son and a Caucasian woman were eating breakfast. White linen, shellfish omelets and toast wedges on gilded china, sterling flatware, floral centerpiece, champagne in iced bucket. The Hickorn Sporting Club, Kiet thought.

Jean-Guy wore a silk robe. "Hungry?" he asked, gesturing at the spread. "I can have more food sent up."

"No thank you," Kiet said, looking at the woman. She had on loose-fitting clothing, a white blouse and gray slacks. Her hair was short and blonde, not Binh's blue-hair blue, although blue was the color of her eyes. Nor was she old, not a day older than thirty-five. She wore no makeup, no jewelry.

Kiet regarded Caucasian women as not especially attractive. They were afflicted with long noses and coarse features. Their hips were wide, their breasts bulbous. No shaving regimen could conceal the reality of prolific body hair. But this young woman was as pretty as the most delicate Luongan. She matched his image of "Western angelic," and there was nothing fundamentally wrong with that.

"You policemen rescue damsels in distress every day, don't you? You lead exciting lives. I had the pleasure of rescuing my first damsel a while ago," Jean-Guy said, gesturing again. "Gentlemen, Miss Mary Beth Applebee."

"How nice to meet you," she said. "Mister LeClerc was wonderful. I was at my wit's end, making a fool of myself, and if it hadn't have been for Mr. LeClerc . . ."

Her melodic voice vanished in a whisper. She dabbed an eye with her napkin, absorbing a tear at the instant of secretion. A single, perfect, tragic missionary's tear, Kiet thought cynically.

He looked at Binh, who was looking at Mary Beth Applebee. Oh no, he thought. He had seen that melancholy lip-licking expression before. Binh's groin and heart were receiving mixed signals of lust and worship, a confusion of dark wet treasures and pedestal placement. Yet another complication to this hellish mess of a week.

"No, no, Mary Beth," Jean-Guy said quickly. "None of it was your fault. And, please, I am Pierre."

"I was frazzled and got on the up elevator when I should have been on the down," she said, ending on a musical sigh.

118

Jean-Guy said, "She was being harassed all evening by customs at the airport. She was so upset she couldn't sleep. She was going to the restaurant off the lobby for breakfast and landed on my floor instead."

"You rescued her," Kiet said, wondering where the implied heroism came into the story.

"To an insignificant degree," Jean-Guy said, shrugging.

"Oh, don't you listen to Mr. Le—Pierre's modesty," Mary Beth said, patting the gallant crown prince's hands. "That little boo-boo was the last straw. I just went to pieces. Pierre heard my awful hysterics. He came out and talked to me and asked me in to eat and I feel much, much improved. He is so sensitive. He picked my mood right up. That is a God-given talent."

"Miss Applebee, at great personal sacrifice, was endeavoring to aid the Luongan people and she was outrageously abused by government officials," Jean-Guy said, glowering, flushing in anger and/or rapture from Mary Beth's angelic hand pat. "I'm going to get to the bottom of this. Believe it!"

Kiet glanced at Binh, presuming that his adjutant would take command, would say that they were in The Victorian Suite to investigate this very problem. But he remained locked on Mary Beth Applebee, virtually catatonic.

Kiet said, "We came to the hotel to interview Miss Applebee on that very problem and were directed to this suite. Miss, you are a missionary?"

She kneaded her napkin. "A pathetic excuse for a servant of the Lord. I represent a coalition of Christian charities in Seattle. Alone they are too poor to afford to do the Lord's work overseas. They read of your drought, pooled their funds, and selected me to deliver our humble offering. Every cent we had was tied up in the airplane charter and the food I bought in Bangkok. I was in a fool's rush to complete the Lord's task before I ran out of money."

"Not to worry, Miss Applebee. Do you have influence with customs, Superintendent Kiet?" Jean-Guy said.

"Some."

"Excellent. I suggest that it would be preferable for you to

119

demand of them the return of the airplane and foodstuffs. Because I'm merely a private citizen, my methods might not be as effective. I'm willing to push as hard as I have to, but time is of the essence. If you fail, I'll step in. How does that sound to you?"

"Splendid. A good plan."

"Please do everything possible," Mary Beth told Kiet. "Starving Luongans are depending on us."

Kiet said he would and went to the door, wondering how hungry he would have to be to eat creamed canned corn. Binh had sufficiently regained his wits to follow him into the anteroom.

"Superintendent, if it's all the same to you, I'll stick around. I am, after all, special security liaison to Jean-Guy."

Kiet did not reply.

"Isn't she gorgeous?" Binh whispered.

"Indeed."

"Well, Jean-Guy's reputation, you know, as smooth an operator as he is, Superintendent, Mary Beth hasn't got a chance." Binh's whisper had assumed the tone of escaping steam.

"A chance of what, please."

"Five'll get you ten she's still a virgin. She's a lamb trapped in a pen by a wolf, pun intended. Jean-Guy, he'll be playing hide the salami the minute the champagne's gone. Mary Beth won't have a prayer, pun also intended."

The relevance of salami? And weren't the omelets filled with crab and shrimp anyway? The lad had been knocked silly by his own hormones. Kiet clapped his chivalrous, lovesick shoulders. "Captain, permission granted. Guard Jean-Guy's life and Mary Beth's chastity."

He rode to the lobby and saw the reporter contingent swarming the red Ferrari. Several were jotting the automobile's French license plate number into notebooks, including a representative of the *Mind*. Once they had that number, they would make inquiries and soon have Jean-Guy's. *Mind* reporters were particularly resourceful and they enjoyed a fat budget. They could spend all day on the phone chatting with French motor vehicle registration employees.

Speaking of telephones. Kiet was without transportation and was not in a reckless enough mood to ride a motorized pedicab to Hickorn International. He could stand outside and hail a taxi or he could phone for one. The technologies integrated in the Luong InterPresidential were, yes, stupendous, but probably somewhat apocryphal. Hot water on demand was preposterous. Functional telephones were surely science fictional.

The Hickorn telephone network had been installed by the French earlier in the century. The governor general who dedicated the system cut the ribbon at Hickorn Metro headquarters and ceremoniously dialed the first number, the number of his office telephone. He received a busy signal. The major improvement since had been modification of pay phones to accept coins of larger denomination. To this day it was easier to call Greenland than across the street.

Kiet asked the desk clerk to please summon a taxi. The clerk handed him a telephone that had neither a cord nor a rotary dial.

"Cellular," he said. "Do it yourself, sir. You will get through the first time, every time."

The device was black plastic and rectangular. Numbers one through zero were on an array of tiny squares that Kiet likened to Lilliputian throat lozenges.

"Trust me, sir. The InterPresidential is on the leading edge of consumer science. We have one of Hickorn's two cellular transceivers on our roof. The second is at the airport.

"The number of custom's main station, please."

The clerk consulted a crumpled Hickorn directory that had the dimensions of a weekly newsmagazine. "46 . . . 810. You are expecting a shipment, Superintendent?"

Kiet, forgetting that he could walk to privacy with the toy telephone, glared. "Never mind."

The clerk took the hint and sidled out of earshot. Kiet, possessor of pudgy fingers, punched the baby buttons with a pencil eraser.

121

"Chief Customs Agent Ninh Tho speaking."

"Tho, you're still on the job. I thought you would be in a Hong Kong penthouse, tapping your Swiss bank accounts. What is it? Greed for the sake of greed? I've heard of that sickness, the accumulation of the fortune superseding the enjoyment of it."

"Hello, Kiet. I can assume you are still at *your* job, living the miserable, impoverished life of the stupid and honest cop. A sackcloth moron of a martyr as per usual, I'm informed. Too dumb to grab what is there to grab. How have you been?"

"Splendid, Tho. Thank you. Yourself?"

"Couldn't be better. Thanks for caring."

Kiet and Tho had years ago abandoned pretenses. Chief Customs Agent Ninh Tho was out of Superintendent Bamsan Kiet's jurisdiction, and the latter accepted the impossibility of converting the former to decency. They were at an impasse, a symbiotic impasse. Kiet tolerated Tho's contraband on Hickorn's black market. Tho reciprocated by responding candidly and thoroughly to Kiet's inquiries.

"Tho, the woman missionary's charter last night from Bangkok. Talk to me, please."

"She's cute for a white girl."

Ninh Tho had so many mistresses that Kiet thought of them as concubines, a loose-knit harem. "Why did you refuse the airplane?"

"You should've seen the shit they had, Kiet."

"Creamed canned corn."

"That's not the worst of it," Tho said. "Cranberry sauce. What the hell is a cranberry?"

"I do not know."

"She's bringing stuff to help us, she should be bringing stuff we can use, like Scotch whiskey and American cigarettes. Or perfume. Perfume is good too if it's a European name nobody can pronounce."

"Good for your black market, Tho. Commodities very useful to hungry people."

"We could've worked something out, Kiet, the missionary and myself. A cash money deal. There's rice out there, Kiet. You just have to cough up the wherewithal to buy it."

Ninh Tho was bald and roly-poly. He had body odor and he glistened with sweat, as if he perspired mineral oil. Kiet asked, "Worked something out? Did you expose yourself to her?"

"I offered to, in my office. She wasn't buying."

"Then?"

"I went by the book. I performed my duty according to the manual and with the best interests of the kingdom of Luong foremost."

"Amazing."

"Amazing to me too, Kiet. Her paperwork was screwy and the garbage she was transporting wouldn't bring fifty zin altogether downtown. Any hungry person who ate it would barf his guts out. Cream of asparagus soup. What the hell is an asparagus?"

"I don't know."

"The situation was suspicious, Kiet. I was tempted to tear the cartons apart one by one."

"How did Miss Applebee react?"

"She fussed and whined."

"Vigorously?"

"No. Not as vigorously as I would've if I'd gone halfway around the world and was told I couldn't do what I set out to do for whatever god it is I happen to worship. She's mousy, but maybe not as mousy as she pretends to be. It kind of bothered me that she gave up so soon. A pretty lady always has something of value to barter with me, and I'm not referring to whiskey or smokes."

"She is perhaps a virgin, Tho."

"She is? You've seen her?"

"Yes."

"Do you think she is a virgin? A virgin of her age and attractiveness is extremely exotic, isn't she?"

"I don't know if she is a virgin. I don't care. I am not her boyfriend. I am not her gynecologist."

"Kiet, listen, I have a contact who has a contact to the cousin of this Arab oil—"

"Next question, Tho. An earlier arrival from Paris—"

"Is the Ferrari owner the crown prince? That is the rumor going around."

"No," Kiet said. "His name is Pierre LeClerc. He sells, uh, air conditioners."

"Really? Red Williams could take notes from him. Red rides in taxis. LeClerc drives a Testarossa."

"You and Red Williams are friends?"

"Acquaintances. He's giving me a window unit for my office. I close my eyes to import duties. Uh-oh, Kiet, sorry, you of pure heart and clean hands. You don't think any less of Red for that, do you?"

"Of course not. My opinion of him is unchanged."

"He played American football. They say he was a terror. I've watched films on television. Those guys collide and the stadium shakes."

"I too am in awe of Mr. Red Williams. Did you inspect Mr. LeClerc's airplane?"

"No."

"Why not?"

Ninh Tho sighed. "Because we were bribed not to. Kiet, I worry. Old age is gaining on you."

"Excuse me. I apologize for my ignorance. Bribed by whom, please?"

"The Ministry of Agriculture. Who else? This assistant deputy something who can hardly stand up on his rubber legs because he has to lose at tennis constantly to Houphong Duc and convincingly fake it. He's Duc's bag man."

"Why do you say 'who else,' please?"

"Kiet, you're so fucking righteous and principled, the goodness is dissolving your brain."

"Please humor me."

There was a pause. Kiet visualized an exasperated head shake. "Tho, how can a head swivel on shoulders without benefit of a

124

neck? When you pass on, and I shall mourn inconsolably, your remains should be willed to a museum of natural history."

"You're not what I'd call an anorexic either, Kiet."

"Tho, I am an understanding person. The new strains of venereal disease, I realize, affect one's mental processes, so I shall repeat slowly—why did you say 'who else?' A straight answer would be appreciated."

"The Ministry of Agriculture chartered the flight and paid in advance. I saw the papers. Logical?"

Kiet said it was very logical, wished Tho the Western neologism "have a nice day," and attempted to hang up. There was no hook to follow the cord he didn't have. The gizmo had the heft of a bird's nest, yet the sound was strong and crisp. He laid it delicately on the front desk.

The two uniformed officers guarding Jean-Guy Pakse walked out of an elevator. Kiet motioned to them.

"You were on when the American lady entered the suite?"

"Yes sir."

"Yes sir."

"I have a dirty mind," Kiet said. "I am therefore wondering whether she went into the Victorian Suite long before breakfast was served."

"Yes sir."

"Yes sir."

"Ah. Before breakfast was *ordered?*"

"Yes sir."

"Yes sir."

"What time of the morning, please? Only one of you should reply. Echoes are distracting."

"Nine-thirty, sir," an officer said.

"The wall clock reads nine o'clock," Kiet said. "Shouldn't you consult your log?"

"No sir," said the other officer. "Nine-thirty P.M. Yesterday evening."

125

FOURTEEN

Luong University was established by the French in 1909 to train upper-class natives of dull intellect and refined manners for the civil service. Until independence it manufactured clerks and little else. The era and the curriculum changed, and social barriers fell. It was possible today for a farmer's or shopkeeper's son to also be educated as a petty bureaucratic tyrant.

Half the student body still enrolled in the College of Government Administration. Quin often complained to Kiet, "We in the med school are fighting brain death while Admin teaches it as an academic major."

Of the colleges besides Administration, the College of Medicine was inarguably Luong University's most distinguished. Its parasitology department was among the Far East's finest. An adjunct to the parasitology department's research and treatment center was the recent study of nutritional disorders.

Kiet was en route there, walking through stucco, tile-roofed classrooms and a baked memory of lush green grounds. As he headed for the College of Medicine and Quin Canh, he rehearsed his lie, which wasn't precisely a lie at all, but rather what he considered a partial omission of information.

The non-lie pertained to last night's cancellation of their tryst. He was a policeman and things happened. He had tersely cited excessive paperwork at his office.

He had not precisely said that he would be working late, attending to backlogged paperwork. He just said that it existed. That was the unmitigated truth—past, present, or future.

The partially omitted fact was that he knew he would have been unable to perform. Madame Saravane's curse, however preposterous, had whammied his subconscious mind.

Quin was a nurse, a dedicated healer with a touch of scientist sprinkled in. This witchcrafted severing of his libido would not amuse her. It wasn't that she would be unsympathetic to a temporary flameout of his ardor. She was, after all, no nymphomaniac. But she was a modern woman and the medieval aspect would appall her.

That he had stood her up to peruse himself with a mirror for lesions, implying instead that he was shuffling documents would probably alter their relationship forever. That is, if she believed him at all and did not leap to the conclusion that he had spent his passion elsewhere.

A mess. A genuine mess.

Kiet went into the College of Medicine building burdened by an unfair amount of guilt. The twin surprises garnered in the Luong InterPresidential lobby did not much soothe. How could one clarify a convincing semitruthful non-lie, sell it, when bombarded with two instances of important skulduggery?

The virginal Mary Beth Applebee sequestered throughout the night with Jean-Guy Pakse, debaucher of the Mediterranean region. The wealthy playboy Jean-Guy, his immigration subsidized by the Ministry of Agriculture. By Houphong Duc, that little Yuppie-MBA-NICster-suspendered snot.

It was too much, an overflow of evidence for a nonexistent crime, a glut of stimulation. He was feeling hot and bloated, as he did when he overindulged in rich food and/or Golden Tiger.

"Bamsan. What on earth are you doing here?"

The building was cross-shaped and they had nearly collided at right angles in the center. Kiet said, "Six reports are due by the end of the week."

She had him by the arm pulling him along in the direction she was headed. "Bamsan, what does that mean?"

"I don't know," Kiet said. "Where are you dragging me?"

"I was buzzed. An emergency. I was teaching a medications

delivery class. We have call-boards in the lecture halls. We'll have to talk on the run."

"Four of the six reports are to be completed in triplicate."

"Bamsan, have you been drinking? Your ears are as red as pomegranates."

"No."

"Have we had you in for a blood pressure test lately?"

"No. Useless. A waste of time. If I had no blood pressure, I wouldn't be alive. I am in the pink."

"Your face says you are in the crimson."

"Never mind. It is the hot weather."

"Why are you limping?"

"I am not limping. What sort of emergency?"

"A beriberi case. An adult male from Foh Ten. He was in an advanced stage of acute beriberi, barely conscious and partially paralyzed. He has neuritis, edema, and an irregular heartbeat."

Foh Ten, Kiet thought. Better known as Dragon's Bile. Hickorn's hideous slum on the west side of the Ma San River. Your nose told you when you were there. It had no sewage system and garbage was constantly picked through, too precious to be trucked off. Streets were not worthy of alleys, and dwellings were a hodgepodge of cardboard and tin and mud. Foh Ten was a warren of the hopelessly poor, the displaced person, the petty criminal, and the army deserter. No police officer entered it alone, day or night. Ever.

"Quin, how did he get to the hospital?"

"Somebody brought him and left him at a door," Quin said. "You know how Foh Ten people avoid Hickorn proper. His friends and family must have seen how gravely ill he was and how he was worsening."

"Malnutrition?" Kiet asked, adding, "Sorry. Stupid question."

"Not technically a stupid question, Bamsan. He wasn't getting enough to eat and the nutrients of what he did eat weren't benefitting him because of alcoholism. Alcohol interferes with the body's absorption of thiamine."

"Foh Ten Punch," Kiet said.

129

"What is Foh Ten Punch?"

"Whatever you have that is laced with alcohol. Absolutely anything. And the alcohol could have been distilled to drink or to degrease machine parts," Kiet said, inexplicably thinking of the Hickorn Sporting Club's mysterious salad bar and of his missing cat.

Kiet followed Quin into a room. An emaciated man with swollen ankles was prone on a bed. He was an old man who might have been twenty or sixty. He wore only shorts. A tube ran from his arm to a suspended bottle. A perspiring doctor was bent over him, massaging his chest, grunting at each thrust of the heels of his hands. He was using a motion and a force that Kiet associated with pushing a stalled car.

"Defibrillator, Nurse!"

"Yes, Doctor." Quin ran into the hall.

The patient's eyes were wide and unblinking. They seemed to focus on Kiet. The man was like a face on a poster, not quite alive, eyes staring straight at the camera, eyes that stared right into his, regardless of the angle from which the poster was viewed.

Kiet edged to his side, careful not to impede the doctor. The man's eyes fluttered. He exhaled and the fluttering stopped. His gaze remained on Kiet, but that special luminescence from within was gone.

The doctor ceased work and wiped his brow with a forearm.

Quin rolled a castered cart into the room. On it was a machine. Attached by cords to the machine were two black cups.

Quin hurriedly plugged in the machine and unrolled the cords.

The doctor refused the cups.

FIFTEEN

Kiet went to headquarters, shaken by the death. He had seen stiffs, yes, each corpse one too many, but nobody except his beloved Tien had ever expired at such an intimate distance. The Foh Ten wretch, a stranger, had made it personal. By his fixation, he had chosen Bamsan Kiet as the last human being he would see in this world.

Further, in an unfortunately timed exhalation he had gasped his last and Kiet had felt the warmth of that final breath. What was the significance? Was he jettisoning his soul? Had he drawn Kiet close for a lifesaving purpose? Was Kiet supposed to snatch the man's spirit out of the air like one of Red Williams's footballs, intercepting it from the man's ancestors?

Kiet thought of Feng Vu. Two men in a week and a lifetime would die before him. The moment was correct for a follow-up interview.

The head jailer was on duty at the jail dispatch anteroom. He jumped off his stool and saluted. He had been reading an English-language magazine that glorified mercenary soldiers. Kiet was familiar with the publication. Its editorial slant was weaponry and troublemaking. He imagined that it appealed to sissy boys with violent fantasies.

The young sergeant had promise, but apparently needed guidance. Kiet made a mental note to take the lad aside for a chat when circumstances were less hectic.

"Who is on Feng Vu watch, please?"

Kiet's question was answered by a guard who stumbled through the inner doorway, clinging to the handle for support. His white uniform was spattered red. An eye was shut, already puffy and bluish. The officer was holding his jaw, attempting to speak, his lips rounding into the "oo" diphthong.

Kiet filled in the preceding "V," and told the head jailer, "Up front! Have them send for medical care for this man. Bring extras. Not all the blood is his. Then send as many officers as they can spare me."

Kiet ran through the main jail and into the isolation block. The painful promenade of the beaten policeman had excited the prisoners, had agitated them giddy and insolent. They hurled insinuations at Kiet about his mother and little boys, but he heard not a one.

Feng Vu was seated on his plywood bunk, a goofy look on his face that struck Kiet as a beatific sneer. His arms were on his thighs, palms up. His wrists were meat, his slacks beneath stained red. A rivulet of blood had dried at a corner of his mouth, affording him the appearance of a postprandial vampire.

It dismayed Kiet that an officer of his had apparently smuggled a razor or a knife in to his celebrity prisoner.

Vu's cell door was closed, automatically locked. The jailer's key was on the floor. Kiet picked it up and walked over to the cell.

Feng Vu said, "Kiet. You solved the crime against me and you are coming to free me? You recovered the rice? You are going to, instead, on Monday shoot the persons who framed me?"

Kiet twisted the key in the lock and said, "No."

Vu stood and made fists. "You have no right to prevent me from taking my own life."

"You said you wouldn't, Vu. You said you wouldn't cheat me."

"I lied. A man of my pride and stature cannot, will not, shall not, be killed for the amusement of a lunk mob."

Kiet opened the cell door.

"You're acting like a village idiot if you think you can subdue me by yourself. Ten strong men would be required and you're

132

nine short. But you can't wait for your reinforcements, can you? I'll have bled to death. Such a dilemma. What will you do?"

Kiet could not conceive this man possessing a spirit. But there had to something within that escaped at death. He pictured the Chinese's essence departing like a fighter pilot ejecting from a stricken jet.

Would Vu's ancestors then refuse a soul so crude and obnoxious? If Kiet had been superstitious, he might have feared the possibility of the man's shrill rejected soul being eternally snared at headquarters. Haunting him. Sneering beatifically at him.

Kiet walked into the cell and slammed the door. "What I will do is act like a lunk village idiot."

Feng Vu stepped forward one pace in the tiny cell and brought himself within range. He swung a right cross. Kiet, never quick and no brawler either, ducked. He had counted on Vu's loss of blood to dizzy him, slow his attack, and it had.

His face was in Vu's chest when the next punch came. A left hook rustled air behind Kiet's head. He lifted upward with all his strength, lifting on the tips of his toes, ramming his fist into Vu's jaw.

Teeth cracked. Feng Vu's head jerked. He tumbled backward, bouncing off the wall and then onto his plywood bunk. His tumble from fist to floor sounded to Kiet like an automobile accident.

Kiet looked down at Vu and rubbed his knuckles. The rice czar was unconscious and Kiet could, miraculously, move all ten fingers.

"You saved Feng Vu's life by knocking him out, Superintendent," said the doctor. "Your pulse rate slows during loss of consciousness, and he could do no additional harm to himself."

The physician was wiry and intense. His clinic was located three buildings east on Avenue Alexander Loubet, above a tattoo parlor and a purveyor of incense. He had practiced emergency medicine for the Hickorn police department before, but his specialty was the embarrassing infection. Captain Binh referred to the doctor as a "chancre mechanic."

Feng Vu's wrists would not fester due to contact with a prostitute, but it comforted Kiet to know that antibiotics had been administered competently, by a highly experienced penicillin injector. Vu was taped, medicated, and upright on his bunk, semiconscious, coming out of sedation. Kiet had been both elated and horrified to learn that Vu had damaged his wrists by chewing though them.

Kiet's elation was due to the knowledge that his guards had not betrayed their oaths by smuggling Vu a sharp object. His horrification was the awareness that a creature capable of gnawing through its own flesh had not become extinct during the last ice age.

"I can't relate to what he did," the doctor said to Kiet. "It's beyond my comprehension and training. I've had patients procrastinate too long before visiting me, mortified by their afflictions, their wives suspicious about chronic headaches, that they were agonized to an extraordinary depth of psychological miasma, but Mr. Vu's masochistic—"

"Thank you," Kiet said. "His physical condition, please."

The doctor coughed and said, "He severed minor arteries and a hundred capillaries."

He lighted an Emerald Queen. "I forget the medical name for the gushers. We studied the terminology in med school. Anyway, he missed them."

"Nobody cares about terminology," Kiet said. "And?"

"His front teeth are jagged, Superintendent. Your pugilistic legacy. He could chomp through, an effortless piercing of skin once the tape is removed."

"I am doubling the guard," Kiet said. "I appreciate your advice, but we will be on alert."

"I'll instruct your men on changing his dressings twice a day and I—scratch that."

"Excuse me?"

134

"I was going to say that I'd examine Vu in a week, but he doesn't have a week, does he?"

Kiet did not reply.

The doctor dragged on his Emerald Queen and said, "Superintendent, might I prevail on our professional relationship for a favor?"

"You may ask."

"Execution tickets."

"Excuse me?"

"Just two tickets. For my wife and me. I am not a naive man. I know that the front rows are committed to officials, senior army officers, and the rich. A middle section with a moderate sight angle would be satis—"

"No execution tickets," Kiet interrupted. "No seats. No ice cream and popcorn. Vu's physical condition, please."

The doctor accurately read Kiet's frame of mind and did not persevere. He coughed and said, "Well, at least there will be a firing squad, thanks to prompt action by you, Superintendent, and to my humble medical efforts. I pronounce him fit for execution."

"Ironic," Kiet said.

"Poetic," said the doctor.

"Send us your bill," said Kiet.

Kiet chased out his reinforcements too. He waited patiently until Feng Vu was lucid. "Vu, I came to interview you and I intend to interview you despite the unfortunate delay."

"Kiet, you took from me the right every man has, to decide when his life is too intolerable to continue. I am alive. I am in pain. I am defeated. I have lost face. I have nothing to say to you."

"Vu, you have never been defeated. You are scheming whether to overpower me and escape, or whether to just spit at me. Do either and I will have you kept groggy on morphine until . . . Monday."

Vu looked at Kiet and spat on the floor the blood-veined saliva

135

that had been allotted for Kiet's face. "You know me too well, Kiet. And I know you well. You cannot say 'when we shoot you until dead.' You say 'Monday.' Your stomach churns at the expectation of discharging a ritual bullet into the back of my head. You won our skirmish. You are a police chief. You are not a weak man. This is a contradiction that makes no sense to me."

"You are not a weak man either, and you are twice as contradictory as I. Suicide is a weak man's ultimate escape. You have never done anything that wasn't calculated to the tenth of a point, and you have never been motivated by anything but profit. Where is the profit in bleeding to death? As long as you are alive you have a chance of escaping your . . . Monday fate. That is how you think. So why, please, this itinerary to your ancestors who are certainly in no rush to welcome you?"

Vu responded with silence and his profile, his Mussolini pout.

"All right," Kiet said. "Very well. I cannot force you to talk. You have turned into a stone. Splendid. Talking is not presently in short supply in Hickorn, though. Rumors and gossip travel faster than light in Hickorn, don't they, Vu?"

Vu looked at him.

"The streets and shops and offices are buzzing with Feng Vu's botched suicide. Half the stories will be accurate, half will be false. The false stories will write you off as a successful suicide. Dead. I wonder how they will be reacting. I wonder if they will be joyous or whether they will be angry."

"Angry?"

"Yes. Angry that you denied them a public execution. The event of the decade is scheduled and the guest of honor inconsiderately cancels by dying. I wonder how Minister of Agriculture Houphong Duc is taking the news."

"Why did you mention his name, Kiet?"

"He stole your rice, did he not? Two hundred metric tons of Thai rice. He framed you. He charged you with hoarding and he hand-carried you through the swiftest trial in Luongan history.

136

Without the zeal of Houphong Duc, Vu, you would not be sitting on plywood, arms taped, being uncommunicative." Kiet shrugged. "I was merely curious."

"You haven't recovered my rice yet?

"No."

"Four hundred and forty thousand pounds of milled paddy and the Hickorn police department couldn't find it if it were dumped like an avalanche and smothered every man on the force."

"Rice grains are not cattle, Vu. They are not individually branded. Minister Duc tells me that your contraband was—let me remember his wording—was immediately distributed to every food seller in Hickorn at below-market price."

Feng Vu laughed.

"Do you dispute his version?"

"Do you? You've been setting me up for a rebuttal."

"Tell me your theory."

"*Certainly* Duc sold the rice on the marketplace at under whole-sale. How much did it cost him? Zero."

Kiet nodded knowingly, feeling stupid.

"What has Duc done with the rice money, you ask?"

"Since you asked, I ask."

Feng Vu shook his head. "Kiet, I endlessly remind myself that you are dumb, poor, and honest. What would you do with a pile of small, untraceable bills received from a hundred merchants? You would pay off your leg men and convert the cash into dollars or yen or marks or Krugerrands or commodity futures."

"Vu, does Duc have affiliations in France?"

"What are you suggesting? Does he bank his money in France?"

"That, yes. And miscellaneous affiliations too."

"You're the detective, Kiet."

"And Houphong Duc with his suspenders and his MBA and his salad bar and his NICs is your archenemy. An archenemy as formidable as Feng Vu should know him minutely."

"Salad bar," Vu said. "The salad bar at the Hickorn Sporting Club is legendary. Naturally this is secondhand information.

137

Chinese are discouraged from applying for membership and are blackballed when they do."

"My question, please?"

"Kiet, you're jabbing and poking for a story, a clue."

Kiet nodded. "I saved your life, Vu. You owe me."

Feng Vu's eyes brightened, ignited by the superintendent's cynical humor. "And you shall receive. Are you superstitious?"

"No," Kiet lied.

"Me neither. Still, there are forces we cannot comprehend. Are you a believer in an afterlife?"

Kiet shrugged.

"You are going to kill me Monday, Kiet. I have no earthly way out."

"Madame Saravane," Kiet said, giving up on wringing further information about Duc.

"Astute deduction."

"How much, please?"

"There are, of course, no guarantees beyond this life."

"Of course not."

"On the other hand, who has ever crossed that border and returned to tell of it."

"Nobody I know," Kiet said.

"Madame is honest with me. I have seen her for years. Her horoscopes and numerological analyses have been very good to me. Oh, my cunning and hard work are primarily responsible, but Madame gave me times and days when to do this and when not to do that. How can I say she wasn't right and that my achievements were entirely my own?"

"You cannot," Kiet said indifferently.

"Exactly. She is guessing, but she has an edge no one else is privy to. Her comet—"

"Please, leave Madame's comet out of this. How much for what?"

"She is majority owner of the Luong InterPresidential. I see by your raised eyebrows that you didn't know."

"I am not surprised," Kiet said coolly.

"Madame came to my cell and we recited incantations. She will place an amulet in my coffin, on my chest."

And also kill a chicken, Kiet wondered? "The purpose of the sorcery, please?"

"Safe passage through the demons who wander the netherland between this world and the next. Don't give the fish eye, Kiet. I don't necessarily believe. I can't take it with me, you know."

"That is a relief."

"I refuse to voluntarily leave anything to anybody, so I was generous with Madame. Her magic is insurance. Considering my bleak future, cheap insurance."

"How generous?"

"As I said to you Tuesday, I bought the land under the InterPresidential low and sold it high. To Madame for a smooth ride to a prosperous and immortal life after you kill me."

Friday, May 22
Hickorn
High 96, Low 77
Clear

SIXTEEN

"Superintendent, have you been at your desk all night?"

"No," Kiet said, technically truthfully, though lying in principle. He had been at his desk for only an hour. The remainder of the night had been spent outside Feng Vu's cell, like a mother with a sick child, on vigil until a fever broke. Vu would not be allowed to die before Monday, thank you.

"Well, you're in your office rather early. That's why I made the assumption."

Assumption not drawn exclusively because of bloodshot eyes and rumpled clothing, Kiet thought. Being middle-age weary and the antithesis of a clotheshorse gave him the aura of being slumped in a car for three days on surveillance duty.

"Is it the straight skinny, Superintendent?"

"Excuse me?"

"You know, you coldcocking Feng Vu. The story's spreading around town."

"I did what was necessary to subdue him," Kiet said modestly. "He had lost blood and strength."

"Oh, man, *subduing him*. Talk about the understatement of the year! The scuttlebutt is that you hammered him, lifted him off his feet with one punch. He was seeing birdies before he hit the ground."

Kiet massaged his knuckles. "An exaggeration," he said snappily, to disclaim Binh's account yet not discourage the praise.

"Wow. I'd've loved to have been there. Boom! Feng Vu flat on his ass. I've got to tell Red about this. I'll put the hit you laid on Vu against any damage Red did to any humungous Big Eight fullback. Your hit would make anybody's highlight film."

Lest he overheat in the glow of Binh's admiration, Kiet changed the subject, gesturing to the newspaper rolled up in his hand. "Interesting to us?"

"Read it and weep, Superintendent," Binh said, giving him this morning's *Hickorn Enquiring Mind*.

Kiet scanned the headlines: YOUTH MARRIES HIS GRANDMOTHER—OCTOGENARIAN'S FIERY PASSION WINS HIS HEART. ELVIS DONATES KIDNEY SAYS RECIPIENT—HOSPITAL STAFF AT LOSS TO EXPLAIN NOCTURNAL TRANSPLANT. CROWN PRINCE JEAN-GUY PAKSE IMMIGRATES TO LUONG—VOWS TO SIT ON HIS RIGHTFUL THRONE.

"The wording," Kiet said. "As if young Mr. Pakse traveled to Hickorn to sit on a toilet."

"This is unadulterated bat guano, Superintendent. I've practically lived with Jean-Guy and he's said diddly-zip to the press. You're talking reporters, hell, he dives under tables. He hates those media pukes."

Hates them enough to come to town with an alien spaceship of an automobile, Kiet thought. He paged to Madame Saravane's column. Gemini and Sagittarius were unusually compatible and the zodiac, in general, was magnanimous. Jupiter arced the Sun and the Moon with gentility and deference. Any number but six was opalescently lucky. A personal number of six was not so bad either unless you rode a pedicab to your wife's lover's home or quit your job. In addition, Madame had looked out her window last night and had been bathed by a meteor shower.

"The gods of fortune have kissed and fondled the kingdom of Luong," Kiet said. "A sudden and happy twisting of the fates. Celestial philanthropy. Splendid."

"Madame and her bullshit," Binh said. "The old douche bag sees this comet and things are out of whack and Prince Pakse is the fall guy. Now the planets are copacetic."

144

"Coinciding on the very day Jean-Guy Pakse is confirmed to be in the country," Kiet said, chucking the *Mind* into his wastebasket.

"My eyes and ears have been on red alert, Superintendent. Jean-Guy hasn't had contact that could be remotely regarded as subversive. If he's in cahoots on a coup, he's plotting in his sleep. Madame is whipping her black magic on him."

"What has he been doing besides staying in his room and sleeping?"

"Well, we sort of went out last night," Binh said.

"Sort of?"

Binh stretched eyelids with his fingers. "A roadmap drawn in red. Excuse me for saying so, but I'm almost as bloodshot as you are. Jean-Guy was restless and asked me to show him the town, which I sort of did. He's some kind of awesome party animal, Superintendent. He can drink me under the table with one arm tied behind his back."

Kiet wondered why a healthy, undisabled, young fellow would require two arms and two hands to consume alcohol. Bamsan Kiet guzzled Golden Tiger ambidextrously. He said, "You patronized nightclubs?"

Binh moaned. "Chalk up another understatement of the year. Name a joint with live music and single babes on the prowl, and we made the scene, bending our elbows, bopping and schmoozing. Jean-Guy is astounding. He had them eating out of the palm of his hand."

"They knew who he was?"

"Some maybe recognized him. Jean-Guy wears those shades inside and out. He definitely wasn't taking advantage of his pedigree. Uh-uh. He wasn't doing any crown prince number. He played Pierre LeClerc to the hilt. Good looks, charm, and a Testarossa at the curb. What else do you need? You can't score with that going for you, you've got a severe problem, right?"

"Right," Kiet said. "So you and Jean-Guy ingratiated yourselves with the prettiest girls in Hickorn, recited standard lies, and took them to the InterPresidential for sex, yes?"

"Nope. Wrong," Binh said. "Abnormal and sick as it sounds, we didn't cut a pair from the herd. We just drank and socialized and danced and went home alone. We had a great time."

"Peculiar," Kiet said.

"Yeah," Binh agreed, wincing as he nodded. "Jean-Guy's rep precedes him, and, well, you know, I'm not exactly a slouch in the chippy-chasing area myself. Not bragging, mind you."

"No," Kiet said.

"I'm stating a fact, a fact I'm not always proud of. I wish I had a zin for every time a woman I've treated shabbily has said that my dong overrides my brain and my heart."

"On a less confidential note—"

"I'm glad we're having this talk, Superintendent," Binh went on. "I have to confide in you and ask your advice. Those days of sowing the wild oats, they're in the past."

Oh no, Kiet thought. Binh and the American missionary lady. A father-to-son chat. He hated the confessionals nearly as much as their son-to-father sessions, in which Binh lectured him for shortcomings such as unprogressive obstinacy, being a fuddy-duddy, etc.

"Please," Kiet said. "Go ahead."

"Well, I don't know what Jean-Guy's hang-up was. The action was like you wouldn't believe. Thursday nights are usually not swinging."

"Peculiar," Kiet said, taking his adjutant's word for sexually lackluster Thursdays.

"Jet lag is a possibility."

"Possibly."

"When I flew to and from D.C., you know, I wasn't sure what week it was after I landed. Your normal bodily functions are screwed up. You can't eat, sleep, or take a dump. You're a zombie."

"Yes."

"Except I'm gonna rule out jet lag. I think he's really fallen hard for a girl. I tossed a bunch of leading questions at him, but he didn't bite. I guess you know what's next, huh?"

"Yes?"

"Me too. Like a ton of bricks. Guess who."

"Who?" Kiet unfortunately knew the answer.

"Mary Beth Applebee."

"Ah."

"It just sort of happened," Binh said. "After they finished breakfast yesterday morning, her and Jean-Guy, I accompanied Mary Beth to her room. I was worried about the amount of champagne she'd belted down. She isn't a boozer and she never drank before noon in her life, I'd stake my life on it."

"Jet lag," Kiet said.

"Yeah. 8:00 A.M. in Hickorn is like, you know, suppertime yesterday in Seattle."

"The champagne was, then, an after-dinner libation or three?"

"Yeah, chronologically speaking. Well, one thing led to another. I had no intention of going into her room with her, but she wanted somebody to talk to, after the rough time and the ration of shit she had at customs. She was grateful to Jean-Guy for taking her in, but she figured good ol' Pierre LeClerc was trying to get her drunk, which was obvious to a man of the world such as myself, but surprisingly perceptive for a babe in the woods like Mary Beth.

"Anyhow, Mary Beth and me, you wouldn't imagine that two different people from two different sides of the world, two divergent cultures and races, two diametrically opposed backgrounds, would have so much in common, would you, Superintendent?"

"No," Kiet said. "No."

"Well, we do. Me a ho-hum Buddhist, her an evangelical Christian. Me a world-weary cop, her a naive do-gooder. You'd automatically assume she'd be hounding me to accept Jesus Christ as my own personal savior, which is the language they use and they stay on your butt till they close their sale. None of that. We accepted each other for our differences too, and this chemistry we had, the instant simpatico that wouldn't quit, on a one to one basis. Go figure.

"The one thing leading to another, Superintendent. Mary Beth

147

and I were together throughout the day. No man and woman have ever been more intimate in the entire spectrum of a relationship. And you know what else, what has me feeling sort of guilty as hell, except that since we're in love, it's probably okay?"

In spite of the question's convolution, Kiet was sure he knew, and even surer that he didn't want verification. He said nothing.

"Well, I'm fairly positive she was a virgin. I didn't examine the sheets—I'm not that crass—but the way she would scream—"

"Yes, yes," Kiet said. "Never mind. I don't doubt you."

"Superintendent, am I embarrassing you?"

"No," Kiet lied.

"I'm really mixed up. Cupid nailed me betwixt the peepers with his maximum arrow. A fifty-fucking-caliber hollowpoint of an arrow. I didn't think a man of the world like yours truly could fall like a ton of bricks, but there you are. What do you think I ought to do, Superintendent?"

"Proceed cautiously," Kiet said.

Binh looked at him.

"Obey your instincts temperately."

Binh raised his eyebrows and sighed. Kiet recognized that he had mimicked a fortune cookie; he should apply for employment at Madame Saravane's. But he could not resist. How could he guide this lad who was madly in love and/or lust with a stranger, a Caucasian missionary lady who had yielded her virginity to him immediately following a night in the penthouse suite of an international playboy? If he could not counsel ably, he would hedge.

"We might, uh, confer. Socially. The three of us. Someday."

"We'll do lunch," said Binh, brightening and snapping fingers.

"I shall treat. Fried shrimp and Golden Tiger beer on the Conti terrasse."

"We'd really like that, Superintendent, Mary Beth and I."

"You and your woman side by side, I can observe and perhaps counsel you. Whichever, congratulations."

"Thanks. Okay, fantastic. When?"

"Soon," Kiet said. "Where is Mr. Pakse?"

"Outside huddling with Kham. Jean-Guy's kind of a police buff.

148

We were coming to headquarters when we all of a sudden had car trouble. The Testarossa began sputtering like a ruptured popcorn popper. We couldn't've been running out of gas. We'd just filled up. We had to push it into the courtyard."

Kiet revealed Jean-Guy's charter payment flight by the Ministry of Agriculture and that Madame Saravane was Miss Luong InterPresidential Hotel. He did *not* reveal the virginal missionary's sojourn in The Victorian Suite, nor did he mention the beriberi death that continued to distress him.

"Holy shit," Binh said, shaking his head. "This is the straight poop?"

"Reliable sources," Kiet said.

"C'mon, Jean-Guy and Houphong Duc? Nah. Nope. They're finagling an underhanded deal, they're playing it damn tight to the vest."

Machine gun fire brought Kiet out of his chair. Civil disorder? Food riots? Armed mobs on the march, demanding rice?

"Relax, Superintendent. The Testarossa's backfiring. It's some kind of hurting when you can hear it through these thick walls."

To save face, Kiet converted the frenzied leap to his feet into a brisk and natural stride around his desk and out of the office. "Come, Captain."

"Where's the fire?"

"We cannot have a VIP's expensive car exploding on department property, can we?"

The rear hatch of the Testarossa was raised. "Identical to the department Volkswagen Beetle, Captain. Its powerplant is also inside the trunk."

Binh sighed heavily. "Identical? Not quite, Superintendent."

Kham was smoking an Emerald Queen and saying to Jean-Guy Pakse, "A car like this won't run on the gas they sell in Hickorn."

Jean-Guy's arms were folded, jawline jutting, aquiline nose canted upward. "I'm not a mechanic, but isn't gasoline gasoline? What I know about the internal workings of this car is that it'll exceed 150 miles per hour on the Autobahn."

"Wow," Binh said softly.

Kham was not as impressed. He was Kiet's age, underweight and prematurely wrinkled. He swam in coveralls that had not been laundered lately. He was the Hickorn Police Department Maintenance Division. He kept the department's motorbikes running and made sarcastic remarks whenever a headquarters pipe burst or wiring caught on fire inside a wall, comparing the failed systems to terminal illnesses. Commentary done, however, he usually managed to render first aid. When Kham retired, Kiet vowed never to report to work without an umbrella, crash helmet, and oxygen mask.

The mechanic slammed the Ferrari's engine lid, flicked his cigarette butt between thumb and forefinger, and said, "I don't give a shit if you broke the sound barrier. You won't get around the block in this rig on Hickorn gas. It's low octane. Rotgut. I can tweak the fuel injection and the ignition so it'll halfway run, but you won't go ten kilometers before you bend a valve."

"Bending a valve is bad?" Jean-Guy asked.

Kham's cigarette butt landed by a row of department motorbikes, in an accumulation of sludge and dripped fluids. Kiet wondered why auto mechanics could smoke around fuels and oils. Ninety percent did. Flames should erupt, roofs should blow off garages, but remarkably didn't.

"Bending a valve," Kham said gravely, "is like taking a kidney punch or swallowing a nail. It's rough on the system."

"I shouldn't drive the car?"

"I wouldn't if it was mine. I'm no goddamn idiot," Kham said with grinning contempt. "You can't park it here either. It's blocking traffic."

Kiet surmised that Kham had not recognized Jean-Guy. He was not a *Hickorn Enquiring Mind* reader. His reading taste began and ended with automotive service manuals.

Kiet had an idea, the germ of an opportunity. He said to Binh, "Does the InterPresidential have an underground parking garage?"

"Yeah. Three levels of concrete dungeon."

"Kham," Kiet said. "A stout rope, please."

SEVENTEEN

Kham wrapped rope around and around the Volkswagen's rear bumper and mounting brackets as if weaving a cocoon. Flat on his back, he groped under the nose of the Testa-something, cursing ground clearance while he wound the other end through the molded rubber nose. The coil of hemp had appeared ridiculously long when Kham brought it from his shop, but when he climbed to his feet and wiped his hands on his coveralls, Kiet saw that there was none to spare.

"Remember," he said to Kiet, "You're pulling a rig that weighs twice as much as the rig you're pulling it with."

"Yes."

"This tin can isn't a tow truck."

"No."

"Keep it in low gear and hope you don't overheat and seize up. That wind-up motor of yours is air cooled and you'll be straining along slower than I can walk on a day like today that's hot as a charcoal grill."

"Yes."

"I looped ten meters of my finest rope over every semisolid part. They don't build cars like they used to."

Kiet started the Volkwagen. "We appreciate your effort, Kham."

"Try not to jerk. You may yank off your own bumper or that dumb, red, lemon-sucking, plastic piece of dog shit that masquerades as a bumper on the rig you're pulling."

"And if I do jerk?"

He lighted an Emerald Queen and looked away. "Same as cooking your engine. Don't call Kham. I already have a week's work to finish by quitting time. Your cops drive on flat tires until sparks fly off the rims. And I have to rewire the headquarters fuse box because some goddamn imbecile ordered air conditioning!"

Kiet began to protest his innocence, his identical scorn of artificially cooled air, but Kham was already skulking away. Splendid, he thought. Guilty without a fair hearing. Like Feng Vu.

Kiet let out the clutch, easing the car forward until the rope went taut, and gunned the engine. The Beetle quivered and howled in vehicular pain, but inched forward. Kiet ignored the odor of scorched machinery.

"Can we make it to the hotel?" Jean-Guy Pakse asked.

"Indeed," Kiet said without faith.

"Binh is a nice fellow," Jean-Guy said.

"Yes."

"Before I immigrated, I worried whether I would make compatible friends."

"Compatible?"

"Buddies, comrades of my age, men who are—I apologize, Superintendent Kiet, I fear that I am insulting your Luonganness—hip and cosmopolitan. We have to face reality. Luong is a third world country. Binh was in the U.S. for a year. He is a man of the world. Binh and I relate. We communicate."

"I am not insulted," Kiet lied.

He was actually too engrossed in the opportunity he had arranged to be too angry at the brat. It had taken no salesmanship to insert Binh at the wheel of the stricken sports car. Though being pulled like a plow behind a water buffalo, his Ferrari-impassioned adjutant was indubitably fantasizing a three hundred kilometer per hour romp on a European throughway. Kiet was pleased with himself, having manipulated a private chat with the prospective crown prince. Now, how to cajole the lad to talk?

Jean-Guy was twisted in his seat, looking back. "I can't see well through the smoked windscreen, but it looks like Binh is uncomfortable. His head and shoulders are bobbing."

"He is fine. He is enjoying a kinetic daydream."

"I hope my Testarossa will be fine."

"It is just a car that you can replace," Kiet said.

"No, I can't. You make it sound easy."

"Easy, no. Possible, yes."

"Easy, no. Impossible, yes."

"The Testarusta is a scarce model not presently available for sale?"

Jean-Guy resumed a sitting position. "This junker has air conditioning?"

Kiet raised a hand as Jean-Guy's touched the on-off switch. "Please. The gizmo will drain our towing power."

"Superintendent Kiet, could we have a confidential discussion on a . . . delicate subject?"

Ah, Kiet thought, there are gods. "Yes, splendid, indeed. Of course."

"Well, I am a man of the world. I am not bragging. I am what I am. I'm known as a lady's man. The older and more mature I am, the more I understand that it isn't a badge of honor. I've taken advantage of so many women, I can't remember them all."

Kiet did not much care for the path of Jean-Guy's confidential discussion. He did not much care to hear about the lad's conquests. And the whiny timbre in his voice was irritating.

"You are an immigrant to Luong," he said. "Forget your past."

"My past is as impossible to forget as my Ferrari would be to replace. Frankly, my attitude regarding women was unchanged. France is full of willing ladies who believe their lives would be enriched by a night with an Asian crown prince. I'd scored in every country in Western Europe too, and several in the Eastern Bloc."

Kiet sighed. "Is there a point?"

"The point is, my attitude changed the night before last."

Out in the congestion of Avenue Alexandre Loubet, the towing had became hard, tricky work. Kiet's concentration was diffused, but Jean-Guy's statement registered solidly. "Oh no" formed silently on his lips.

"This will come as a surprise to you, Superintendent Kiet, but the American missionary, Mary Beth Applebee, came to my room not yesterday morning, but rather the previous evening."

"Oh?" Kiet said.

"The facts of our hallway encounter are as we related them. The timing was the lie."

"Amazing," Kiet said.

"Please don't tell Binh. I think he's sweet on her."

"It is our secret," Kiet said.

"I didn't intend anything to happen. Attractive as she was in her fresh, chaste way, I wasn't interested in seducing a religious humanitarian. I gave her some champagne to steady her nerves after her airport experience. I drank champagne too. I'd wager every franc I have that she never drank as much as she drank Wednesday night."

"Jet lag perhaps caused her to be intoxicated quickly," Kiet said.

"It probably did. You're probably right."

"One thing led to another."

"Yes. You're old and wise, Superintendent Kiet. We talked and we held each other and we made love until the sun rose. You wouldn't dream that two people so different would have so much in common."

Old and wise? "I would. That is possible."

"She was a virgin. She had been saving herself for the right man."

Kiet replied by clearing his throat.

"Of all the women on earth, a suave rake of a man like myself falls madly in love with an innocent missionary. How do you figure?"

Kiet remembered that virginity was significant in the Christianity dogma, but he couldn't recall why. He might have to ask the maidenly Miss Applebee. "Some phenomena are simply beyond comprehension."

"What do you think I ought to do? Should I begin a new life committed for life with a woman I scarcely know?"

"Proceed cautiously," Kiet said.

154

"What else?"

"Obey your instincts temperately."

"What else?"

Kiet shrugged. Beware of double virgins, he resisted saying.

"I could have cracked open a fortune cookie," Jean-Guy said.

"Sorry."

"Maybe I'm being unfair. You are a policeman not a psychologist. I have a bad habit of demanding too much from people. Have you jumped on customs about what they did to her and her shipment?"

"The airplane is gone," Kiet said. "We cannot reclaim the canned corn and cranberry sauce."

"You leaned on those customs crooks?"

"Yes. I spoke to the chief customs agent on a telephone without a cord. The reception was wonderful."

"It seems odd to me that a man in your position couldn't apply pressure to a common thief."

Binh must have tapped his brakes. Kiet's neck whipped backward. He was hot. His shoulders, legs, and arms ached from the tension of concentration. Now his neck and back were sore.

"Don't use that snotty tone on me or I'll take you over my knee."

"Are you forgetting who I am?" Jean-Guy's protest lacked arrogance. It was the complaint of a spoiled child who was being chastised for the first time.

"I am not forgetting who you allegedly are," Kiet blurted, reining his anger one syllable from the addition of "bastard."

"You're my father's friend. Your attitude toward me is his!" he said in a high quavering voice.

It was not Kiet's intent to induce pouting and tears, but he nearly had. He had gone for the groin with a hard-toed shoe. He felt like sewage.

"Listen, Jean-Guy," he said gently. "I inquired to the chief agent on your charter flight too. Who do you know at the Ministry of Agriculture, please?"

"Nobody."

155

"Minister Houphong Duc? You know him, yes?"

"I don't know him. I recognize his name. He's an important man."

Jean-Guy's denial puzzled Kiet and it was convincing. "Who paid for your charter flight from Paris to Hickorn?"

"You're insinuating that I didn't. Do I look like a pauper?"

The shrillness had left the boy's voice. Good news. Perhaps, he thought, an earache will not compound my various discomforts. "Who paid for the charter, please?"

"Mother. She and I had been quarreling. Her new husband and I don't get along."

A retired Wall Street wizard, "the sweetest of her seven sugar daddies," so reported the *Mind*. Logically, the boy cramped the Frenchwoman's gold-digging style. Kiet said, "Jean-Guy, forgive me for my 'allegedly' gibe. You are His Royal Highness' son. Unmistakably. You came off the airplane, I skipped a heartbeat. You could have been your father stepping out of a time machine. Except for the green eyes, of course. I lost my temper and I am sorry."

"It's my fault you blew up. I deserved it. Not to worry."

Kiet, conscience again pristine, contemplated Jean-Guy's patriotism and his pitiful incognito. His return to the world of his ancestors. In his country's hour of need. The racial logic of immigration, he a mulatto, dusky and proud. Kiet genuinely liked Jean-Guy, but he remained distrustful of his airport proclamations. He might decide to attack them, though later.

"Have you contacted His Royal Highness?"

"Not for lack of effort I haven't. I've telephoned and sent notes."

"Do you play billiards?"

"I learned the game to please him. It's fun, Superintendent Kiet. I was pleasantly surprised. I played three or four nights a week for several months. I shoot a good stick."

"Challenge him to a match, in writing, by messenger. I have never known him to refuse billiards."

156

"Thanks. Outstanding idea. I will."

"Are you familiar with Madame Saravane or her work?" Kiet asked.

"Word of mouth. Binh says she belongs on a broomstick. Astrology is medieval and stupid. I'm not superstitious."

"Nor am I." Kiet felt a jab of pain in the prostate region. He prayed to any deities tuned in that only his seat belt had pinched. "I agree. Stupid. Ridiculous. Has word of mouth mentioned political manipulation in her columns?"

"What is this, a quiz show?" Jean-Guy asked.

"It is your Luongan naturalization test. Identification of our foremost citizens. You shall not pass until you can gossip proficiently."

Jean-Guy laughed. "No. Everybody's afraid of her. Binh says somebody should pound a wooden stake through her heart, but politics haven't entered into it as far as I know."

A lie, Kiet thought. Madame's vile, wretched comet was as famed a celestial body as the moon. "Feng Vu?"

"Is it true?"

"Excuse me?"

"Don't be modest, Superintendent Kiet. You're faking."

"Oh. That."

"Binh idolizes you."

"He does?"

"Doubly since you knocked Vu out. He says that if you were American, you would have been a football star."

"He did?" Kiet paused to sop up the flattery, then said, "Next to last question. Red Williams?"

"Nifty dude. Binh's words. I haven't met him yet."

"What is beriberi?"

"Binh says he's a lounge lizard. I won't argue."

"Excuse me?"

"He sings and plays the piano at a club we had a drink at in our travels. He wears his hair in a greasy pompadour and does bad Sinatra. Barry Barry Kim, a Korean."

Kiet groaned. So did the Volkswagen. The oil light winked on. The engine sputtered and quit.

Kiet got out and lifted the engine lid. He hadn't an inkling what he was doing, although inspection somehow seemed mandatory. Oily smoke drifted from the exhaust pipes. Dead, he thought. An aspiring pimpmobile cum detective cruiser en route to automotive Valhalla.

Binh and Jean-Guy had dismounted too, exchanging shaken heads and downward-pointing thumbs.

"And they say close only counts in horseshoes," Binh said inscrutably.

"Translation, please."

"We're close enough to push."

They were close enough, Kiet observed. Their bizarre caravan had wholly obstructed the intersection of Mu Pakse and Avenue George Bush. The black maw of the Luong InterPresidential Hotel parking garage was on the southwest corner, fifteen meters distant. Pedestrians and cyclists and pedicab drivers waited patiently at the plugged intersection. Mouths gaped like the garage entrance at the spectacle, not to mention the attendance of the future monarch. The Ferrari, the crown prince—this was an event.

Kiet wagged a finger at the liveried Indian doorman. When he had quickstepped within earshot, Kiet asked him to please recruit several strong backs.

Binh kicked a Volkswagen tire. "I can't honestly say I'm gonna shed tears over this shitbox."

Kiet said. "For that I am grateful."

"What are we gonna do for wheels?"

"Pedicab?"

"C'mon, Superintendent. We deserve a staff car. We *need* a staff car. You've essentially dumped the execution in my lap, let me remind you, and while I am not bitching, I've got a zillion details to attend to that require reliable transportation."

"I shall look into the matter," Kiet lied. "Top priority."

The doorman had brought two bellhops dressed like miniature

Nehrus and three kitchen employees sloppily clad in undershirts, shorts, and aprons. He addressed Kiet as sahib and stood poised for a tip.

Kiet thanked the Indian in behalf of the Hickorn police department.

Binh said, "How about the Vee Dub?"

"In the garage too?"

"I don't know, Superintendent. They charge three thousand zin a day to park. What do we do if they say we abandoned it on their property and whip a humongous bill on us?"

"Same as the average Hickornian would do. Call the police and report it retroactively stolen."

Binh smiled and winked, and directed the removal process, he steering the Beetle, Jean-Guy the Ferrari. A portly Luongan wearing a Western business suit and a jittery smile came from the hotel to Kiet in the comical gait of a frightened waterfowl. Kiet knew him by sight to be the InterPresidential manager.

He bowed and said, "I humbly request five of your valuable minutes, Superintendent?"

The bow was vaguely Japanese and therefore annoyed Kiet, who wondered yet again why Luongans could not behave like Luongans. "Five private minutes, I assume."

"Yes sir. The issue is touchy."

Kiet trailed the manager inside and to an unoccupied end of the front desk. "Who is he, Superintendent?"

"Who is whom?"

The manager forced a smile. "Mr.—ahem—Pierre LeClerc."

Kiet lifted a shoulder, eyes wide and uncomprehending.

"Superintendent, the InterPresidential is among the classiest hotels in Southeast Asia. Every afternoon, after a maid cleans a room she puts a chocolate mint on the bed pillow and a flower in a cut-glass vase on the dresser. Early every morning, before guests have awakened, we lay a complimentary copy of the *Mind* outside each room. I also read the *Mind*, Superintendent. You can't deceive me. Pierre LeClerc is Crown Prince Jean-Guy Pakse."

Kiet looked at him. "You requisitioned five private minutes to boast your knowledge of trashy gossip?"

The manager flinched. "I meant no disrespect."

"But you would be delighted if I confirmed your suspicions."

The manager smiled. "The Victorian Suite, isn't that a silly name for a penthouse in a tropical hotel?"

"A colonial flavor to it," Kiet said, his mouth puckered by the sour taste.

"The Crown Prince Jean-Guy Pakse Suite, Superintendent. I love the ring to it. Verify what everybody in Hickorn suspects and I will have the name changed and a new plaque—"

"I shall investigate and you will be the first to know," Kiet said. "Verify something for me, please."

"Anything, Superintendent!"

"Who is paying Mr. LeClerc's bill?"

"The hotel."

"The hotel is whom, please?"

The manager motioned to a computer terminal. "The secretive consortium that owns us. His reservation was specially coded. Charges are automatically credited as they're debited, instantaneously zeroing out."

"Who is the consortium?"

"I don't know. My paycheck is computerized and mailed from a post office box in Bangkok."

"Paid or not, is there a record of exceptional charges, say, room service or telephone calls?"

"Yes. I'll demonstrate."

The manager thunk-thunked the computer's keyboard, summoning text onto a green screen. He said, "Room service, yes. Expensive meals and drink. No outgoing telephone usage."

"Speaking of which, may I use that magic telephone?"

The manager brought it to Kiet, who asked, "Is it capable of a transpacific call? Oh, for instance, to Seattle and Los Angeles?"

"Certainly, Superintendent. The airport cell is directly linked to Metro overseas operators."

"Final question."

160

"Anything, Superintendent," the manager said spreading his hands.

"Anything?"

"Anything."

Kiet punched the zero button. "May I charge a few calls to Mr. LeClerc's bill?"

EIGHTEEN

Kiet's telephone inquiries were inconclusive. He placed ten calls, five apiece to the American cities of Seattle and Los Angeles. Two to each were regarded as cranks and/or persistent wrong number pests. The clicks of receivers slammed down eight thousand miles away registered in Kiet's ear, marvels of rudeness and technology. Two to each were regarded as orders and/or donations, and when it became obvious they weren't, Kiet was advised that they would "be in touch and to have a nice day." One to each, a charity in Seattle and a Los Angeles air-conditioning distributor elicited concern. These were serious people who pledged investigations and answers, and asked for a return number. Kiet informed them that his access to cordless cellular cells was temporary and recommended cabling instead.

He trudged three long blocks to the ministry of agriculture, feeling not a little sorry for himself. His Royal Highness's throne was imperiled by a spoiled illegitimate child he was entrusted to baby-sit and by a female fakir who saw noncomets and cast her evil eye at his superintendently crotch. The kingdom was short on rice and half a million pounds of milled paddy had gotten legs. In three days he would be expected to fire a bullet in the back of a suicidal Chinese's head. His cat was missing and people were dying of nutritional diseases, the theoretical correlation of which was not lost on him. His staff car was dead and he was ravenously hungry, for he had been too busy to eat breakfast. These days he felt guilty complaining of hunger, but tell that to his growling stomach.

Compounding the entire mess was his adjutant's infatuation. Twice in twenty-four hours Mary Beth Applebee had been ravaged and made a woman. Kiet cringed at the thought of intimate contact with another man's semen. What did this Christian missionary, this career virgin, want? What?

Naturally Houphong Duc was not at the ministry. He had played morning tennis at the Hickorn Sporting Club, a match that went into extra sets. Tennis had segued into luncheon. I should have known, he told himself as he walked to the club.

The same Luongan doorman who could not speak his native language to Kiet was jabbing an angry finger at a young lady, yelling in French that she was unwelcome. She was a pretty young woman in slacks and blouse who had once been pointed out to Kiet. He didn't know her name, but her *Hickorn Enquiring Mind* byline was "The Dragon Lady." She wrote flying saucer stories. Her typical viewpoint was the interviewed victim, who narrated the hair-raising tale of teleportation aboard a UFO for a biopsy and kinky alien sex.

"You're Superintendent Kiet?" she asked over the clatter of the slammed gate.

"Yes. You're having trouble?"

"That little worm," she said, shaking Kiet's hand. "I'm the Dragon Lady who writes for the *Mind*."

"I am a fan of yours. I especially liked your piece on the seven-foot-tall female Alpha Centaurians, although I usually disapprove of bondage."

"They say you're an honest man. You are. Most people lie and pretend they never read me."

"I'll lie about it to others, but never to the author herself."

"I'm writing a science fiction novel in my spare time," she said. "Meanwhile, before my book is published and I'm rich and famous, I'm trapped at the *Mind*. I'm writing at home at night what I write at work during the day, and I'm going insane. I asked to be reassigned as a muckraking reporter. My editor says I can be if I prove myself worthy."

"Thus your trouble here?"

164

The Dragon Lady's head was hanging, her spirits low. "Yes. Luong is suffering a famine and Hickorn's rich are gorging themselves in the club."

"Please don't say famine. You tried to gain entry to report the gluttony and excesses firsthand?"

"You saw what happened. Say, would *you* grant me an interview?"

"No thank you. I am very boring."

"You're at the heart of the Jean-Guy Pakse matter, Superintendent. You prevented Feng Vu from committing suicide. You have the inside dope. Please!"

"You're a trained journalist," Kiet said, ducking her. "You are entitled to accessibility to wherever your story is. Come."

Kiet went through the gate, badge held like a torch, the Dragon Lady at his heels. He said to the doorman, in Luongan, "Official police business. Must I repeat myself in French and English?"

"No sir. The—her?"

"My deputy, sworn-in thirty seconds ago. Open the door, please."

The doorman was standing so stiffly he had gained an inch in height. "Sir, I'm confused. Nobody except club members and proper guests are admitted. They aren't criminals."

The Dragon Lady grinned and covered her mouth, sealing in the guffaws.

Kiet said, "Young man, you are a doorman. You're not a detective."

His eyes bulged. "Crime at the club? You're kidding!"

"I am afraid I am not," Kiet said grimly.

The doorman pivoted and grasped a brass knob that gleamed like topaz. "I'll alert the manager."

"No," Kiet said.

"The element of surprise," said the Dragon Lady, whose tears were not of sorrow.

"Sir, please take me into your confidence. Are you investigating a murder or what?"

"Pilferage of dining room silverware."

165

The doorman was horrified. "Murder is one thing, sir. Stealing the silver. *That's* tacky."

Kiet extended an arm behind him, clasped fingers with the Dragon Lady and entered an atmosphere of money and expensive cooking aromas.

"Where, I wonder, is the salad bar?"

"Don't ask me. People associated with the *Mind* are barred. I'm the first to break the barrier, but I've heard their salad bar is the finest in all Asia."

A passing waiter overheard Kiet and responded, "No salad bar on Fridays, sir. Friday is international day. The salad bar is converted into a buffet at which sushi, barbecue, and crepes are served. The wide doorway to your left."

"What day isn't an international day?" Kiet mumbled.

"A gigantic Caucasian is waving at you, Superintendent," said the Dragon Lady.

Red Williams was filling a plate at the buffet table. "Hey, Bam-sand, come and get it while it lasts. Bam-son. That's your first name, isn't it?"

Kiet groaned. "Bomb-sawn."

"Yeah, Bomb-san, like I said. Hey, who's the cutie?"

"Try Super-in-ten-dent, Mr. Williams. You just might conquer the phonics."

"Yeah, okay, be a hard-ass, see if it's any skin off mine," Red Williams said, showing Kiet a plate heaped with beef ribs and chicken quarters that had been slathered with a red sauce and blackened as if blowtorched. "Good groceries, huh? I got my doubts about that raw fish the Japs are so goofy over and those crepes, far as I'm concerned that's fairy food for ladies' tea parties. The club chef, though, he whips up some kind of vicious barbecue sauce. Friday's the day to chow down here, I'll tell you. They chuck the rabbit food and lay out some serious vittles. Where I played college ball, we had ourselves a righteous training table, but it was bush league compared to this spread. Your office a.c. unit is due in any day, by the way."

"Splendid."

166

"Who are *you?*" the Dragon Lady asked Red.

He leered at her, tipped an imaginary hat, and said, "Honey, you're gazing fondly at the hummingest, rootin-tootinest air conditioner salesman this side of Wilshire Boulevard. Red Williams is the name, environmental comfort is my game. You got me at a disadvantage."

The Dragon Lady stared at Red Williams, licked her lips, and unbuttoned her top blouse button.

"Whoa!" Red said. "Show time."

The Dragon Lady exposed not her breasts but a miniature camera, reeling it up and out by the straps. She then retrieved a note pad from the front of her shapeless slacks.

"Red Williams," she said, pen poised. "What is a Red Williams? Who is the man inside the immense body?"

Kiet sidled off to the dining hall, although not before a careful study of the buffet. The sushi, Mr. Red Williams's Japanese raw fish was decoratively arranged on trays, bordering on fine art. A chef cooked individual crepes over a gas flame. Diners selected their filling from a dozen choices. And the barbecue! Piquant and greasy, the charred meat whetted Kiet's appetite.

He counted the calories available at this International Day buffet to Hickorn Sporting Club members. It was guesswork, decidedly unscientific. He computed in his head, assisted by his nose and salivary glands. He figured the feast would feed Foh Ten for thirty-six hours. His appetite suddenly departed.

Minister of Agriculture Houphong Duc sat at his courtside table. His luncheon companion was Lieutenant Commander Tuon Tran, commandant and chief of naval operations, Royal Luongan Navy. Tran, ovoid in his dress whites, struck Kiet as a candied pear dipped in powdered sugar.

Duc saw Kiet and rolled his eyes. Tran looked quizzically at Duc, saw Kiet, and shot to his feet. Kiet had been squinting beyond, through the screening at the tennis courts. Heat waves shimmered above the playing surface. Eight of eight were vacant. Good, Kiet thought. An oddly sensible crowd today.

"Please don't let me chase you away, Commandant."

"You didn't," Tran said, taking his hand. "Nice to see you, Superintendent."

"Commandant Tran is late. He was kind enough to stop by and say hello," said Houphong Duc.

"Late?" Kiet asked.

"We're setting sail upriver on patrol at 1300 hours. I'll never make it in time, a bad example to my sailors."

Kiet patted Tran's shoulder and occupied his chair. "Shoot a pirate for me, Commandant."

"You are utterly devoid of savoir faire, aren't you?" Duc said.

The food before Kiet was warm and untouched. Crepes wrapped around sauteed chicken chunks. On the side, a dish of sliced strawberries and cream. And a plate of ribs. And a smaller plate containing butter and a freshly baked roll. Wonderful as the meal appeared, it smelled even better. Kiet's appetite returned.

Kiet cut into a crepe with a fork and said, "Tuon Tran stopped by to say hello and run, not to eat lunch. Ergo, the food is not for him, it is for me. Very thoughtful, sir. I thank you."

"Oh, my pleasure, Kiet! I trust this encounter won't be a total washout. You came to report on execution progress?"

Kiet chewed, swallowed, and said, "I did?"

"My compliments, incidentally, on subduing Feng Vu."

"My pleasure," Kiet said, glancing at a border of red suspender behind tropical pinstripes. He thought of Quin. Of how he would so much rather be with her than this manicured little monster.

"Arrangements for Monday are tracking properly?"

"Certainly. No glitches or diverted flow patterns. Your chink shall die on schedule."

"You're having fun at my expense, Kiet. Fine. But do me the courtesy of telling me why you're usurping my space. God, watching you slurping and smacking your lips, it's like having a wild, woolly animal rummaging in my kitchen."

Kiet laid his fork on his plate. He glared at Duc, who gulped and blinked, finding himself at the mercy of the uncouth and angered brute who had knocked Feng Vu unconscious.

"I will continue slurping and usurping, Mr. Minister, until you tell me why you chartered Jean-Guy Pakse's flight."

Duc stroked his chin with a finger, looking at his verbal assailant without quite targeting his eyes. The twerp was regenerating his composure, Kiet thought. A made-in-the-shade, MBA-taught craft.

"A car doesn't run satisfactorily, Kiet. What do you do?"

"Requisition a rope and tow it behind a Volkswagen."

"The Ferrari breakdown was sad," Duc said. "Jean-Guy is really attached to that big red machine."

Jean-Guy Pakse. Recognizing the name of Houphong Duc, an important man. Not knowing him personally, knowing nobody at the ministry of agriculture. "Sad," Kiet said. "Very said."

Duc formed his right hand into a pistol, pointed the gun at Kiet, and winked. "I'm not referring to automobiles, am I? I'm speaking metaphorically."

"Obviously," Kiet said, wondering what next.

"The car is the kingdom of Luong. The car's engine is Uncle Novie."

"Ah, you replace the old Uncle Novie engine with a new Jean-Guy engine."

"Unless the old engine can be rebuilt. Suppose the old engine is facile, suppose it is intelligent."

"No. Engines have no intelligence." Kiet resumed eating.

"Kiet, don't be obtuse. You understand."

"Metaphorically?"

"Yeah. Suppose the intelligent old engine does not desire to be wrenched out of the car and relegated to the scrap heap."

"It sees the new engine in the crate and says, no thank you, and permits rebuilding?"

Duc smiled. "You've grasped the concept."

"His Royal Highness accepts your vision of NICs and geo-political Pacific rims and foreign aid to erect dams and your sound business practices and enlightened management or else, yes?"

"Foreign countries with deep pockets have us under a micro-

169

scope. They'll bankroll a nation's advancement on the condition that leadership is stable and modern."

"Prince Pakse has ruled since 1954," Kiet said.

Houphong Duc smirked. "The law of diminishing returns applies to stability, Kiet. When stable goes musty and shriveled, stable crumbles to the touch. That isn't the message you want to send."

Kiet squeezed his thighs, an alternative to Duc's neck. "Again, His Royal Highness is encouraged by the threat of overthrow in favor of a youthful playboy or else? Duc, what possessed you? And don't continue your foreign aid lecture. Something more than that is behind it."

"Kiet, calm down. Jean-Guy is symbolic. He represents youth and progress. Uncle Novie will catch on."

"If His Royal Highness does not 'catch on,' then what have we on our hands?"

"We would be evolving into a sophisticated political situation, which is a bit deep for you to—"

"A coup d'etat?"

"Politics isn't your business, Kiet. Keep your distance."

"People killing people on the streets of Hickorn for whatever reason *is* my business, the business of crime."

"Lighten up," Duc said, smiling bleakly.

Kiet stood. Anger repulsed his peripatetic appetite. "Think carefully. If the nightmare begins, I am coming after you, Mr. Minister."

Kiet waited outside in the refreshing heat for the Dragon Lady. The air was blistering, yes, but at least it was fresh. The Dragon Lady emerged in twenty minutes.

"Once I ditched Red—he kept calling me sweet pants—I shot a roll of film and scribbled two pages of notes," she said. "Thank you, Superintendent. I guess it's the red meat Western men eat that makes them so horny. Does he have a wife in Hickorn?"

"Not that I'm aware of."

"Don't get me wrong. I'm not interested in him. I'm between relationships, but I'd never stoop *that* low."

170

"Why do you suspect he has a wife in town?"

"He asked me to have dinner and drinks with him, but the cafés he suggested are on the edges of downtown. He wanted a late dinner too, after dark. Like he was sneaking out."

"Interesting," Kiet said as Captain Binh and an inspiration came to mind. He pictured Binh married to Applebee, converted to her faith. "You are between boyfriends, yes? You are eligible?"

The Dragon Lady smiled at him.

"Oh no, not me."

She shrugged. "Too bad. I don't discriminate on the basis of age. Not against you."

His vision of Binh persisted. He and his bride heading a mission. Her dragging him around the countryside, preaching the word of somebody's god. He remembered the French proselytizers. Strong women, weak men. He imagined Binh in ten years, hangdog and meek, domineered by virgin-plucking guilt and avenging angels.

He shivered and said, "Do you know my adjutant, Captain Binh?"

"We've never met, but I've seen him. He's a doll!"

"Ah," Kiet said. "He is also between relationships."

NINETEEN

"Well, brunch tomorrow, Superintendent? Can do?"

"Of course," said Kiet, whose jaws opened and closed faster than a camera shutter, a precaution against ingesting insects.

"Good. I took the liberty of making reservations at the Hickorn Continental *terrasse*. Reservations aren't ordinarily mandatory, but it never hurts to nail things down. My impression is that you've been sort of lukewarm on the situation, as busy as we are with the execution coming up and everything. You love the *terrasse*, Superintendent. Their fried shrimp is your favorite. Mary Beth says anything's wonderful with her, that's the kind of gal she is. I hope Quin can come. I don't recall us ever double-dating, Superintendent. Tennish? You can drink all the Golden Tiger you can hold, you can get totally hammered, and I won't say a word. Ten A.M. in the early mañana, ten-thirty, somewhere in that ballpark range?"

Captain Binh's head was cocked at a grotesque angle. He was yelling rapid-fire out of a side of his mouth. He was not palsied or deranged. He was driving a Hickorn police department motorbike at speed, addressing his passenger, Bamsan Kiet, who while pleasantly cooled by the slipstream was scared senseless.

"Yes, yes," he said. "Tennish."

"Okay, good. That's not too early for me, us, Mary Beth and me, despite it being a weekend," Binh shouted as he turned right at Avenue Alexandre Loubet and Rue Ho Chi Minh, simultaneously S-curving between a pedicab, a vegetable cart, and a cadaverous dog who had paused to scratch.

"Splendid, splendid."

The choice of transportation had been the adjutant's. Kiet knew he was doing atonement, risking death and dismemberment, for failing to instantly replace the staff car. Which was inadequate and undesirable anyway. As Binh would say: Go figure.

"Speaking of the execution, Superintendent—"

"Watch out for the taxi!"

Binh veered right. "No sweat. Missed him by a mile."

Either an insect large enough to have tattoos or the taxicab's door mirror had nicked Kiet's elbow. He saw no blood, so he held his tongue.

"I'm going to draw names out of a hat for the firing squad, Superintendent. That's the only fair way."

"Fairness is vitally important," Kiet said.

"I've got a sandbag detail going and they're making progress. We certainly don't want anyone hit by a ricochet, you know. Crowd control is the big remaining bugaboo. We're gonna need to have us a skull session, Superintendent. We gotta get our ducks in a row."

To shoot a Chinese rice hoarder *and* aquatic game birds? "Soon."

"Our assignment, where we're headed, well, don't get me wrong, I love scams and stings. However."

"Yes," Kiet said. "However."

"What you say regarding Madame Saravane's financial interest in the InterPresidential, her majority ownership, and the hotel picking up Jean-Guy's room and board tab, that's damned intriguing."

"I thought so too."

"Minister Duc picking up Jean-Guy's charter, that's also interesting. Jean-Guy, a rich playboy, he's getting a free ride."

"We should be so fortunate, Captain."

"Okay, it's explainable. Everybody's cozying up to him, to position themselves if the unthinkable—"

"And unspeakable."

"Going to Madame Saravane's is worth a shot, Superintendent.

I'm not holding my breath till she confesses this humongous conspiracy you think she's up to her ugly puss in. Your plan of you saying you're sorry for accusing her of lying and paying her cash to ask forgiveness and tell a fortune, that'll knock her for a loop if anything will. Red, when he played ball for the Cyclones, they utilized a lot of misdirection plays, you know, where they showed tendencies that made the opponent think they were concentrating on the opposite direction they really were, which spread the offensive line into gaps you could blitz through."

"Excuse me?"

"But please do us both a favor, Superintendent."

"Yes?"

"Don't mention Feng Vu, okay? And whatever you do, don't call the old douche bag a liar. You remember what she claims she did to you? Not that we believe in curses and any of the rest of her happy horseshit, right?"

"Yes, yes." Thanks to the motorbike's rocklike seat, Kiet was practically numb between the navel and the knees. "I am fine, I do not feel a thing."

"Well, good. Stirring up a hornet's nest in there would be counterproductive, you know. What's her place like, Superintendent?"

"Unique."

Binh parked in front of the noodle soup café on Rue Dan Quayle and dropped the kickstand. Kiet dismounted and successfully fought the urge to collapse on his knees and kiss pavement.

"I have time to kill today," Binh said. "Why not a new and bizarre experience, right? Mary Beth has been tracing down her donated food and coming up blank, which gave her a brutal headache. She has these nasty migraines, you know. She broke our date on account of it, so I guess I might as well stay at my desk and plow through the paperwork that's been piling up since you made me special security liaison to Jean-Guy Pakse, no offense, Superintendent, just stating a fact. Jean-Guy's kind

175

of under the weather also, a combination, I think, of last night's pub crawling and a dose of the blues over the Testarossa crapping out."

The lad's lung power, Kiet marveled. "He is, of course, well guarded."

"Goes without saying, Superintendent. I've posted crackerjack officers. I don't want to nag, but I can't emphasize how critical it is that we maintain civil tongues, no matter how difficult the old bitch makes it for us to keep our cools. Diplomacy is the operative word."

Kiet ignored Binh's nagging and led him up the stairs, pondering the coincidental maladies of Jean-Guy Pakse, international playboy, and Mary Beth Applebee, virgin emeritus.

"You learn your lessons well, Kiet," Madame Saravane said, studying them through a twilight of bad lighting and tobacco haze. "Sending a policeman on to request an appointment was sensible."

"Madame," Kiet said with a nod that was not quite a bow.

Binh scanned the dingy room, then Madame and her black silk and overdone jewelry. He wrinkled his nose at the must and cigarette smoke, and whispered out of the side of his mouth, "Jesus, Superintendent, this sucks."

"I see you clearly, young man. My aging ears detected every word."

"Oops," Binh hissed to Kiet. "Slipsies."

"Captain Binh, isn't it?" Madame Saravane said, lighting an Emerald Queen from the one she was smoking. "Don't answer. The question was moot. I know everyone and everything in Hickorn. You, my insolent whelp, doubt your own masculinity. Your insecurity has turned you into a lothario."

Madame spat a piece of tobacco from her lip and clucked her tongue. "Those poor girls. You ensnare them with pretty looks and a white smile and smooth words, and then you cannot perform."

"That's a crock of shit!"

"Captain—"

Madame pointed an index finger to the ceiling and bent it at the first knuckle, tsk-tsked, and said, "How sad, how disappointing."

"You shriveled old cow, what do you know about love?"

"Captain. The operative word. Diplomacy," Kiet said, maneuvering him by a forearm to the bamboo guest chair and pushing until he sat.

"Superintendent, it's happened to every guy. You know, you've been out late and you're super beat and you've been hitting the sauce and maybe you're a little keyed-up. You've been there, haven't you? Jean-Guy, I'll bet he has. Red maybe. You don't make All Big Eight if you're not all man, but Red's only human."

"All Big Eight *second* team," Kiet corrected.

He stood behind Binh, patting his shoulders, saying yes yes. This was not entirely a gesture of brotherhood and empathy. Should Madame aggravate Binh further, Kiet was positioned to clasp clavicles and restrain.

Madame didn't see all, know all, he reminded himself. Tien and the house numbering. Binh and his postadolescent sexuality. Madame was a knowledgeable busybody, yes, but Madame was not omniscient, Madame was shrewd and cruel. Madame was a psychological monster. Madame had an instinct for the soft spot. If this was not sorcery, it was a facsimile.

"State your business," Madame Saravane said.

"The money, please," Kiet said to Binh.

Binh dug an envelope out of a pocket and slapped it onto Kiet's outstretched palm. "We shouldn't be giving her money, Superintendent. We should be giving her a broomstick so she'll have appropriate transportation."

Kiet handed her the envelope and said, "We are honest and therefore poor policemen, Madame. This is what we can spare. Please accept this and a profound apology for my conduct two days ago."

177

Madame tore it open, shook Luongan zin—currency and coin—into her lap, and droned a deprecating "hmmm."

She separated bills, stacked coins, and pulled a pocket calculator from her bodice.

"A modest sum, yet a sacrifice," Kiet said, elongating the lie. The money was a portion of the Hickorn police department petty cash fund. Pickpockets and other sneak thieves were the primary donors. Upon arrest, the suspect's cash was confiscated on the reasonable assumption that every zin was ill-gotten.

Madame Saravane exhaled smoke the color of nuclear winter and said, "Conversion at the going rate is 54.86 dollars, U.S. To ask me to remove the curse I imposed on you for such a paltry sum is insulting, Kiet."

"No, no. You misunderstand, Madame."

"Fifty dollars and change," she said thoughtfully. "For that much, I would be willing to prolong your end a week or so."

"No," Kiet said. "No thank you. We brought the fee not to offend you, Madame, but in the ardent hope that you would perform a service for us."

"A service?"

"A prediction, please."

"You know where she can stick her crystal ball, Superintendent."

"Captain."

"Where the sun doesn't shine is where."

Madame Saravane said, "A prediction? Scores of next week's soccer matches? Crass, stupid men come to me one upon another to gain a wagering advantage. I refuse. My gift is too precious to waste on games."

"Of course it is, Madame."

"Fifty dollars and change does not buy you a prediction of consequence."

"You owe me an expensive prediction, Madame. I am returning the prediction you gave me on my prior visit. A faulty prediction. A defective prediction. It burns excessive oil and it unravels at the seams. I demand a refund. Apply it with the money and it becomes an unpaltry sum."

178

Madame Saravane's eyes seemed to dilate at the accusation of fallibility.

"Jean-Guy Pakse," Kiet said. "He is not in France, courting the Marseille blonde sports car heiress. He is in Hickorn. You are a *Mind* columnist and the *Mind* uncovered his immigration, in press terminology scooping the story."

Kiet clucked his tongue. "Tsk-tsk. Extremely careless and unprofessional of you, Madame."

Madame returned the zin to the envelope and held it out to Kiet.

"No thank you. I forgive your error. Keep the money."

Madame's eyes were glazed, locked on a nonexistent horizon.

"Please rejoin the conversation at your leisure," Kiet said.

"Jesus H. Christ, Superintendent, look at her! She's branching out into new age. This is their routine, those channelers. Their eyeballs roll up like window shades, their voices go deep, and they pretend they're some ancient caveman who's possessed them to dispense his wisdom, which is big-league nutso if you think about it, since the dude is ten thousand years early to the party where they invented the wheel, which means the dumbshit can't even cart kindling wood into the cave to burn to keep himself warm because they haven't invented fire yet either. These suckers who shell out big bucks, this guy's gonna clue them in on the mysteries of the universe? Go figure."

"Yes, yes," Kiet said, patting Binh's shoulders, thinking that he had better remove him from the premises directly. On the off chance that Madame *did* possess magical powers, he would shortly have a frog for an adjutant.

Madame Saravane lighted an Emerald Queen. "I was resting my eyes."

"My prediction, please."

"On Wednesday my prediction was a lie. On Friday it is incompetence. Which?"

"You tell me, Madame. You are the seer."

"Neither."

There was less than the usual arrogance in her voice, less

179

confidence. Fallibility was *her* soft spot, Kiet thought. He said, "Impossible. Jean-Guy Pakse is in Hickorn. Either you lied or you forecast incorrectly."

Madame said nothing. Kiet wondered whether he should prompt her with Duc and the InterPresidential. No, he thought. No. Patience.

Finally she said, "There is a third alternative. You inquired regarding his immigration. Jean-Guy can visit Luong and not immigrate, can he not?"

"Ah," Kiet said.

"Huh?" Binh said.

That evening.

"Thank you for the lunch invitation, Bamsan."

"Brunch, Quin. Brunch."

"We seldom go out to eat. We cook for each other."

"Are you complaining?"

"No, but it's a nice change."

"Tomorrow is in the line of duty too. Fun, food, and work."

"I feel like a spy."

"Are you complaining, Quin?"

"No. It'll be fun. Binh and an American missionary? I can't picture it."

"Peculiar yet true."

"True love?"

"Not if I can successfully intervene."

"She may be genuinely nice."

"Hah!"

"May be, I said. Losing your virginity twice—I must bring Miss Applebee to the attention of our chief of gynecology and obstetrics. At the Conti *terrasse*, Bamsan, you said I should accompany her to the lavatory?"

"Yes. According to Binh, on an American double date it is customary for the ladies—"

180

"Women."

"For the women to simultaneously powder their noses. They giggle and gossip and confide their intentions."

"Intentions?"

"Whether or not they'll sleep with their dates."

"Bamsan, we're sleeping together in the broad use of that expression. Binh and Applebee have slept together."

"Learn what you can learn, Quin."

"I'm gla-ad you re-vealed to me the curssse."

"Very theatrical, very funny."

"Madame Saravane. You really do believe that Jean-Guy isn't in Luong for good?"

"I do not know if anybody has informed him, but yes, I do. Madame hates being wrong. She will jeopardize her plans to prove she is inerrant."

"The curssse. Does this tickle?"

"Yes."

"And this? What does this do?"

"Ah."

"Bamsan, I pronounce you cured."

Saturday, May 23
Hickorn
High 95°, Low 82°
Clear

TWENTY

ELVIS WINS LOTTERY—DARES NOT COLLECT HIS $5.5 MILLION. Exclusive: LECHEROUS SPACE ALIEN JOINS HICKORN SPORTING CLUB—GIANT FAIR-SKINNED EXTRATERRESTRIAL VOWS TO FATHER EARTHLING BABY. LUONG'S RECORD-SHATTERING INFERNO CONTINUES.

Kiet read the *Mind* headline at a newsstand, but declined to buy a paper. He would after brunch. He would read the Dragon Lady's muckraking debut in depth.

Brunch consumed him now, and he zestfully and guiltlessly consumed brunch. Fried shrimp, exquisite fresh water shellfish netted from the floor of the Ma San River. Cooked with sesame seeds in peanut oil. Iced bottles of the mellow Golden Tiger, which was peculiarly nicknamed "amber death" by Westerners.

Captain Binh kept his promise and did not criticize Kiet's beer drinking, not even after the third. Quin, on the other hand, was giving him that look. He sipped number four, prolonging both its nectarlike tang and congenial relations with his love. Order a fifth and he'd have to brace for a kick in the shin and Quin's ensuing headache. No thank you.

Quin was exceptionally beautiful in an Indonesian batik sarong printed like a tropical aviary. Captain Binh in uniform (heavy starch) had never appeared more lustrous and heroic. Mary Beth Applebee wore formless slacks and blouse, perhaps her uniform. She smelled of soap and goodness. Kiet wore his usual slacks and white shirt (clean and pressed), and sandals, and consequently felt under dressed.

He was not particularly chagrined by his sartorial understatement, however, as only he had selected a normal meal; he had a social edge on his companions there. Quin was eating a raw vegetable salad—no visible salad bar origins—and *nothing* else. In an effort to meet the InterPresidential's challenge, the Conti had expanded the *terrasse* menu, billing it "Cosmopolitan and International." Binh and Mary Beth were questionable beneficiaries of the competitive move. They had chosen the American Drive-in Groovy Number Six: bacon cheeseburger, french fried potatoes, chocolate milkshake.

Binh was dominating the conversation, chattering, it seemed to Kiet, nervously prattling about general topics. Sports, cars, work, politics. His bland small talk, Kiet sensed, addressed to the group, was a barrier to Mary Beth, a sexual headache in the making. Quin was baffled too. Glances at one another, the ESP of lovers, confirmed such. What was going on?

"Complications grow by the minute," Binh was saying. "The dimension of the thing is awesome. You figure you've got your bases covered and a new situation crops up. Journalist credentials, a nightmare and a half! I'm getting a ton of requests for interviews and photo opportunities. How do I establish accreditation policy in under two days? Take my word for it, you have to use kid gloves on the media. You offend some reporter and don't even realize what you've done till you get zapped in the neck somewhere down the road, you know, dumped on big-time in an editorial or something."

Binh had shifted to the execution. Kiet wanted very much to shunt that subject "somewhere down the road." Shrimp from his second helping was spoiling in his mouth. He needed an innocuous subject. The weather. No, no, no. Stupid. Weather was not innocuous, not nowadays in Luong. Quin came to Kiet's rescue.

"Mary Beth, how do you like Hickorn?"

"It's swell," she said, after a ladylike licking of hamburger sauce

186

on her lower lip. "My mission and I are off to a rocky start, but the people are as nice as pie."

"I'm sorry about the loss of your supplies. Have you had luck in recovering them?"

"No. None," Mary Beth said, sighing. "Lord willing."

Creamed canned corn, Kiet thought, chewing slowly.

"How does the loss affect your missionary plans?" Quin asked.

"It's too soon to say. Oh. Mr. LeClerc. Has everybody heard the rumor about Mr. LeClerc—Pierre? He's royalty in disguise? Is he?"

Binh looked at Quin. Kiet looked at Binh. Quin looked at Kiet. Kiet finally said, "Yes, he is."

"The good Lord must be watching out for me," Mary Beth said, smiling blissfully. "Jean-Guy Pakse? Is that his name?"

"Yes," Kiet said.

"He's Luong's crown prince?"

"Perhaps."

"He said he would get to the bottom of my lost supplies. You fellas, you were there. You're still investigating for me too?"

"Yes," Kiet said, nodding feebly.

"I pride myself as a pretty good judge of character. The Lord gave me that ability. I take no credit myself. Jean-Guy or Pierre, I believe in my heart he's sincere."

"Jean-Guy's a stand-up dude," Binh said, nodding energetically.

"I remained in my room last night. I had an excruciating headache. I left word at the desk to be rung if somebody special in my life called. You, dear, headed the list."

Kiet was certain Binh tensed when Mary Beth caressed his arm.

"The Mr. Le—Mr. Pakse too. I was too ill to receive visitors, but I would talk to the savior of my cargo if I were on a bed of coals."

"He didn't contact you?" Quin asked.

"No," Mary Beth said with a disappointed whine that made the fillings in Kiet's molars ache. "I'm not a quitter, but I'm not optimistic my cargo will—"

187

"Mary Beth," Binh said. "You spilled a glob of catsup on your blouse."

The glob was a speck. Kiet could barely see it. He looked at Quin. She raised eyebrows, saying: Binh beat us to our signal. Why?

"My uniform's cotton, same as your blouse, Mary Beth," Binh said. "What you have to do is dab cold water on."

"Oh, dear. I didn't pack many clothes," Mary Beth said. "And I can't afford to discard what I did bring."

Quin said, "I have to powder my nose. Let's see what we can do."

Mary Beth laughed. "You're delightful, Quin. I didn't know Luongans had that expression too."

"I didn't either," Quin whispered to Kiet.

The women went into the lavatory for their arcane nose-powdering ritual. Kiet said, "Explain, please."

"Huh?"

"Captain."

Binh leaned forward and took Kiet's beer out of his hand. "Superintendent, thanks. If ever in my life I crave a snort, this is then."

Binh inverted the Golden Tiger. Bubbles rose in the bottle. The liquid level fell as if a dam had burst. Binh's Adam's apple bobbed. Splendid, Kiet thought. I shall be accused of guzzling. Quin sees a fifth brew on the table upon returning from her powderless nose-powdering, she will commit me to an alcohol sanatorium.

Binh put the empty bottle on the table and burped. "That hit the spot."

"I am glad," Kiet said.

"Mary Beth, she saw me drinking like that, like a lush, she'd have a shit fit. She'd be hurt and I want to, you know, minimize hurting her."

"Please proceed."

"Madame Saravane should've seen me last night, Superintendent. I'm not bragging, mind you."

188

"No."

"Are you familiar with this *Mind* reporter who goes by the name Dragon Lady?"

"Vaguely."

"Well, I was in my office shuffling paper like I said I was gonna do and in she walks. Superintendent, she's a living doll. Nothing dragon or draggin' about her. She said can she have an interview and I said okay, fine, as long as you don't portray me patrolling Hickorn's streets in a flying saucer. She got a big chuckle out of that. We really hit it off. She's also got this thermos full of mai tais and would I care to have a drink while we interview, as kind of a reward for me putting up with her questions. Would I! You've got to hand it to her, knowing mai tais are my favorite drink. That was a classy touch."

"Tenacious journalism," Kiet said, avoiding eye contact.

"Well, what happened next, it's kind of hard for me to spit it out."

"One thing led to another?"

"Yeah. Sure did. I locked my door, cleaned off my desk, and wow! She ought to change that nom de plume from Dragon Lady to Tigress. You can use your imagination."

"Indeed." Kiet said, thinking that he shall henceforth judge less harshly the pimp and his profession.

"The Dragon Lady—funny, I don't think she told me her real name—she's between relationships. I don't read her stuff, I don't read the *Mind* unless police business requires me to."

"Of course not."

"Those stories she writes, so they say, have to do with aliens and bondage."

"So they say."

"She was probably super horny and hot and bothered and repressed from typing about big Martian cocks all day long and those mai tais were super strong too. Anyway, my point is that I'm not ready to settle down. Mary Beth, as great a gal as she is, I can't escape the fact that I've got wild oats left to sow."

Bushels, Kiet hoped.

"It wouldn't be fair to put her in the position of me chippy chasing on her every time some little honey in a miniskirt whips a winning smile on me."

"No, of course not," said Kiet, who was smiling too, hopefully a mild fatherly smile, not the triumphant grin of a conspirator.

"Her missionary career is the apex of her life, her reason for existing. I'm not exactly what you'd call an ideal helpmate in her mission. I mean, I can't visualize myself tramping through the boonies with a trunk full of giveaway bibles on my back. Uh-uh. And I have my own career. What deserves precedence, God or crime? We'd have ourselves some big-time lovers' spats on that issue, some donnybrooks."

"Yes," Kiet said. "I agree."

"You guys, when you finish brunch, and split, I'll stall around, dump the news on Mary Beth. Breaking her heart is the bottom line, but if I do what I have to do in private, who knows what might happen?"

"Who knows," Kiet chimed, observing the approach of Mary Beth Applebee and Quin Canh. Mary Beth beamed at Binh, tapping the spot of the former catsup spot. Quin was not beaming at Kiet. She was saying with nary a twitch, a tic, a grimace, a grin, in the expressionless language of telepathic lovers, saying "we have to talk." Kiet nodded and winked, saying "very well."

Twenty minutes later.

"Bamsan, are you sober?"

"Yes, Quin, yes, of course."

"Bamsan, you drank five beers in just one hour."

"Four beers. Four and a fraction. I told you. Binh—"

"That quickly?"

"He perfected the technique in America, at parties. They term it chug-a-lugging."

"All right, Bamsan. If you say so."

"How long do you plan to keep me in suspense, Quin?"

"In your condition, I'm surprised you remember."

"The nose-powdering, please. Do not omit a word."

"There weren't a lot of words to omit. I applied cold water to the catsup spot, she said thank you, and we brushed our hair. She said isn't it hot, I said, it surely is. She complained about airline food on her flight and said lunch was tasty and I said my salad was excellent too. She smoked a cigarette. She inhaled deeply, like she craved nicotine. She asked me not to tell anyone. Bamsan, I think she's a phony. I think she's an actress."

"Excuse me?"

"She changes. She wasn't the bubbly missionary in there. I think she felt she could relax around me just a little. I think she's been so engrossed in the missionary role she had to let down, to temporarily revert in order to release stress. Smoking is no crime, but when she lit the cigarette she became a Western woman who could be hard, worldly, and unhappy. I saw bitterness and cunning in her face, Bamsan. I tried to be discreet, but I couldn't stop looking at her. She saw me staring at her through the mirror and instantly shifted back into the missionary woman."

"A professional actress? Perhaps. In Jean-Guy's suite she cried a single, perfect tear."

"She's capable of crying on demand. She could be a professional. I've seen worse acting in live theater."

"Ah. Los Angeles."

"Los Angeles?"

"Yes. I telephoned Los Angeles about Mr. Red Williams and Seattle about Mary Beth Applebee. I should be speaking to Los Angeles regarding her as well."

"Why Los Angeles, Bamsan?"

"Not Los Angeles, Quin. Los La-La Lotusland Hollywood Angeles."

Two cablegrams awaited Kiet at headquarters. Each reply was negative. He was elated. He was in such a rush to make additional

191

cordless cellular telephone transmissions that he drafted Binh to drive him to the InterPresidential on a motorbike.

"How did Mary Beth take it?" he yelled.

Binh cocked his head. "Like a trooper. I told her in the context of me not being good enough for her, which is, you know, basically the truth. A tear fell. She blew her nose and said she would always be my friend. She's one helluva gal, Superintendent."

"Splendid."

"Then she asked me for a favor."

"A favor?"

"A teeny little favor is how she phrased it, which it is. Figuring that you wouldn't have objections, I okayed it."

"How am I involved to object, please?"

"Well, it sort of concerns the department."

"I am listening."

"That we kind of collect money for her cause."

"Kind of?"

"You know, not from poor people. Whenever an officer answers a squeal by somebody rich or well-to-do, after police business is handled, he could let it be known that the department is endorsing a worthy charity. Food for hungry Luongans is as worthy as it gets. Before we know it, Superintendent, Mary Beth will have aid planes streaming into Hickorn International. I routed a memo to street personnel and supervisors. Any objections?"

"No," Kiet said, too angry to summon the proper words of objection. The scheme smacked of shakedown, and as far as Kiet was concerned a money pitch for whatever cause was still a shakedown. Collect your thoughts, he told himself. Discuss it with the lad when you are calm and rational.

They rode the rest of the way to the hotel in silence. Once there, Kiet borrowed the magical telephone from the hotel manager. It was late in the day, much later than when Kiet had telephoned across the Pacific yesterday. Because of a nine hour time difference, he spoke to the answering machines of sleeping Los Angelinos.

192

TWENTY-ONE

His Royal Highness, Prince Novisad Pakse, ruler of the kingdom of Luong, motioned to Kiet, inviting him to take a seat. Kiet obeyed, picking a cushioned recliner beside the prince.

This and other leather lounge chairs were arranged in an arc facing a forty-five-inch color television receiver. The set was on, but the picture was mute. When Kiet was shown into the room, Prince Pakse had killed the sound by flicking a button on a remote control gadget that resembled the InterPresidential's supernatural telephone.

Prince Pakse did not immediately speak, and etiquette forbade a commoner from initiating the conversation. On the screen were two billiards players in tuxedos. An older man with a fat gut pocketed, in numerical sequence, nine balls that had been arranged in a diamond pattern. The diamond alignment was repeated, but no ball fell on the break. His opponent, a younger man with hollow cheeks and a cigarette hanging in his mouth, disposed of all nine balls. The scene transferred to a barroom. Pretty young Caucasian men and women were gaily drinking a brand of "light" beer.

Prince Pakse was watching a videotaped billiards tourney. The original program had been transmitted by an American sporting event network. Prince Pakse had scooped the signal out of the sky via the satellite dish that blighted the royal palace's roof. Technological wizardry, Kiet thought.

Prince Pakse flicked the button-encrusted remote controller. The screen went black.

"Bosha, you threatened my nephew."

Kiet was unafraid. *He* had requested this audience. If Prince Pakse intended to punish him, he would have summoned Kiet. "Yes, Your Highness."

"May I ask the reason?"

"Your Highness, I respectfully ask that you first relate to me Minister Duc's version."

"You will not like what he said about you, Bosha."

"And you will not like what he said about you, Your Highness."

"Shall I be blunt?"

"Please."

"I can't remember verbatim, but he did brand you as an 'oaf' and a 'crook.' He said you crashed the Hickorn Sporting Club, brought a female tabloid reporter along with you, made considerable noise, took a guest's place at my nephew's table, ate that man's food, then insulted and threatened my nephew. Are you guilty of those indiscretions, Bosha?"

"Yes, Your Highness. Guilty on every count."

"Excellent. My brattish nephew and that pompous enclave of snobbery are overdue for a dose of humility. The 'crook' label was his response to what he says is your hedging on the Feng Vu execution. My overeducated high-achiever of a nephew accuses you of accepting a bribe from Vu. For a fee you'll manufacture evidence that proves he's not guilty."

"Nonsense," Kiet said.

"I know it is. How did I fare with the brat, Bosha?"

Kiet had decided beforehand to spoon-feed Duc's cruelty, to edit it. He told his tale, excluding the Uncle Novie references and the old engine analogy, but withholding no relevant facts.

Houphong Duc and his ministry of agriculture chartering Jean-Guy Pakse's flight from France. The Luong InterPresidential Hotel paying Jean-Guy's room and board. Madame Saravane's majority ownership of the InterPresidential; her acquisition of the hotel land from Feng Vu for a ticket to a heavenly Disneyland. The speculative alliance of Duc and Lieutenant Commander Tuon

Tran. Jean-Guy Pakse's mysterious part in the conspiratorial drama, providing he had a part and there was a drama.

Prince Pakse, an octogenarian with not a gram of surplus flesh, seemed to shrivel. "Bosha, I've been apprised of some hazy rumors, but I had no idea that it had gone this far."

"So, Your Highness, you do agree with me that mischief is in the making?"

"I have no choice but to agree. The drought has my people restive. The Feng Vu execution is a potential catalyst. The populace could react like a domestic animal tasting warm blood. Bosha, what do you suggest we do?"

"Promote Tuon Tran."

Prince Pakse looked at Kiet.

"Tran is a component in the mess. The weakest, yes, but a component nevertheless. Perhaps when we remove this component the entire structure will collapse."

"Removing him by buying his loyalty, Bosha?"

"Yes, Your Highness. By buying him with something no amount of money could buy. By buying him his life's dream."

Prince Pakse said, "Our constitution authorizes me to raise or lower the rank of a chief of service—army, air force, or navy—without consulting the National Assembly or the Ministry of Defense. But you're aware of that clause, aren't you, Bosha?"

Bamsan Kiet smiled.

"To which rank do you recommend we elevate him?"

"Admiral."

"To four-star fleet admiral?"

Kiet shrugged. "The happier our chief of naval operations is, Your Highness, the stronger his loyalty to us."

"You have an ulterior motive, don't you, Bosha? Didn't Tran participate in the Feng Vu raid?"

"Yes sir."

"I'm not going to lecture you on accepting what the court decreed, Bosha. You listen to no man when your mind is made

195

up, and you've convinced yourself that the Chinese rice hoarder is innocent."

"Your Highness, I have convinced myself that he may have been unjustly tried and convicted."

"I won't dispute you. I myself just said that the execution could be a catalyst. All right, I'll promote Tran to full commander."

"Vice admiral," Kiet countered.

"Captain. A four-striper."

"Rear admiral."

"Commodore."

"Rear admiral, sir."

"Bosha, to promote an undeserving individual ridicules one of my strongest beliefs. I become a hypocrite."

"The promotion is, we hope, for the good of the kingdom. What could be more noble?"

"We promote him. What then?"

"After the ceremony, you and I and Captain Binh and Admiral Tran shall have a chat."

Prince Pakse shook his head. "My army generals are going to be peeved at me."

"The joint chiefs can still shun him, Your Highness. They can and will continue to exclude him from staff conferences. How can Tran protest? Lob water balloons at them from his cabin cruisers?"

Prince Pakse sighed. "All right, Bosha. Rear admiral. We'll stage a ceremony tonight. I'll issue the order, you supply the uniform. Luong has never had an admiral in its history."

"Thank you, Your Highness. One other item of business, please."

"Thanks to you, Bosha, this is turning into an extraordinary day."

Kiet ignored the royal sarcasm and said, "Jean-Guy."

"Yes?" Prince Pakse said tensely.

"Has he attempted to contact you?"

"No. Neither my secretaries nor the palace guards have received appointment requests."

Ah, Kiet thought, you have been monitoring the log books. "Your Highness, have you contacted him?"

"Certainly not."

"Would you, sir, please? At your earliest convenience."

"To forward your investigation, your premise, which to say the very least is rather indistinct?"

Kiet knew that His Royal Highness would rather burn his cue sticks and drop his billiards table into the Ma San River than befriend his alleged, reputed, court-decreed illegitimate son of the elegant French tramp. Despite imminent peril, Prince Pakse would play the ostrich. "Indistinct, yes, Your Highness, but menacing."

"Menacing," Prince Pakse said. "I admire your facility for the right word at the right time."

"Captain Binh, my special security liaison, is at your disposal, Your Highness. He will deliver the boy to you discreetly and expeditiously."

Prince Pakse reactivated his billiards tournament. Through a complicated series of cushion rebounds, the older gentleman sank three balls with one shot.

"Experience," Prince Pakse said. "The youngster possesses more talent now than the older man had at the peak of his career, but the older man possesses the seasoning and the poise to make that sparkling combination. The kid has been psychologically crippled. He is mortally wounded. I've seen this tape a hundred times, Bosha. The boy was leading six games to four, but the veteran took the last five games and the match. The three-ball parlay was the turning point."

"Is this a parable, Your Highness?"

"No, just an observation. Get out of here, Bosha, before you think of anything else for me to do."

TWENTY-TWO

"You're pissed at me, Superintendent. Your nose is so far out of joint, if you sneezed you'd snot-shower the dude behind you."

Kiet and Binh were at the royal palace, seated on an antique bench in the receiving room outside Prince Pakse's study. The bench was gilded teak, a beautiful and priceless example of seventeenth century Luongan craftsmanship. It was as hard as iron, and Kiet's buttocks tingled.

"Excuse me?"

"You've been in a big-time snit, but, hey, I'm just second in command. What do my feelings matter? I ran my ass all over town to come up with Tran's admiral uniform. One store in Hickorn had something appropriate. I showed three minutes after he shuttered his door and I damn near had to draw my weapon before he'd reopen."

"Very much appreciated, Captain."

"Except for that goddamn snipe hunt you sent me on, that's three words more than you've spoken to me since brunch, and don't think I haven't a theory or two on what's bothering you, as if it's all *my* fault."

"Very well, I won't."

"That little outburst of mine at Madame Saravane's, which the old douche bag provoked. No sweat, in case you are. Sweating, that is. Speaking for myself, she's shooting blanks with whatever hex she put on us, and you can take it to the bank that she did, despite you doing a slick piece of work of putting her on defense toward the end. At least nothing's fallen off yet."

"No."

"Not it? Okay. The Dragon Lady and I getting it on in my office? I already admitted I was a jerk, but I have hormones, I'm only hu—"

"No."

"Mary Beth?"

Kiet did not reply. The royal palace was no venue for a battle on the charity shakedown.

"Aha! I knew it. You think I'm a heel, right?"

"Excuse me?"

"For taking advantage of Mary Beth, then breaking up with her."

Kiet remained speechless. The Mary Beth Applebee/Seattle and Red Williams/Los Angeles cables were folded in his back pocket awaiting a correct moment. Binh could not be notified and entirely save face. The missives and Binh's ego were at opposite polarities. But Kiet would pick his spot with the hope of mitigating the pain.

"You're laying the silent treatment on me, Superintendent. You couldn't be any more transparent. I'm sort of touched. I never got the impression that you were fond of Mary Beth, but I guess you are. I was super gentle with her, I really was. In the sack and on the *terrasse* when I cut her loose. Honest, Superintendent."

"I am relieved," Kiet said.

The royal protocol secretary opened the door of the study and asked Kiet and Binh to enter. Prince Pakse was shaking hands with the other witness to the promotion ceremony, the Royal Luongan Navy Deputy Chief of Naval Operations, a lieutenant. A saucily happy fellow, giddy with visions of also rocketing in rank, Kiet thought. Too bad, so sorry.

The grinning lieutenant pumped Kiet's and Binh's hands, and departed with the secretary.

Rear Admiral Tuon Tran patted lint from his jacket and said imperiously, "Welcome aboard, gentlemen."

The jacket was dark blue and long. Its buttonholes and collar were embroidered gold as were tassels that fairly poured from epaulets. Vest and trousers were white, and too snug to flatter Tran's physique. The ornate three-pointed hat recalled sails and cannonballs.

Tran was wearing the fruit of Binh's frantic shopping expedition. The costume store had identified it on the invoice as Nelson at the Battle of Copenhagen.

"Congratulations, Admiral," Kiet said.

"Thank you. This is a wonderful uniform. His Royal Highness said that you gentlemen provided it. Thank you, Superintendent. Thank you, Captain."

"Our pleasure," Kiet said, eyes forward. Trade glances with Binh now and they would be on the floor howling.

"It is a dress uniform and as such should be confined to parades and high-level staff meetings. I'll have to assign the problem of an everyday uniform to my stewards. Khaki like American task force admirals wore at Midway maybe. I loved the movie."

"Superintendent Kiet was instrumental in your promotion," said Prince Pakse. "He has been a champion of yours."

Kiet shrugged. "Talent and loyalty should be rewarded."

"Yes, of course they should," Prince Pakse said. "I value loyalty to the utmost. It is the uncommon man who combines ability and allegiance. You are that man, Admiral Tran."

"Thank you, Your Highness," Tran said, choking on emotion, gorged on pride.

"How do they phrase it in the United States, Captain Binh? A team player?"

"Yes, Your Highness."

A splendid act of priming the interrogation subject, Kiet thought. His Royal Highness is a born detective.

"Team player. It has a nice sound. Superintendent Kiet, a team player, regardless of personal risk, would not hesitate to give honest testimony if the team were threatened, would he?"

"Indeed not," Kiet said.

"Offense, defense, and special teams, pulling together," Binh said, raising a fist. "Overcoming adversity, regaining the momentum."

Prince Pakse, Kiet, and Binh were looking at Tran. The commandant of the Royal Luongan Navy finally realized he had been jobbed. Color and euphoria drained from his face.

"Are you ill, Admiral?" Kiet asked, thinking that rather than Nelson at Copenhagen, Tran's pallor suggested Nelson at Trafalgar, after a sharpshooter's bullet had felled him.

"No."

"Splendid. You can answer a few questions, please."

Tran turned to Prince Pakse, who was nodding affirmatively.

"The raid on Feng Vu's Sincere Rice Company. You told me earlier that a naval detachment aided the army."

"Yes. I remember telling you."

"But you did not state whether you participated. Did you participate?"

"Do you mean, was I, myself, physically present, or was I referring to my naval unit in a third person sense?"

Kiet groaned.

"Yes."

"Yes what?"

"Yes, Superintendent."

"No, no. Were you there? Yes or no?"

"Yes. I led the detachment."

"Houphong Duc asserts that the confiscated rice, two hundred metric tons, was milled Luongan paddy that Vu was hoarding until the price rose. The rice was in fifty-kilo bags. Duc and the ministry of agriculture sold it to local vendors at below market price, thus inducing a short-term reduction in market price. True?"

"Yes, Superintendent," Tran said eagerly. "Exactly true."

"Yeah, sure, right," Binh muttered. "So is the March Hare and the Easter Bunny. Oops, sorry, Your Highness."

Prince Pakse smiled and winked at Binh.

"Very peculiar. Feng Vu's version differs substantially."

"Vu is condemned to die," Tran said. "Condemned men have been known to lie."

"Feng Vu says the rice came from Thailand in a recent shipment. It was packed in one-hundred-kilo bags. A hundred kilos is too heavy for Luongan hand labor, so Vu's employees transferred the rice to fifty-kilo bags printed with the logo and name of Sincere Rice Company, Limited. Vu claims that Duc took the rice and disposed of the empty one-hundred-kilo bags and the bills of lading."

"Ask Feng Vu's coolies," Tran said. "They'll confirm that Vu lied. Ask a soldier or a sailor who took part in the raid. They'll confirm that Feng Vu is a liar."

"An effort was made prior to Vu's trial to locate a friendly witness," Binh said. "Uh-uh. An average citizen is gonna stick his neck on the chopper for some rich Chinaman who's hated worse than Hitler? Gimme a break. I'll be upfront with you, Tran, I'm not too gung ho, you know, about my boss's Feng Vu hang-up. The thing is, we're here having us a circlejerk when we could be spending our valuable time assigning execution day press credentials and drawing the names of the lucky shooters, but hey, I'm smelling something funny at this point in time and it ain't a skunk's armpit."

Tran asked Kiet, "What did he say?"

"He said you are the liar, Admiral."

"The kingdom of Luong is in its third millennium," Prince Pakse said. "You are her first admiral, her first lord of the seas. Rear Admiral Tuon Tran will appear in history books. You bear a tremendous responsibility."

Captain Binh puckered his face. "Benedict Arnold. Quisling. Tran. The plot thickens and the odor ripens."

"Ah, the advantages of obscurity," Kiet said to Binh. "No school child in the year 2500 A.D. will fill in the examination paper blank by my name or yours with 'twentieth century traitor.' "

"Right on," Binh said.

Tuon Tran slumped in his chair and inhaled deeply. A coat

button popped free and shot across the room as if grenade shrapnel. "I live in shame or die a hero. Pardon me for having trouble choosing."

"Dying for speaking the truth? No, Tran. Who do you fear?"

"I don't know who I fear. Pardon an old familiar gripe, but nobody confides in me. I can't verify a plot, but I feel it palpably. I don't know what it is and who is in it, but my instincts see it in every shadow."

"Paranoia City," Binh said.

Kiet said to Tran, "My advice is to patrol upriver as you said you were when you bolted from the Hickorn Sporting Club. Or, if you prefer, I can hold you in protective custody. Do not be afraid of retaliation."

"Tran, do you consort with that pack of snobs?" Prince Pakse asked.

"I'm not a member, Your Highness."

"In the event I do not reduce you to ordinary seaman, save your zin for the initiation fee," Prince Pakse said. "All my generals belong."

"Admiral Tran was having lunch with Minister Duc," Kiet said. "He was the guest whose place I rudely and crudely appropriated. Tran, was Feng Vu's story accurate?"

"To the letter."

"And Minister Duc is the principal menace in your life?"

"Menace, menacing," Prince Pakse said. "Bosha, you use the words as if you invented them."

"Bosha?" Tran said indignantly. "Who's the runt? I'm short, but I'm too plump to be a runt."

"Never mind," Kiet said. "Again, is Minister Duc the principal menace in your life?"

Tran lowered his head. "Duc has a knack for selling people on doing his bidding."

"How did he sell you?"

"He claimed that Luong was on the verge of revolution. He said that Feng Vu's hoarding was causing thousands of people to

204

die of starvation. He said that the men who brought Vu to justice would be on the forefront of tomorrow's Luong."

"Did you believe him?"

"I wanted to. I wanted to be—superior to a lieutenant commander. I did not want to retire as a lieutenant commander, an old sailor in the rank of a young officer in most navies. Duc implied that I would be an admiral in tomorrow's Luong. Here I am, admiral in today's Luong and I may not live long enough to see tomorrow's Luong. I'm confused and I have a headache."

"The two hundred metric tons of rice, please."

"The rice in Vu's warehouse wasn't hoarded. I *am* a sailor. I am on the river. I saw the rice unloaded on the Ma San docks a week prior to the raid. Feng Vu is a no-good, hateful bastard son of a Chinaman swine. He may have planned to hoard that Thai rice, but we took it and him before he could."

"Forefront of tomorrow's Luong" sounded to Kiet like a fascist slogan. It had a cold metallic ring. He imaged Houphong Duc, suspenders under pinstripes, hair and teeth gleaming, haranguing a mob from a balcony.

"Where is the rice?" Kiet asked.

"Duc spoke the truth. The rice was sold fast and cheap to Hickorn food sellers. Soldiers, sailors, and Vu's coolies lugged it to their shops and awoke them. Duc let them keep the cash. It was a staggering windfall. The troops and laborers made more money that night than they earn in four years. Eighty or ninety men altogether, Kiet, and you couldn't unseal a single man's lips with a crowbar. Don't waste time trying."

"The paperwork?" Kiet asked. "Bills of lading and account notations?"

"Duc collected every scrap of paper, every ledger, and disposed of them. Have you seen Vu's godown? It's empty and clean. His friends and neighbors have forgotten his name."

"Feng Vu is bad luck," Kiet said.

"Lucky as an earthquake," Binh said. "Lucky as syphilis."

"Captain," Kiet said.

205

"What is to become of me, Your Highness?" said an extremely apprehensive Tuon Tran.

"For the time being, sailing upriver like Superintendent Kiet proposed is excellent advice. Take several months of provisions and your most trustworthy sailors. Make no contact with the villages, however. You're on special assignment. Explore the Ma San River's remote tributaries. Be the Luongan Vasco Da Gama. We'll send for you at a future date, and you and I can reevaluate your naval career. Your deputy is capable of commanding pirate patrols. I'll promote him to commander for the interim."

"Have I a choice?"

Prince Pakse looked at Kiet, who said, "Criminal charges once this mess is sorted out. Perjury, conspiracy, mopery. We have no dearth of charges."

"It so happens that my flagship is provisioned, ready to leave port immediately," Tran said. "I maintain it in a constant state of red alert."

"Splendid," said Kiet. "A few extra questions, please. Did Duc mention names of major coconspirators?"

"No."

"Madame Saravane?"

"No."

"Jean-Guy Pakse?"

"No. Duc, like I stated, treats me the same as the army generals. He doesn't confide in me."

"Why did you jump like a rabbit when I saw you with Duc at the Hickorn Sporting Club?"

"I was startled. I didn't know you were a member."

Kiet groaned. "Admiral."

"Duc was nervous. He was giving me a speech on the importance of sticking to the agreed-upon raid story. A lot of good it did."

"A pep talk," Binh said. "Straightening their row of ducks."

"Duc disposed of the rice paperwork, Admiral," Kiet said. "What became of the bags, please?"

Tuon Tran did not reply.

"Captain, how bulky is two thousand rice bags?"

"High as an elephant's eye."

"Quite bulky," Kiet said. "A conspicuous bonfire. A large hole in the ground. Any ideas, Captain?"

Binh snapped his fingers. "Davy Jones's locker."

"Excuse me?"

"The bottom of the Ma San River."

"Indeed."

Prince Pakse jabbed a bony finger at Tran. "You have a mission before you embark on your sabbatical. Do not insult our intelligence by asking what it is."

Sunday, May 24
Hickorn
High 89°, Low 82°
Scattered clouds

TWENTY-THREE

The clouds fooled nobody. They looked like dumplings floating in blue broth. There wasn't enough moisture in one puff to moisten a person's lips. The air was as dry and prickly as yesterday and the day before yesterday and the day before the day before yesterday. The southwest monsoon teasing us, Kiet thought, cruelly tormenting, a deity's meteorological deviation on the Chinese water torture. The *Mind* did not publish on Sundays, so Kiet could not read a forecast, nor whether Madame Saravane had a goofy vision on the meaning of the minor weather change.

Kiet walked through the InterPresidential lobby to the far hallway and the banquet rooms to which it led. The rooms varied in capacity from a handful to a multitude. Their inclusion in the hotel design was inspired by Western boosterism and clubbiness and by the desire to attract tourist conventions.

Kiet had booked the smallest for brunch, but he could have had his pick. Luong as a convention hub was weak competition to the carnal glitter of Hong Kong and Bangkok. And Hickorn merchants were too busy eking out a livelihood to meet on the third Wednesday of the month, pick at mediocre food, and listen to a worse speech. The hotel's most faithful clients were federal civil servants who congregated for long, long luncheon bridge tournaments.

Kiet came to his reserved room. While suites such as Jean-Guy Pakse's were illogically named for eras, the banquet rooms were, in his opinion, logically named for celebrity gourmands. He stopped at the Norodom Sihanouk room and checked a hallway clock. He was precisely twenty minutes late. He smiled. His timing was faultless.

He walked in on Mary Beth Applebee and Red Williams, and said good morning. They were at opposite ends of a round table, hands folded, expressions blank. They repeated his greeting in concord, like schoolchildren to their teacher.

Kiet sat between them. He knew his hunch was dead on.

"No coffee yet? This is outrageous," Kiet said cheerfully.

"We were waiting for you," Mary Beth said, smiling sweetly.

"I am sorry to be late," Kiet said. "I ask two strangers, albeit American countrymen, to brunch, and Hickorn traffic delays me. I of all people should know the whims of Hickorn traffic. I trust you overcame the awkwardness of the situation and introduced yourselves in spite of my inconsiderate tardiness."

"Yep," Red said with a wink and a wide grin. "A pretty lady and brainy too, but, shoot, she's a missionary. Gotta be watching my language around Mary Lou."

"Mary Beth, Mr. Williams."

"Yeah, gotcha. Hey, coffee."

A waitress brought a pitcher and three cups. Red poured and said, chuckling, "Nothing beats a hit of caffeine to kick-start the ol' ticker."

"Mr. Williams was a college football star," Mary Beth told Kiet. "He sells air conditioners."

"Yes," Kiet said.

"Oh, silly me," Mary Beth said in a coquettish tone. "You know that, Superintendent. Mr. Williams said you invited him to brunch to speak to him regarding air conditioners purchased for your police station."

"And I invited you to discuss your errant shipment of famine relief. Mr. Williams and Miss Applebee, whatever your real names are, I lied. As you have lied from the very instant you alighted on Luongan soil."

Red squinted at Kiet. "Am I hearing right? Are my ears playing tricks on me?"

212

"I neither know nor care whether you have hearing problems, Mr. Williams. I called you a liar. I can repeat, louder."

"I'm a man with things to do," Red blustered. "I got no time to be getting my chain jerked and my good name dragged in the mud."

"Oh goodness," Mary Beth said. "You're being dreadful to us, Superintendent Kiet."

"Stop it! Quiet!" Kiet took the cablegrams from his pocket. "I investigated the pair of you. I don't completely know who you are, but I damn well know who you're not. You are not what you have represented yourselves to be."

"Oh yeah? That's what those measly little scraps of paper say?"

"It is what they omit, Mr. Williams. Not what they include. Mary Beth Applebee is unknown to any foreign Christian mission operating out of Seattle in the American province of Washington. No air conditioning wholesaler in La La Angeles is affiliated with a Far East salesman named Red Williams."

Their eyes darted back and forth. Red spoke first. "So how'd you connect the dots between me and her."

"Shut up, dummy," Mary Beth said.

"Two American hustlers coming to Hickorn within two weeks of each other, collecting money. Air conditioner down payments and famine relief aid. Monies fraudulently collected from and solicited by the Hickorn police department. You cannot begin to conceive my loss of face.

"I had no proof, however. I was purposely twenty minutes late so you could confer. You didn't disappoint me. If you were true strangers, given what I've observed of your true natures—"

"Hey, like what true natures? Are you insulting us?"

"Gregarious and venal and randy."

"I can live with that," Red said.

"Jesus Christ," Mary Beth said, lighting a cigarette.

"Instead of spontaneity, I was greeted by contrived strangers."

Red lifted his coffee cup in a toast. "Tricky-slick work, Blamsand. I reckon that's how come you run the marshal's office in this hick town."

"Indeed," Kiet said.

213

Mary Beth exhaled smoke with a sigh of nicotine bliss. "Red, you and me, we'd be happier campers if you could just keep your mouth shut and your pants zipped."

"She's starting on me again," Red pleaded to Kiet. "Some god-damn bimbo girl reporter for this sicko tabloid, she writes me up as this spaceman who invades the Hickorn Sporting Club and puts a move on every honey with a pulse. Sister Bernadette here, she gobbles it hook, line, and sinker. I haven't had a minute's peace since."

"Hire that reporter to write your autobiography, toots," Mary Beth said. "She read you like a book."

"Bam-saw. I'm gonna sue that rag for every zin they got. You can sue in Luong, can't you?"

Kiet had no interest in or knowledge of civil law. Binh had regaled him with unbelievable tales of proliferating American lawyers, a litigious and greedy pestilence that gridlocked U.S. courtrooms. "No. You cannot. Luongan courts do not award money for slander or injured feelings."

"Damn. Well, hell."

"Sue somebody for printing the truth?" Mary Beth said, smiling. "Her only mistake was the planet you're from."

Red cocked a thumb toward Mary Beth and said to Kiet, "That coming from a little cookie whose heels are so round she has to stuff newspaper in her shoes to stand up straight."

"I do what I do for business, you asshole. *Our* business."

"Excuse me," Kiet said. "Are you married?"

"Divorced," Mary Beth said.

"Twice," Red said. "Married and divorced twice."

"I'm a slow learner," Mary Beth said.

Kiet consulted his cablegrams. "You are also a professional actress?"

Mary Beth set her coffee cup down hard. "What gave you that idea?"

"I inquired at the actors' union you La La Landers belong to," Kiet said, not clarifying that his inquiry was yet unanswered.

214

Red laughed. "*The Suck Sisters*. She co-starred."

A domestic comedy? Kiet wondered.

"*Trixi and the 69th Infantry Division*," Red continued. "Top billing in that Tinseltown classic."

A war epic? Kiet loved John Wayne and Paul Muni war movies almost as much as anything by his favorite Western actor, Sydney Greenstreet. "Filmed in a Hollywood silver screen studio?"

"Nope," Red said. "A Van Nuys motel room."

Mary Beth said, "Since we're airing the dirty linen, you know the big man's football career is phony, don't you?"

"Indeed," Kiet lied.

"Hey, where'd you dig up all this dirt you have on us, anyways, Bon-some?"

"Interpol."

"All-world college linebacker, isn't that what he told you? It's the line he feeds everyone. He gets away with it because he's a big tub of lard."

"The Iowa Typhoons," Kiet said. "Eighth team, All-Big Two."

"Close enough," Mary Beth said. "We were born and raised in Ames, home of Iowa State University."

She poked a finger in her mouth, a gesture of vomit inducing. "We were high school sweethearts. I still can't believe it."

"Ah," Kiet said. "Young love."

"Red never attended State or any other institution of higher learning, unless the Story County jail qualifies. Burglary, wasn't it, honey? Busted in an alley in the process of cleaning out an appliance store."

Red Williams blew Mary Beth Applebee a kiss. "We were made for each other."

Mary Beth Applebee batted her eyelashes and gave Red Williams the finger.

"Are you using your given names?"

"Yeah. Mary Beth Applebee's her maiden name. They nab you with fake i.d. in some of these countries, you're in a world of hurt. Interpol, huh? If you were wired to Interpol, you'd have my

215

hat size and fourth grade penmanship grade. I think maybe I ought to be wearing hip boots."

"Excuse me?"

"I'm sloshing in manure up to my knees, boy, and the poop's rising by the minute. Don't bullshit a bullshitter."

"I am not a boy," Kiet said evenly.

Red made the peace sign. "Whoa. No offense. You're a mean motor scooter and I'm not in the market for the kind of hurt you laid on the chink."

"I am not a lunk."

Williams swiveled his head, as if in search of the last fair-minded human being on earth. "God, what the hell did I say? This Feng Vu son of a bitch eats live babies. He's about as popular as Ghaddafi in Jerusalem and you're shooting out his lights tomorrow. You act like I said you were a nigger and I didn't call you a frigging thing."

"Feng Vu is a chink. Feng Vu is Oriental. I am Oriental. We are inferior to your race. I am therefore a lunk."

"Never in a million years will I ever figure you people out," Red Williams said. "You let me outta this room alive and I'm hauling ass to some place you don't get the inscrutable trip laid on you by every Tom, Dick, and Fu Man-chew."

"Children, children," Mary Beth said, clapping. "Brunch."

The waitress served steaming plates of individual layered combinations, bottom to top respectively: English muffin, sliced smoked pork, fried hen's egg, yellowish sauce. Eggs Benedict.

Rigid and semiedible banquet menus were inviolable, Kiet had been informed when he transacted the Norodom Sihanouk room. The manager, however intimidated by Kiet, regardless of the charge he would thunk-thunk into Jean-Guy Pakse's computerized tab, would not yield, would not substitute fried shrimp and Golden Tiger.

Eggs Benedict. Kiet wondered if the dish was named in honor of the American traitor. He nibbled politely, positive that it must have been. Mary Beth and Red wolfed theirs, Red saying that

216

Brokaw and Rather and those guys preaching that the world was a global neighborhood were on the button when, you know, you're halfway around the world in some country that doesn't have a supermarket or an NFL team but can dish up Eggs Benedict second to none, Mary Beth saying hers was delicious too but for Red to please shut the fuck up.

"Mr. Williams, you have sold air conditioners you have no intention of delivering in other countries too?"

"You betcha. The rule of thumb is if you can fry Eggs Benedict on the sidewalk, you got yourself a prime territory." He laughed at his own wit and said, "Stock up on brand name brochures, print up some official-looking order forms, and you're in business. You know that saying about selling refrigerators to Eskimos?"

"No."

"Well, anyhow, I'm good, but I ain't *that* good."

"Not air conditioners to Eskimos either?"

"Nope. Space heaters, though. Made me a killing a few years back up in the Great White North. Hopped a plane just in the nick. They were mushing their dog teams out on the runway when we broke ground. Ninety seconds later I'd've caught me a harpoon through the ol' gizzard."

"Your honesty is commendable. You are confessing to crimes far removed from my jurisdiction."

"Know why?"

Kiet shook his head.

"Remember LBJ's saying? If you have 'em by the balls, their hearts and minds are sure to follow. I think you got me cold, Bum-shawn. I'm being your basic cooperative felon in the sincere hope you'll grant me mercy and that ain't no shit."

Mary Beth sighed. "Old age is creeping up to you, snookums. You used to have such wonderful survival instincts."

"What are we supposed to do, sugar, bop him over the head and make tracks? This man's not stupid, for Chrissake. He wouldn't be jacking us up like this if he didn't have the hotel surrounded. You think he's an idiot? We'd be eating lead for dessert, right?"

217

"Yes, surrounded," Kiet lied, feeling himself redden from the neck up.

He swallowed a mouthful of saline and mushy food, and said to Mary Beth, "I apologize. I misjudged you."

She dropped her fork.

"I confess I disliked you intensely."

"I'm a sweetheart now?"

"Relatively. You aren't a Christian missionary. You're a generic criminal."

"Er, uh, thanks."

"The source of your ill-fated air shipment, please?"

"You're not into foreplay, are you? Okay, Red arranged it el cheapo with these guys he knows in Bangkok. The pilots owed him a favor and he bought the stuff on the black market for a song. I was living back home in Ames with my folks, when he enticed me with a foolproof plan. Foolproof. Ha ha. My acting career was going nowhere and Red, silver-tongued devil he is, talked me into this gyp. He said it hadn't rained lately and rice wasn't growing. Out of the clear blue sky he calls me after skipping on the alimony payments three years ago."

"Bam-sa, don't ever ever split the sheets and remarry. Her shyster lawyer, honest to God truth, he dings me for a second alimony payment. Divorced twice to the same broad and I'm paying a double dip. In-frigging-credible."

"Jean-Guy Pakse?" Kiet asked Mary Beth.

"We were playing it by ear. I was in Bangkok, waiting on the plane and all the cargo, reading the bible like crazy in case I had to quote verses. For God so loved the world he gave his only begotten Son. Stuff like that, you know. Then bubblebutt phones breathing like an obscene caller, he's so excited, saying forget what you haven't loaded on the airplane, get the hell to Hickorn ASAP. The Crown Prince has arrived and he's richer than Solomon."

"He has donated?"

Mary Beth shoved her plate aside and lighted a cigarette. "He promised me the moon."

218

"Has he paid you?"

"No, he hasn't yet."

She tilted her head upward, rounded her lips, and blew a perfectly circular smoke ring.

"Will he?"

"I don't think so. I don't think he can. His assets are frozen or something like that. He was uncomfortable talking about it, but that's what I think the problem is.

"For what it's worth, Kiet, I like Jean-Guy and Binh. They're sexy, sweet boys."

"Splendid," Kiet said.

Red belched softly, wiped his lips with a napkin, and said, "Good grub. Guess it's time we pay up?"

"Brunch is my treat," Kiet said.

Red said, "Uh-uh, nope. That's not what I mean. We're smokin' and jokin' in Hickorn's swankiest hotel instead of at your slammer, where we'd probably be lunching on fishheads and rice. We're talking serious payback, aren't we?"

"Restitution."

Red nodded morosely. "We'll refund what we haven't blown."

Kiet said nothing.

Red looked at him and said, "Okay, what else?"

Kiet smiled. "Now that you mention it, your assistance on a small dilemma might be useful."

219

TWENTY-FOUR

"It's one damn thing after another, Superintendent," Captain Binh said. "Execution glitches are snowballing. I had to break up a fight between two of my officers. One said the other cheated on the drawing and won a firing squad slot. How do you cheat? Sour grapes was what that was all about.

"Then there's press credentials. I sure wish you'd pitch in and help me out. The media's jockeying for prime photo opportunities and sound bites. Less than eighteen hours to go and I haven't even been able to draw up firm security plans.

"Compound that with Prince Pakse's project regarding the admiral. Yeah, I know it was implied and it's your thing anyway, but if I'm gonna be a whipping boy I might as well go all out. No half-assed abuse heaped on this kid, right? It's big-time or nothing. Now this situation lands in my lap. Like I'm not spread thin enough to begin with."

I should be spread thinner, Kiet thought. At minimum thirty kilograms thinner. He tugged on Binh's sleeve and answered with a gasp.

"Okay, we'll take a short breather so you can catch your second wind, Superintendent, but we've got a major emergency on our hands. I could've handled it alone, but when Jean-Guy, who I was personally baby-sitting, by the way, me with all the time in the world, when he drops the bombshell on me that Madame Sara-vane's bopping on by to introduce herself and to tell his fortune, Madame Saravane who make house calls as often as American doctors do, I figure something's fishy and I hustle out to retrieve you. Don't bother to thank me."

They were on the fourth floor stairwell of the Luong Inter-Presidential Hotel, the fourth of six. Kiet pointed limply at the door.

"The elevator?"

"Uhhh," Kiet said.

"No can do, Superintendent. The media'll be on us like a bad smell. They patrol the hallways of all floors except the top, which we've sealed. That's how come we're flanking them on the fire stairs."

"Lie to them," Kiet muttered.

"Nah. The bullshit's reached critical mass," Binh said. "We have no further credibility regarding Jean-Guy. They aren't fooled. They know Jean-Guy and Pierre LeClerc are one and the same, and they're gonna stick to the hotel like wallpaper till they get their story. They're vultures, Superintendent, vultures with delusions of journalistic grandeur. Visions of exclusive interviews are dancing through their heads."

Kiet regained the power of speech. "The Dragon Lady's head too?"

"Okay, okay. I'll have to kind of admit that she's sort of a factor in our flanking move. She's hounding me, Superintendent. If she isn't hanging around headquarters, she's in the lobby here, lying in ambush. She's smothering me. She wants a commitment. I kind of evaded the situation."

"She is a nice young lady."

"I thought you said you didn't actually know her, Superintendent."

"I have captured my second wind, Captain," Kiet said. "Shall we?"

The uniformed policemen guarding The Victorian Suite clicked their heels and saluted. Captain Binh returned the salute and asked if the old biddy had arrived. They said yes sir, ten minutes ago.

Binh said damn it, with the current duties piled on him, he'd probably be late to his own funeral. Chest heaving, Kiet said that they probably could have ridden up the elevator, one car ahead of her.

Binh sighed melodramatically, threw open the suite door, and stopped in midstride. "No lights. What the hell's—Oh my God!"

Kiet galumphed into the darkened anteroom behind Binh. They felt their way to the threshold leading to the corner room at which Jean-Guy Pakse and Mary Beth Applebee had eaten their champagne breakfast. It was an hour past sundown, but the out-of-doors was not quite as black as The Victorian Suite and its rich, dark, ornate decor.

Through the windows, the night sky and lights forgetfully left on in ministry buildings and the spotlights purposely shining on the royal palace and its grounds cast an eerie iridescence on a rather peculiar silhouette.

The postcoital breakfast table had been folded and leaned against a wall. In the center of the carpeting a human figure knelt above a prone human figure. A cigarette ember glowed near the face of the kneeling figure. Emerald Queen smoke stung Kiet's nostrils.

"Holy shit!" Binh cried. "She's killing him!"

"Captain," Kiet said, seeing no movement, no strenuous activity whatsoever.

"Superintendent," Binh said, drawing his pistol. "Find the light switches."

"Captain."

"Freeze!" Binh commanded, elbows locked, the Colt .45 caliber automatic aimed at the kneeler.

Kiet stumbled over a table lamp. He turned it on. Jean-Guy Pakse was alive, but inside his silk robe the bulky, nickel-plated pistol had frightened his limbs as stiff as rigor mortis. Madame Saravane, however, was not visibly alarmed.

"You two ridiculous excuses for gendarmes, are there no limits to your insolence?"

"Madame, what, please, are you doing to him?"

223

There was a pinkish cluster of raw crystal on Jean-Guy's chest. It was the size of an orange. Six-sided sections of quartz seemed to erupt from a core cluster. Madame tapped one with a fingernail and said, "I am realigning his energy plane. His etheric body is kinked. His electromagnetic polarity is turbulent and his personal destiny number is too unsynchronized for an Aries."

"Of course," said Kiet, who was relieved to see Binh twirl his .45 and holster it.

"I told you before, Superintendent, she's branching out into the New Age scam. In the States, gurus have really done a number selling the rubes on crystals."

"Advanced technology. I am a healer and a psychic. My clients are sophisticated. I do not close my minds to Occidental methodologies. I have no qualms about utilizing them in my integrated modality."

"Another jigger of snake oil splashed in the brew is the name of that tune," Binh said, smirking.

"I hesitated when Madame contacted me and insisted on coming to the suite, Superintendent Kiet," Jean-Guy said. "I haven't forgotten what I said to you regarding astrology, but Madame has an impressive reputation in Hickorn and my mood needed a boost."

"You're riding a downer, buddy?" Binh asked.

"A woman I was devoted to severed our relationship."

Binh whistled. "Sorry, no flippancy intended, Jean-Guy, but Jean-Guy Pakse being dumped by a babe, hey, that's gotta be a brand-new experience."

"It is. I console myself that she didn't desert me for a lover. She's dedicated her life to God and Jesus Christ. She gave me up because she has assured herself that there would always be a conflict. She couldn't be thoroughly devoted to me and to her religious faith too. She would be shortchanging her man and her Lord. She loves me and always will. She hurts more than I, she says. I believe her, although that is small consolation for my loss."

"Wow," Binh said, "we're gonna have to have us a skull session over a few snorts. I had a hunch that night we barhopped that you were carrying a torch. I just underwent a similar situation except that things were reversed, you know, me being the dump- or, not the dump-ee, and my gal's in Hickorn, not Fran—"

"Captain," Kiet interrupted.

Jean-Guy said, "No, my woman is also in Hick—"

"Gentlemen," Kiet said firmly. "Please. Once again, Captain, we are demonstrating to Madame our absence of couth. You two are bemoaning your love lives. I was typically abrupt. Madame, accept our apologies. How, by the way, was the electromagnetic adjustment proceeding?"

Before Madame Saravane could answer, Jean-Guy removed the quartz chunk from his chest, rose to his feet, and said, "I definitely feel better. My sadness lingers, yet it's a brighter and warmer gloom. I'm energized."

"Splendid. Enough magnetic repairs. On to your fortune telling, Madame, please."

Madame had deposited her cigarette butt in the crotch of the crystal and moved to an ornate wing chair. "I refuse to practice my craft in the presence of barbarians."

"Hey, why don't you put a sock in it," Binh said.

"Madame, I apologize for Captain Binh. We shall henceforth behave, I promise. You insisted on offering your services to Jean-Guy, he mentioned. Did you sight another comet invisible to any mortal but yourself?"

Madame lighted an Emerald Queen and said, "Sarcasm will bear you bitter fruit, Kiet."

"Answer my question, please."

"I released my curse on you out of the goodness of my heart, Kiet, and I did not place a curse on the boy captain in spite of his vulgar tirade in my salon. Leave us immediately. My patience and charity have expired."

"You will hex us if we don't?"

"With all my might."

"Deadly curses then, yes?"

225

"Slow, painful death, Kiet."

"What did you just hear, Captain?" Kiet asked.

"Some of her same-same voodoo shit, a double dose."

"Besides the magical aspect. Did she not threaten duly appointed law enforcement officer?"

"Hey, yeah." Binh unsnapped his holster.

"We shall assume that her curses are effective. Ergo, she is discharging a deadly weapon at policemen who are performing in the line of duty."

Binh drew his pistol. "We're hauling her in?"

Kiet winked. "Captain, in the event that a citizen uses deadly force against a police officer, how is the officer trained to react?"

Binh aimed the pistol at her. "Okay, should I shoot to kill or wing her?"

"She is not fleeing, Captain."

Binh squinted and pulled back the hammer. "Gotcha. Right between the peepers."

Madame Saravane sat impassively, but Kiet saw a flash, a psychic flinch when the hammer clicked.

"I am a practical person," she said. "Not even I always possess the advantage. Your curses are in abeyance."

"For that we are grateful, Madame."

Jean-Guy wiped sweat from his forehead. "I'm grateful nobody's bleeding in my suite. A drink would taste great. Anybody else?"

Binh twirled and holstered the Colt. "I'll mix the mai tais."

After they had gone into the kitchenette, Kiet said, "Madame, when we spoke at your salon, you implied that Jean-Guy is visiting Luong, not immigrating. Elaborate, please."

"I perceive future uncertainties."

"A vague answer."

Madame Saravane lighted an Emerald Queen from the one she was smoking. She did not reply.

Kiet closed his eyes. "Allow me then, to attempt clairvoyance. Crown Prince Jean-Guy Pakse will ascend to the throne when His Royal Highness Prince Novisad Pakse soon abdicates. Your ominous comet, the ongoing drought, and increasing anti-Chinese violence compel him to retire. The new monarch will be controlled by advisors and his reign might well be brief and tragic. He would subsequently be replaced, perhaps as the result of a fatal accident, by a half cousin named Houphong Duc."

Kiet opened his eyes and gave the bluff of his life. "Please be advised, Madame, that I shall not allow that to happen. I will kill the principals in the scheme and blame the murders on thugs and anarchists."

Madame shrugged and said, "For a novice mystic you predicted accurately."

"Thank you. In payment for a cushy afterlife, Feng Vu deeded you the land underneath this hotel. How much of the structure do you own?"

Madame looked at Kiet and blew a smoke ring. "The Chinese are superstitious and fatalistic. They hedge their bets."

"No direct comment? Perhaps I should digress from *how much* to *why*. We already recognize your phobia of fallibility. Madame the Omniscient. I don't think you relish mortality either. You can't live forever, magic or no magic. You have made a lot of money telling fortunes. The money could be accumulating like the assets of your wealthy clients, in Swiss and French banks, but I think not. You have invested in Luong, although patriotism is doubtlessly on the bottom of your list of motives. The Inter-Presidential is to be your posthumous shrine. But why the ownership secrecy?"

Binh and Jean-Guy were grinding liquors, fruit juices, and ice cubes in a blender. Madame leaned forward and whispered while the machine ran. "Afford me *your* magic, Kiet."

"A deal?"

"Yes. Immunity from prosecution. And your boy stallion with the periodic sexual dysfunction does not shoot me."

"A deal," Kiet said. "Speak to me."

"Luxury hotels are expensive, Kiet. I am not as rich as people suppose."

227

"You borrowed the money?"

"I have a 70 percent interest in the InterPresidential. Eighty percent of my 70 percent is mortgaged."

"Who is the 30 percent partner?"

"A dozen different investors. Their names would mean as little to you as they do to me. They were recruited because I was at my debt ceiling."

"Debt ceiling," Kiet said. "The ring of made-in-the-shade MBA-NIC-Yupsterdom terminology."

"Kiet, I am meticulously conversant with the afterlife and the inner self, but high finance baffles me. Houphong Duc arranged everything. He has the best Western and Japanese financial connections in Luong."

"Which he placed at Madame's disposal for a favor or two or three, not to mention a timely comet. Please clarify the ownership secrecy."

"I'm overextended. I was too anxious to sign. Forty percent would have been a share I could afford, but 40 percent isn't majority interest. Duc knew and took full advantage. I was too swollen with pride to refuse. Duc says he has to juggle my loans daily to ward off default."

"He anticipates your continued cooperation?"

"Yes. Within a year, he promises, after the change in government and a public subsidy is signed into law, the hotel will be mine free and clear. The Luong Saravane."

Kiet suppressed a groan. "An eternal tribute. A legacy to yourself. Aside from the hotel computer continuing to erase The Victorian Suite room and board fees, what other cooperation is to continue?"

"Duc didn't inform me beyond tomorrow. He says, and I quote, that the situation is fluid and we'll go with the flow."

"But between now and the execution?"

"An asteroid."

Kiet groaned. "In tomorrow's column?"

"Yes. I see an asteroid tonight. A dangerous omen foretelling another year of drought."

228

"And the asteroid might veer off if Jean-Guy Pakse pleased the forces of the universe by actively cooperating in quest of the throne."

"Yes."

"Did he agree to?"

"I was to broach that topic after crystal therapy," Madame said.

Binh and Jean-Guy had shut off the blender, were pouring their mai tais into glasses. Kiet spoke in a hush, quickly, "Our deal, you and I, is for you to develop writer's block and call in sick tomorrow."

"And?"

"Enjoy your drink," Kiet said, taking two mai tais from Binh and handing her one. "Then take a walk. Go via the lobby and draw the reporters with you. Imply you know something."

"Then?"

"Lead them several blocks, to the west. West, not east."

"And then?"

"Stop and lecture on the benefits of crystals."

Five minutes after mai tais were consumed and Madame Saravane departed with her quartz, Captain Binh excused himself to attend to the extremely pressing obligations concerning the execution of Feng Vu. Superintendent Bamsan Kiet asked Jean-Guy Pakse a two-part question: Have you contacted His Royal Highness, Prince Novisad Pakse yet? Has His Royal Highness contacted you yet?

The replies, respectively, were no and no. Kiet was not surprised. Two royal children, he thought.

They took the elevator down. Kiet trusted that Madame had cleared the lobby. Stair walking was enervating activity, down as well as up. Madame had done her diversion job splendidly. A single reporter remained.

The Dragon Lady stood behind a potted plant, face to face with Captain Binh. She had hooked her index fingers around his belt loops, her talking, him listening. She did not appear to Kiet to be discussing journalism or current events.

Unseen, Kiet escorted Jean-Guy into the night. They jaywalked Mu Pakse onto Avenue George Bush, eastbound. Kiet said, "Minister of Agriculture Houphong Duc and I had lunch at the Hickorn Sporting Club. His tongue slipped."

"Pardon me?"

"Pardon you, indeed. He doesn't know you. You don't know him. You both lied to me."

Jean-Guy's voice quavered. "I have no money."

"Thus your excessive worries about the health of your Testarusha?"

"The Ferrari and my clothing, they are my assets. I couldn't pay a day's rent on this suite. I can't even buy a meal."

"I suspected, but not strongly," Kiet said. "I resisted my suspicions because of your mother's wealth. You and she fought, and she terminated your allowance?"

"She cancelled my allowance because she has no money."

"No money? Seven rich, older husbands, the seventh a Wall Street tycoon, and she has no money?"

"*Six* rich, older husbands," Jean-Guy said. "Mother is older now than her first husbands when she married them. She is aging and can't stand to. The tables and the worm turned.

"Her Wall Street husband is twenty years younger and he is no tycoon. Chip was young and handsome. He swept her off her feet. Mother thought she had snared youth and money, the epitome of a male possession to an aging, vain woman. She was wrong. Chip worked on Wall Street, but he skipped a step ahead of the American Securities and Exchange Commission. He was an arbitrager and inside trader. The Americans indicted him and asked France to extradite. He skipped out on Mother too. With every franc she had."

"The *Hickorn Enquiring Mind*," Kiet said. "Their ignorance disappoints me."

"No doubt they knew, but their silence was bought with money or threats," Jean-Guy said.

"By Duc?"

"Who else?"

"How did they buy you?"

"By promising the status quo. I could move to Luong and eat, drink, fuck, and drive fast. Do what I was told and my life would be easy and unchanged. They are going to install me on the throne and kill me, aren't they?"

"Unless we disrupt their plans."

"Superintendent Kiet, I might be worthless but I'm not a scoundrel."

Kiet patted the lad's back, thinking that it would not be such a bad epitaph. "No, you aren't."

Jean-Guy's eyes were wet. "I do feel Luongan. I want to be Luongan. In France I was a half-breed. I want to be friends with my father."

They had reached the royal palace gates. Kiet motioned to a guard and said, "You shall."

Monday, May 25
Hickorn
High 86°, Low 75°
Overcast

TWENTY-FIVE

"Bamsan, are you sleeping?"

"Yes."

"You aren't awake?"

"No."

"So you've learned to sleep while staring at the ceiling."

Kiet groaned and sat up. "What time is it, Quin?"

"Five minutes after two. About four hours until dawn."

"It isn't . . . being done at dawn."

"You don't like talking about the execution and neither do I, but it is bothering you deeply. We should talk about it."

"Something is bothering me?"

"Don't play those games with me. You fell asleep with your arms wrapped around me. I couldn't get up and go home. Since you're responsible for getting me into trouble with my mother and son, you could have at least let me sleep, but because of your nightmares I couldn't."

"You're a grown woman, Quin."

"Bamsan, we've been through this time and time again. I'm also an unmarried woman. Mother won't speak to me for a week."

Pure bliss, Kiet thought. "Ow!"

Quin had grabbed his spare tire and twisted. "Don't you smirk."

"Did you see me smirk? I didn't smirk. I am no smirker."

"You smirked in your mind. I know you, Bamsan Kiet. Don't think Mother isn't thinking of you too. You're the seducer. My ravager, my despoiler. Some day when you're eating dinner at our home she will poison your food."

Kiet lay down and took Quin's hands. "The execution is at noon. In the phraseology of my young adjutant, high noon. Binh informs me that the execution-at-dawn tradition is obsolete in the electronic age. Camera crews regard dawn lighting as too shadowed, therefore inferior. Significant persons dislike attending important functions at such an hour. Binh says that American college and professional football clubs—not soccer, not bona fide football, their peculiar version in which players wear paramilitary plastic armor and employ an oblong football they seldom kick— their starting times are dictated by the television networks. I am not complaining. I dropped the Feng Vu execution project on Binh's willing lap. Anything that he is compelled to do to produce enhanced sound bites and sharpened, color-brightened photo opportunities is splendid with me. I furthermore permitted him to bring folding chairs."

"Bamsan, you babble like Binh. When Binh babbles, he is Binh. When you babble, you're nervous and tired. Close your eyes and count convicted criminals gamboling over a fence."

"I have to go."

"*You're* going? Isn't that wonderful? Have you forgotten whose house, whose bed we're in?"

"Police business, my love."

"Classified information," she snapped. "I should not inquire about the particulars."

"Thank you."

"Is your mission planned or spontaneous?"

"Yes."

"Thank you, Superintendent."

"Quin, I thought of it in advance but I did not make formal plans. I wasn't sure whether I would follow through."

"What swayed you?"

"I could not sleep."

"Insomnia," Quin said. "Insomnia is a factor?"

"Yes. I'll never sleep again if I do not do what must be done."

"Madame Saravane's influence is shining through. You sound as

236

though you're speaking of omens and predestination. Where is your secret mission?"

"Eight, nine, ten blocks."

"Too far to walk. Borrow my bicycle. I'll try to sleep out the night and take a taxi later in the morning. The timing is better. Mother is awake, waiting. By daylight, she'll be too exhausted to fight."

"I admire your logical mind," he said.

Kiet's cat hopped onto the bed, paid no attention to its human inhabitants, curled up between them, and began purring. It was missing patches of fur and smelled like a cage of rutting monkeys.

"He hasn't been eaten, Bamsan."

"He hasn't," Kiet said. "Not altogether."

"*There* is an omen," Quin said, petting the animal.

Kiet stood and stretched. "Yes, but what kind?"

"Hey, Blam-san. I didn't peg you as a teepee creeper."

Red Williams stepped back and Kiet entered Mary Beth Applebee's hotel room. "Excuse me?"

"Oh, hey, right. You're a detective, you knew you'd find me here."

"Are you being facetious?"

"Not me," Red said. "Not this kid."

Red was unattractively attired in a pair of boxer shorts. Mary Beth wore a wrapped bed sheet. She said, "It's our only compatibility. In the ninety-nine other things that make a marriage fly, we crash and burn."

Red winked at Kiet. "You're looking at the last of the all-American studs."

"Put some clothes on," Kiet said.

"We're going someplace?"

Kiet nodded at a row of suitcases. "You were going someplace?"

"We have an 8:00 A.M. flight to Bangkok and points west," Mary Beth said. "It won't be too soon."

"This small dilemma you said we was gonna help you out on, you didn't say what it was, so I figured you'd maybe changed your mind."

"Not we. You, Mr. Williams."

"Listen, Bomb-some, we already made reservations."

"You won't miss your flight."

"Like you told me to, I gave back the air conditioner deposits we hadn't already spent. What do you want, blood?"

"Get dressed. Come."

Red Williams moaned and stepped into a pair of slacks. "Who do I have to kill?"

"Nobody. You shall burglarize him."

"Is it just me, Blah-son, or is it Americans in general you got a chip on your shoulder the size of a railroad tie about?"

"I have no animosity toward Americans or the United States of America."

"You ever been there?"

"Thankfully, no."

"Yeah? So what jumps in your head when you think of America?"

"Dope fiends, oat bran, and 'have a nice day.' "

"Bom-sut, that's proof positive. You're a racist your ownself."

Kiet paused at an alleyway on Avenue Ronald Reagan, between Mu Savhana and Rue Willie Mosconi. The alley bordered the rear of the ministry of agriculture building. Most lights were on; Houphong Duc's third-floor corner office was a notable exception.

Red gulped. "We're going in there? It's blacker'n a well digger's gonads."

"The alley is vacant. Transients camp elsewhere and the ministry isn't guarded."

"You gotta snoop in this place, why don't you get a search warrant?"

"No."

238

"It's a big hassle like in the States? You gotta get down on your knees and beg some bleeding-heart judge to sign it?"

Red Williams, criminal, past and present, lamenting law enforcement impediments and judicial leniency? Kiet mused. Either the man was deceptively complex or he was even simpler than face value. "No. Luongan judges are too busy dispensing justice. The Hickorn ordinance book grants the superintendent of police the authority to write search warrants."

"So what's your hang-up? What are we doing in the middle of the night in the world's darkest alley? Blah-sown, I gotta tell you, I got me a case of the heebie-jeebies that won't quit."

"Our search has to be a secret."

"You picked me as your partner in crime. Boy, that makes my day. Can't you scare yourself up a Luongan sneak?"

Kiet's bristling at 'boy' was invisible. "Luongans talk, gossip, boast. It is a national characteristic."

"I'm elected, huh?"

"Your knowledge of modern Western burglary technology influenced my choice too."

"Bum-sot, I'm zero for one. They busted me in that appliance store before we hauled out five toaster ovens. I was nineteen years old. Me and these other two guys were shit-faced on a half rack of beer. I knew right then and there I wasn't cut out for that ball game. I was a con artist. I was born for the flimflam. The ol' die was cast."

"How did you gain access to the appliance store?"

Red Williams shrugged unseen. "I was the biggest. I kicked the frigging door in."

Kiet groaned. Red kicked the door in. They headed up the stairs.

"Look at all the paperwork piled up on those desks, Bam-some. Reminds me of offices back home."

"You worked in an office? You held a steady job?"

"Oh, hell no. Wash your mouth out with soap. I'm talking about my parole officer's office."

239

"Please keep your voice down."

"What's bugging you?" Williams said. "These turkeys don't turn a wheel from nine to five and you're expecting company on a Sunday night. Dream on."

"Shhh."

"Yassuh, boss."

Duc's door was ajar.

"The grand pooh-bah's, huh? What are we swiping?"

"Whatever we might find."

"Terrific," Williams said, swinging the door wide and patting the wall for a light switch.

"Don't."

"Lighten up, Bomb-shaw. You worried I'm gonna agitate the cockroaches?"

Minister of Agriculture Houphong Duc, in slacks, white shirt, and suspenders, was at a file cabinet, holding a bulging folder.

"The walls and floors are thick," he said calmly. "I didn't hear anything until you came on to this floor."

"We're naturally talented covert agents," Red said, scratching a temple, gawking at papered and paneled walls, spacious and glossy teakwood desk, leather sofa, and Persian rug. "Hey, not too shabby. Somebody's making out like a bandit."

"Indeed. Working late, Mr. Minister?"

"And you, Kiet?"

"That folder contains urgent business, yes?"

"Ministry business."

"What ministry business, please?"

"Private ministry business, Kiet."

"Hey, what's with you guys? I'm getting bad vibes. One of you been banging the other's girlfriend or something?"

"Madame Saravane alerted you, I presume," Kiet said.

"Unless you have a warrant, Kiet, you're trespassing. You're on federal property."

"Federal property within Hickorn city limits. I also presume that the papers in that folder do not concern Feng Vu's rice

240

shipment from Thailand, the two hundred metric tons. Tuon Tran disposed of the bags, you the manifests. Because of the bulk, his task was more challenging. You could have easily burned or torn up incriminating pieces of paper."

"Hey," Red Williams said, pointing at a machine behind Duc's desk. "He's got a shredder. Whatever you're talking about, he could of made confetti out of it in the comfort and privacy of his very own office."

"A coincidence occurred to me, Mr. Minister. You and Tran attended the same American university in their tropical province of Florida."

"Florida, Florida State, Miami, they got themselves some bitchin' football teams. Top ten ranking and major bowl invitations, year in and year out," Red said.

"While you concentrated on attainment of the hallowed MBA, Tran majored in military science and water-skiing. As Luongan students in an alien land, I presume you were close—"

"Presume, presume," Duc said. "Any competent detective knows that presumption and truth are mutually exclusive."

"Last Wednesday at the Hickorn Sporting Club, you stated that Feng Vu bought paddy from river pirates who robbed grain barges of Luong's last good harvest. Vu held it until the price rose. My memory of your statement is truth, yes?"

"Yes."

"Who, please, converted the two hundred metric tons of contraband raw paddy into the polished white rice you so vigilantly seized?"

Duc spoke slowly, syllable by syllable, instructor to beginning pupil. "Feng Vu is a broker and a miller. The Chinese brokers buy paddy at the villages and ship by barge on the Ma San to Hickorn."

"And you, sir, stated further that a basic responsibility of the Ministry of Agriculture is a health and safety inspection of the milling process and weight measurement for taxation purposes."

"Is there a bottom line to this, Kiet?"

241

"Indeed. The file folder in your grip. Presumably. I would not be surprised if it is a log of milling inspections."

"Vu wouldn't invite an inspector in on contraband processing. Kiet, you're even dumber than you look."

"Whoa," Red said. "Sweet-talking devil, aren't you?"

"Your inspectors, Mr. Minister, virtually live with the rice czars. They have taken an oath to ensure Luongans eat wholesome rice. And it is inconceivable that they would miss their percentage, their salary-supplementing bribes. The two hundred tons are not on the log pages because there was no two hundred tons of bandit paddy. The pages are destined for an accident, yes? A disappearance. A bureaucratic mishap."

"How a man as crude and insulting as you retains a responsible position is beyond me, Kiet."

"The contraband rice is not on the log," Kiet said, extending a hand. "Feng Vu bought the two hundred metric tons of polished rice from the Thais. He is disgusting, yes. He perhaps intended on hoarding said Thai rice, yes. But he did not. He was arrested before he had the opportunity. The log, please."

Duc terminated the debate by striding around his desk to the doorway, the file held to his chest like armor. Kiet snatched across the teakwood slab, snatching air. Red Williams was between Duc and freedom.

"Hey, little lunk fella, I don't think you ought to be scootin', not from the look on Blam-sawn's kisser. Don't make me pick on somebody not my own size."

Red had assumed a boxer's stance, though with palms open to swat the little lunk fella, to slap some of the piss and vinegar out of him.

Houphong Duc, his body rock-hard from a midday tropical tennis regimen at the Hickorn Sporting Club, drove a fist into Red Williams's gut. Red said "oomph" and dropped to his knees.

Kiet, meanwhile, snatched again at Duc, from his rear. He grabbed hold of suspenders and tugged, pulling the surprised agriculture minister backward. Aided by the suspender's elasticity,

Duc slammed into Kiet and the two of them fell onto the desk, slid along its width, and toppled off the edge.

Duc sprang up and opened the top center desk drawer. Knowing what he surely was after, Kiet kicked it shut on his hand and heard bone snap.

Kiet rose to his feet slowly. He reached into the drawer and removed a nine-millimeter automatic pistol.

Though every joint and muscle in Kiet's body throbbed, he did not feel the needle-jab pain of fracture. But he knew he would soon feel the throb of headache.

Houphong Duc was clutching his injured hand and screaming. He was accompanied by Red Williams, who was on his knees, retching on the Persian carpet.

TWENTY-SIX

High noon minus ten minutes.

"I don't know, Superintendent?"

"Excuse me, Captain?"

They were at the execution site, the nameless park rimmed by Avenue Alexandre Loubet, Rue Ne Win, Avenue Charles de Gaulle, and Mu Pakse. They were at the middle of the park, at the rock and waterfall sculpture where it would happen. Sandbags had been stacked against one side of the rocks, which were actually slablike stones, components in an abstract sculpture. Peculiar, Kiet thought. He'd never before noticed that the unnamed park's sculpture was named. A bronze plaque identified it as Minimalist Maximum.

Kiet also noted that a wooden pole had been impaled in the ground in front and at the center of the sandbags. The sandbags, of course, were there to prevent ricochets. Heaven forbid a tragedy at an execution. The fountain was off. He supposed that the sandbags would settle if they became soaked. Not to mention the nationwide water shortage. And the ironic impropriety of Feng Vu being drenched while being shot.

Regardless, Kiet did not care to ask. This was Binh's extravaganza, not his. He had, in fact, asked to command the firing squad and Kiet had happily assented.

"These rice bags, they're bugging the hell out of me."

"These rice bags?" Kiet said, nudging the pile of wet, moldering, one-hundred-kilogram Thai rice bags that were capped with a megaphone. Binh had overseen Rear Admiral Tuon Tran's dredging operation, the fishing of the sacks from the floor of the Ma San River five kilometers upstream.

"Superintendent, quit with the chickenshit jabs, okay? I concede that the bags kind of indicate that Feng Vu isn't guilty beyond a reasonable doubt, but we're between the devil and the deep blue sea here. We're between a rock and a hard place."

"Yes we are," Kiet said, bathed by the shadow of the stone collage.

"We're beyond the point of no return. That's what's really bugging me. Just look at that crowd."

Kiet scanned the crowd. Ropes had been strung on portable stanchions, a uniformed officer standing by each. Their assignment was to keep spectators on their side of the cordons. The makeup of the crowd suggested that the officers might earn their pay. Young toughs had muscled forward, past the average citizenry, the passively ghoulish, and were clutching the ropes with white knuckles. They were primed on beer, eager for the bloodletting, and then a swagger through Chinatown. If execution security proved inadequate, it was due to the extra men Kiet had sent on patrol in Chinatown.

"A group offensive to the eyes," Kiet said.

"I'm afraid to look at the press box," Binh said. "For obvious reasons."

Binh's "press box," a rectangularly cordoned section furnished with folding chairs, was at a corner of Minimalist Maximum. Their photo opportunities and sound bites would be profile and quartering view, close in, death gasps and blood spurts highly up-close and personal, emotional editorial grist and gore. All seats were filled. Kiet counted roughly two-thirds local, one-third wire service. The Dragon Lady looked at Kiet, looked at Binh, looked at Kiet and licked her lips.

"She appears friendly in a sensual way," Kiet said.

"Yeah?" Binh looked at the Dragon Lady. She bared her teeth and thumbed her nose.

246

"Swell, Superintendent. Super. Outstanding. Thanks for the red-hot tip."

"Sorry," Kiet said, imagining romantic vengeance and tomorrow's *Mind* headline. SPACE ALIEN HERPES, SYPHILIS AND AIDS CARRIER INFILTRATES HPD IN NUMBER-TWO SLOT —VOWS TO CONQUER EARTH WITH VD.

"The VIPs. Where are the VIPs?" Binh said. "I have a hundred more folding chairs stacked I can set up directly ahead of the ropes at a moment's warning, but I haven't seen anyone with more weight than a deputy assistant undersecretary and an army major."

"Look at the crowd," Kiet said.

"Yeah, I suppose the big wigs are thinking, hey, why get trampled in some altercation. I'd've thought Minister Duc would make an appearance. He was the prime mover, you know. Him having that mysterious accident to his hand and being stuck in a hospital, it must've been nasty for him to skip this."

"Indeed," Kiet said. "Very painful."

Minister of Agriculture Houphong Duc was indeed in a Hickorn hospital, recovering from multiple metacarpal and phalangeal fractures, under heavy guard and heavy sedation. There would be ample time later to truthfully and comprehensively brief his adjutant.

"These rice bags, Superintendent, why did we have to drag them along anyhow? We haul them out and say this is how come we're cancelling the fun, hell, it's gonna be *us* who're put to death."

"I am hoping the bags will be supplemental evidence."

"What do you mean supplemental?"

"If somebody does not appear, I mean nothing," Kiet said, scanning the outer fringes of the mob.

"Superintendent, pardon me for saying so, no offense, but this is a really big-time shitty moment for one of your famous riddles."

"You are pardoned."

"But he isn't. Look. Here we go."

Their arrival announced by jeers and whistles, the firing squad

247

and their prisoner climbed out of the back of a hearse. Kiet looked at Binh.

"Okay, Superintendent, a hearse is in questionable taste, but I had to borrow something we could stuff everybody into. I don't wanna sound like a broken record, but since the Beetle went tits up the biggest department vehicle in inventory is a scooter."

"Yes, yes," Kiet said, surveying the firing squad.

Five grim policemen, shiny and smart in dress uniforms, marched toward Binh, Kiet, and the sandbags, a manacled Feng Vu inside the human box they had formed. Vu wore clean trousers and shirt. His jaw was thrust, his lips clenched in contempt. Remarkable arrogance, Kiet thought.

Fear had dilated the firing squad's collective pupils. The process of shooting a hated Chinese was no longer abstract. Spectators strained the stout ropes. They were shouting, spitting, cursing, laughing. Turning feral, Kiet worried.

"Your weapon, Superintendent. Where is your weapon?"

"I don't have a gun."

"Certainly you were issued a sidearm—"

"I returned it to supply when I was promoted to superintendent."

Binh sighed, began to unbuckle his pistol belt, glanced at Kiet's girth, and said, "No way."

He instead removed his Colt .45 automatic pistol from its patent leather holster. "I guess you'll just have to hang on to it until—you know. The coup de grace is an honor I shouldn't usurp."

"Splendid. Thank you," Kiet said, shoving the portable cannon into a pocket.

"What are we gonna do, Superintendent?"

"Captain, is the safety in the 'on' position?"

"Yeah," Binh said with a quick smile. "No sweat in regard to Soprano City. What are we gonna do in respect to you know who, in the context, you know, of doing the right thing?"

Kiet saw his answer to Binh's question, his possible answer, who and what he had been anxiously awaiting. An athletic, pin-striped man sandwiched by two Hickorn police officers was forced through the gauntlet. He slapped Kiet's outstretched hand with a manila envelope.

"He was dopey from morphine," the man said angrily. "He wrote his statement under duress. I hope you're satisfied."

"I hope I am too." Kiet tore off an end. The log book pages and a hand-written letter were there.

"Are you through with me?"

Kiet answered the officers, instructing them to escort the man out.

"He's familiar to me," Binh said.

"He is on the federal payroll as a deputy to the minister of agriculture," Kiet said.

"What does he do?"

"Lose at tennis."

Binh was peering around Kiet, reading the letter. "Damn. A day late, a dollar short, but dynamite. Why'd you have Duc's boy do it? Oh yeah, I see, he witnessed. Notarized too. Authenticity, yeah. Still—the crowd, the peanut gallery, it may boil down to Vu or us."

The firing squad clicked their polished heels, stiffened to attention, and saluted. Feng Vu smiled a jagged-toothed smile at Kiet and said, "Do you have the honor of blindfolding me? I am afforded a blindfold option, aren't I?"

Kiet folded Houphong Duc's statement and refolded it. He stared at Feng Vu, wishing he were mean enough to ruin his afterlife guarantee. Tell the Chinese how Madame's curses could be neutralized by a gun barrel. Tell him that her magic was counterfeit. Wished he could. Wished.

Binh nodded sidelong at Minimalist Maximum. Two firing squad members positioned Vu at the post and tied his hands behind it. Vu was tensing, resisting. They perspired from the effort, darkening their shirts under the armpits. The day was hazy and tauntingly humid.

Feng Vu visibly enjoyed their discomfiture. Kiet could not

believe the man, how completely this cunning operator had bought Madame's afterworldly Disneyland.

Binh, in mechanical, military motions faced the prisoner. "Do you desire a blindfold?"

Feng Vu said, "Come closer. The rabble is too loud. I can't hear you."

"Not a chance. You're gonna spit on me. Do you desire a blindfold?"

Vu smiled at Kiet. "I tried. Your boy isn't stupid."

"Do you desire a blindfold?"

Vu glared at Binh. "No. You, all of you, every responsible party shall stare into my eyes. You'll avoid them, but when the rifles are aimed, my eyes will be magnets. None of you have seen a life depart. You can't resist."

A soul fluttering upward, Kiet thought. Oh yes I have. He saw goosebumps on Binh's arms.

"Do you desire clergy?"

Feng Vu laughed.

Binh was clenching his fists, unclenching them, trembling.

Vu said, "I want a cigarette. A condemned man is entitled to a last cigarette."

"I thought of that," Binh said, taking an unopened package of Emerald Queens from a shirt pocket.

"No," Vu said. "Those things are ghastly. I ought to know. I have controlling interest in the factory. A Western filtertip cigarette. A condemned man is entitled to a quality cigarette."

A firing squad member produced a pack of American cigarettes. Binh took one out. Vu shook his head as Binh attempted to insert it in his mouth. "No. Light it for me."

Binh lit the cigarette. Vu refused it again. "No, take a long drag. The match makes the first puff taste like sulfur. My last smoke has to be perfect. I'm entitled."

Binh puffed and coughed. "I don't smoke."

He extended it to Vu, who once again refused. He laughed and said, "I don't either. Smoke it yourself."

250

Binh threw the cigarette down and said to Kiet, red-eyed, "Fuck him. Let's get on with it."

Binh ordered the firing squad to assemble. They marched fifteen meters out, formed a row that was a slight arc, and snapped to attention.

"Port arms!" Binh called out.

The officers brought their carbines to their chests at forty-five degree angles.

"One round, load!"

Five men in unison pulled back the bolts of their carbines, inserted single cartridges, and released the bolts. So quiet had the crowd become that the clacking of machined steel seemed to Kiet hammers striking an anvil.

"Ready!"

The firing squad rotated their gun barrels forward and the stocks to their shoulders. Binh looked at Kiet.

Kiet felt a drop of moisture on his cheek. A tear? Please let it not be.

A velvety sound emanated from the rear of the crowd, Kiet's right front. He had a partial view along Rue Ne Win of the gardens behind the royal palace. Prince Pakse and Jean-Guy Pakse were in the midst of low topiary, eyes and palms upward.

"Aim!"

Five carbine barrels five radii were traced to the center. Deadly geometry, Kiet thought.

Binh looked at Kiet. Kiet picked up the megaphone. Binh smiled thinly and yelled, "Order arms!"

Five carbines came to the ground in jerky synchronization, stock down, barrel up.

"Parade rest!"

Legs parted stiffly. Left arms tucked neatly in the smalls of backs.

"Attention," Kiet said through the megaphone. "Because of an untimely accident, Minister of Agriculture Houphong Duc is unable to attend today's . . . event. As the crime for which Feng Vu has been condemned to death is in Minister Duc's sphere of responsibility, he has the authority to decree . . . changes. Minister Duc has asked me to read a prepared statement. Please permit me to say in advance that I am in complete agreement with Minister Duc's comments. Physical substantiation is in the pile by us and in the logbook beside it."

Kiet felt additional raindrops on his fingers and his nose. Another teaser, he knew, but our first liquid tantalizer. Average citizens remained distracted by the pathetic shower and by the Pakses, who were now arm and arm. The press corps seemed disoriented. Reporters who were pivoting their heads and gaping about at the advent of history, their plates brimming over with news bulletins.

The front-row hooligans comprised Kiet's rapt audience. Some of the cordons were down, evidently severed by switchblades. The young toughs had not been moved by the rainfall or the royal reunion. They were not reflective people, Kiet thought, not the sort who sought natural balances and treasured the beneficence of omens.

Kiet looked at Binh, tilted his head toward the thugs, and spun a finger. Binh said okay, fine, gotcha, and called out, "Detail, attention! About face! Port arms!"

The firing squad complied. The juvenile delinquents, now primary targets of the elite shooters, blended rearward into the mainstream.

Kiet read through the megaphone, "New information has been submitted in the matter of the kingdom of Luong versus Feng Vu. The data is of such a compelling nature that further inquiry should be undertaken. Therefore, it is requested that discharge of the judicial sentence regarding the defendent be delayed until resolution of the validity of the forthcoming information. Signed, comma, Houphong Duc, comma, Minister of Agriculture, period."

Kiet started to unfasten Vu's bonds.

"Kiet, tell me, would you have read that letter if this bloodthirsty lunk mob hadn't been soothed by raindrops and the princes?"

252

Kiet did not answer.

"Would you?"

"We are not releasing you," Kiet said. "You're returning to jail, pending investigation of the new evidence."

"Kiet, you took your time stopping the execution."

Feng Vu's face was oily with perspiration. Perhaps, Kiet thought, at the instant of departure Vu realized that despite magic the voyage to an ethereal amusement park would not necessarily be pleasant.

Kiet jerked the knot to free it.

Feng Vu winced.

Kiet said, "I'm only human."

EPILOGUE

FENG VU was retried and exonerated of treason, but convicted of aggressive nonmarketing, a misdemeanor offense added to the Hickorn ordinance book for the occasion. Vu was fined everything he still owned and released. He swore off all that was worldly and materialistic, and joined a Buddhist monastery, but was soon cast out when he insisted that the order purchase an abacus.

The simpering weather front that deposited the paltry rain droplets on the execution site had lazily drifted northwest to southeast, dribbling on MADAME SARAVANE five minutes earlier. She expediently went into a rainmaking dance/trance and took credit for the monsoon that finally came four days later, and credit was generally given. She raised her rates, had more business than she could handle, refinanced her Luong InterPresidential Hotel debt and moved her salon to The Victorian Suite.

That year's southwest monsoon was so savage that nine important new tributaries to the Ma San River were formed by flood waters and erosion. REAR ADMIRAL TUON TRAN discovered all nine and named them after people who could pull strings in his behalf, but they didn't.

MINISTER OF AGRICULTURE HOUPHONG DUC was asked by his uncle to alter the path of his career. Several recommendations were laid before him. Duc accepted the only one that did not include prison. He became a rural agricultural agent in a village that was experimenting with the cultivation of tapioca.

RED WILLIAMS and MARY BETH APPLEBEE went to southern California. Using aliases, they were accepted as contestants on *The Dating Game*. Mary Beth picked Red (bachelor number two) as her dream date. They spent a glorious and all-expenses-paid weekend in Mazatlan, where Red swindled Mary Beth's chaperone out of $6500 in his latest scam, precious metals futures.

PRINCE NOVISAD PAKSE entertained the brother of the Sultan of Yogyakarta. He played the Indonesian even in straight pool, and would have had the advantage if not for a maddening tendency to scratch on the cue ball.

JEAN-GUY PAKSE returned to France and fulfilled Madame Saravane's prophesy by marrying the daughter of a Marseilles Lamborghini dealer. As a wedding present, his father-in-law allowed a generous trade-in on the crippled Testarossa and sold him a new Countach for 10 percent above invoice. Jean-Guy and his biological father correspond twice a month on videotape.